The Curse of Blackbane

WORKS BY GORDON BREWER

Ray Irish Occult Mystery
A Shot of Irish
(Ray Irish Occult Suspense Mystery Book 1)
Die If You Want Praise
(Ray Irish Occult Suspense Mystery Book 2)
Drink with The Devil at Midnight
(Ray Irish Occult Suspense Mystery Book 3)
No Remedy Against Death:
(Ray Irish Occult Suspense Mystery Book 4)
Ray Irish Occult Mysteries: Omnibus Edition
Death Stalks the Runway: Ray Irish Mystery Case File #1
Reaper Walks the Garden: Ray Irish Mystery Case File #2

Paranormal and Fantasy
Beowulf: Curse of The Dreygurs
Infinite Loop
The Curse of Blackbane

Clovel Sword Chronicles Series
Shield of Skool (Book 1)
Battle for Three Realms (Book 2)
Downfall of the Gods (Book 3)
Clovel Sword Chronicles: Omnibus Edition

Clovel Sword Saga Series

Clovel Sword Saga: Volumes 1 - 2
Skeletons of Nilgava: Clovel Sword Saga 3
The Bleeding Mountains: A Clovel Sword Saga 4

The Curse of Blackbane

GORDON BREWER

Brewer Internet Publishing LLC
2023

Contents

Introduction

In this dark fantasy tale set during the late 18th century, William Marshall carries the infamous name of Blackbane. The rogue buccaneer captain from the Americas currently works for the Ottomans and plies the waters of the Mediterranean.

During a bloody attack on a convent, Blackbane discovers a golden cross and dies at the hands of archangel Remiel. In a cruel twist, the angel returns the pirate to life while giving him a terrible curse. Blackbane becomes immortal and his memories filled with the everlasting suffering of those he's killed.

Now pursued by the Seven Princes of Hell, who intend to rip his immorality and soul from his body, Marshall flees to new waters. Captured in France, the captain meets a strange, bloodthirsty preacher called the Black Monk.

Unable to escape his vicious past, Marshall receives a vision, which may put an end to his curse. With the help of his new friend, the pirate believes he found his escape by recovering the lost relics of saints. However, he doesn't realize that angels carry their own agendas. Like Dante's journey through Hell, the man called Blackbane finds his new destiny remains woven in terror, violence, and blood.

Chapter 1: A Profane Curse

"Curse these blasted fools; we're here for gold!"

Captain Blackbane stepped inside a long hallway with two of his loyal mates. It was the height of the devil's hour. His face darkened at the scene inside the Convent of Santa Clara.

Some of his notorious band of cutthroats ignored his orders. Like wolves, the Diano Marina men descended upon the nuns, already drunk with wine found at a nearby monastery. The screams of women and the lewd catcalls of the sailors hit him like a blast of foul air. Amid the chaotic scene lit by oil lamps hanging on the stone walls, his men were already ravaging their victims. Half-naked victims struggled to escape from their sleeping cells where men shared them.

Blackbane cursed in Arabic at the crew while casually stepped over the bloody body of a partially dressed woman.

"Size orospular erkekler taşıyın! Kadınlardan uzaklaşın, göt oğulları!"

Smartly dressed in a blue wool coat, scarlet vest, and white breeches befitting his status, the captain pushed back his dark brown tricorn hat. The yellow light revealed his pockmarked face. A smattering of black dots showed through his beard on one side of the tan skin.

"Bingham, get these bastards off the women. They'll fetch more when they're chaste." Their leader gave no hints of mercy while his dark eyes surveyed the chaotic scene.

His loyal first mate responded immediately when the captain pulled his flintlock and entered the nearby rooms. Blackbane grimly smiled as he watched Bingham strike one of the reluctant men with his pistol butt after the pirate failed to move quickly enough. He and another comrade immediately joined the pirate captain.

Blackbane directed them toward the stairs, pointing with his captured Polish saber. The blade of his *karabela,* a Polish saber, still glistened with the blood of a monk who lay outside.

"I want every man to scour every spot in this building. No one escapes, or I'll have your guts for the fish." His ominous growl sent the men to their task.

The captain watched his pirates scurry away while he drained a tankard filled with Cachaça, a robust local wine which he held in his other hand. He waved his second mate over while turning over the dead body of a nun with his foot.

"Seymore, help round up the rest of the women. I want them on the ship before morning."

The men immediately hurried away, yelling orders to the other pirates. Bingham continued pulling the men out of the nun's cells while they held on to their screaming prizes. Seymore's men pulled the women away, pushing the women into a group near the entrance to the hall. Seymore order more of his armed men to inspect the various rooms the area.

Blackbane continued the hallway, bellowing orders to the men along the way. Seymore followed along after ordering several sailors to escort the female prisoners toward the entrance. As he came alongside the captain, he saw other men rummaging through the nun's cells. They came out with silver crosses and other religious trinkets found inside.

"It's a meager haul," Seymore complained when he saw the items.

"It's the room I want, damn it. That monk placed his hand upon that damn bible, swearing there was a room of gold." The captain glanced inside a nearby room. He went back and forth, searching for doors to open.

Earlier, the few monks captured by Blackbane and his men swore they harbored no gold inside the monastery's walls.

However, a lay brother who witnessed the torture of the monks told the captain about a room of golden crosses inside the convent. Blackbane forced the man to lead them to Santa Clara. When they reached the convent, the lay brother confessed he didn't know the exact location inside the walls; Blackbane cut the man's throat in rage.

The pirate captain came to the end of the hallway. With a growl, he opened two doors on either side. Inside the second door, he found a crewman raping a nun. The pirate held the pleading woman's ankles as he savagely thrust into her.

Blackbane kicked the bed with his boot.

"You there, get off the wench. I gave you an order to find that gold room!" The captain bellowed.

"When I finish," the drunken naked man growled back.

Blackbane dropped his tankard and immediately struck the man across his naked butt with the flat side of his sword. With a savage roar, he grabbed the crewman by his long greasy hair and pulled him from the woman. As he beat the sailor with the pommel of his sword, blood splattered across the nun. When the wounded man fell unconscious to the floor, the captain stood and pointed his razor-sharp sword blade at his victim's neck. The second mate recognized the danger when he walked by.

"He's a freeman and voted you captain," Seymore yelled out while more pirates gathered around the cell to stare inside.

They watched with bated breath while Blackbane paused. Then he glared at his second mate.

"Seymore, get this man out of her. Tell this rotten crew that I'll flay the next man alive who fails my orders," the captain loudly declared. Still fuming, he pushed through the entrance to the room.

The man looked over at the men watching him.

"Now, get this rabble moving!" He yelled.

"Bear down, men. The women go to the ship, or they're be a cat-o-nine bearing on your back," Seymore bellowed out. Then he smacked the closest pirate with the broadside of his sword blade to emphasize the point.

The second ordered another crewman to take his unconscious crewmate back to the ship. He sullenly grabbed the half-naked nun from the crew, sending her down the hallway to join the others huddled near the entrance.

Blackbane returned after opening another nearby door. He recognized that he'd spoiled his crew's expected entertainment. It was a position that he needed to address or risk losing his position. Pirates were a temperamental group who required diversions.

"Damn ye maggots who forgot our prize! I want that gold room found before sunrise. By Brendan the Navigator's heart, I'll give a chest of silver *reales* to the man who finds the treasure," Blackbane roared out to the surrounding men.

The effect was immediate on the sullen pirates. They roared with approval before they scattered like cockroaches. Blackbane's frown lifted a bit as he walked back to the huddled group of nuns. He waved his second mate over.

"Take the women to the ship," the captain ordered Seymore. "Remind the watch not to molest the young ones, or I'll have their hide. They're worth a lot of silver to the crew. The men can have the old ones for their Fiddler's Green."

Seymore laughed at the thought.

"Aye, captain, they'll think even the old ones are paradise after so long at sea. I'll make sure they treat our cargo well."

"Best take them with your trusted men and be off with you," Blackbane said. He waited, watching until his valuable prisoners were on their way to the *Diano Marina*.

Blackbane turned and walked through the hallway, where he found another passageway leading past a series of opened doors. He followed the trail of destruction left by pirates as they entered the rooms. As he walked past the open doors, the bearded man glanced in to ensure no one was inside.

He heard a couple of pirates cursing at the end of a nearby corridor, and the captain went to investigate. Two men stood by a closed door. The thick wood remained impervious to the pirate's attempts to shoulder the door open. Finally, one man started hacking at the handle with a boarding ax. With growing anticipation, Blackbane stood behind them as he watched their toil.

As the door handle finally splintered apart, Blackbane took the lead and pushed through the doorway. He nearly ran over a small, fearless woman who stood in his path. The convent's abbess had several terrified nuns standing behind her.

"You swine," she savagely told the captain in Portuguese. "This is a holy order, protected by God. He'll punish your blasphemy while the Duke of Gandía hunts you down and rips out your black heart for this insult."

She saw the captain's brown eyes turn cold while he returned a merciless laugh.

"A black heart, you say?" he inquired in her language, then shook his head. "No, you have the name wrong, woman. I'm known as Blackbane."

He enjoyed how her eyes widen in fear at his name.

"I see you've heard of me. I'm honored the Christians on this coast know of my conquests. Now, join the other captives. You'll have a long voyage come dawn."

"Blackbane, I've heard you rape, kill, or enslave Christians for your Muslim masters. You have no honor, and I most certainly don't fear you," she said spitefully.

"You're wrong, old lady! I also rape, kill, or enslave Muslims if the price is right." he looked her over with an ugly smile. "I have no religion. Gold is my crown, and I take crosses of silver for my coins."

He backhanded her. The woman fell back.

"Where is the room of gold in this place?" he exploded.

The woman shook off the help offered by the nuns. She stepped up in front of the larger man.

"You don't scare me, Blackbane. God protects me!"

"He won't protect you from my wrath if you don't tell me where the location of the Gold Room is. I'll leave you alive to sell on the slave market. You might not bring much, but it beats what I'll do otherwise...."

He slapped her. The blow brought a trickle of blood to the corner of her mouth.

Her eyes stared back in defiance. With a scowl at her resistance, the man pointed his sword blade at her chest. Then he looked past her at the nuns with an evil grin.

"You have grit, sister. But are you willing to have your nuns tortured to make you talk?"

The expression on the woman's face softened. Then, the abbess grabbed the blade of his sword. In a flash, she stepped into the karabela's razor-sharp point. The mother superior's blood spurted across the pirate captain before she fell to the floor in a heap.

Gasps and screams came from the nuns who kneeled beside her, praying as she died. A pirate who stood next to his captain crossed himself as a few more men investigated the commotion they heard in the hall.

"You can worry about God on your time," Blackbane quickly gathered himself as he jeered the crewman standing by him. The captain grabbed the closest nun by the collar of her simple bed dress. He pointed his bloody sword at her neck.

"Alright, my sweet virgin, I'll run you through unless you tell me the location of the Gold Room!"

Her big brown eyes widened at the threat, and she recited the Lord's Prayer in Spanish.

Blackbane's fist struck her across the cheek, and she stumbled backward. Blackbane pushed the woman down, forcing her into a crouched position.

"Last warning, wench!" he stated with a menacing growl.

Again, the woman prayed with her head bowed down. With a yell of tormented frustration, Blackbane's sword blade sliced down on the woman's neck. Her head tumbled several feet away.

The captain turned to the next nun.

~~~

As the sun rose in the east, the morning screech of gulls remained unusually quiet. The weather was fair, and a fresh breeze swept in from the ocean. Captain Blackbane paced along the rampart at the top of the convent wall, which overlooked the town of Faro. Covered in blood and gore, the man still carried an inner fury. Despite the torture and deaths of the women, he failed to discover the Gold Room. The rising sun informed him he was out of time. He must return to his ship with nothing to show for the expedition beyond a few barrels of wine and the surviving nuns as slaves. The haul of slaves would bring some silver for him and the crew. However, it wasn't enough.

It would not be enough to satisfy that greedy bastard, Hamidu!

Blackbane convinced the Muslim corsair fleet leader to join him on this invasion of the Portuguese coast. Promises of great riches persuaded Hamidu to bring along his ships. Blackbane recognized his precarious position in the adventure. Hamidu
~~~

would use this failure against him when they returned to Tunis. Both men were under the control of the Beylik, a Muslim who remained wary of the pirate from America. Hamidu was a Turk like the Beylik who made no pretense of his feelings about Blackbane and his men. He hated non-believers. A wrong move would mean the downfall of the captain and his men. As Blackbane wrestled with his limited options, he barely noticed two men passing on the road leading to the convent.

Bingham hurried back to the convent with a message for his captain. A pirate quickly saluted Bingham as he passed by the first mate. Bingham growled, impatiently telling the man to get back to the ship.

Probably scavenging inside for anything his crewmates missed!

The first mate turned his thoughts back to the crew of misfits and outcasts. He held the suspicion that many of the men had no loyalty to their captain. Bingham believed Hamidu made promises that led to unrest among the crew. Since the *Diano Marina* arrived at Tunis, the Turk sent replacements from Hamidu's captured ships. Bingham warned Blackbane that the new men held their loyalty to the Muslim corsair. However, the captain reminded his first mate that there was little he could do. The ship always needed men to replace those killed or who left after successful raids along the coast of Corsica the year before. After all, any buccaneer could leave the ship with their share of a prize as a freeman. Some even stayed in Tunis to become merchants or slave traders.

Arriving at the entrance to the convent, Bingham noticed Captain Blackbane staring out at the ocean from the ramparts. The first mate called out in Arabic from the ground below.

"We need to return to the Diano Marina. Hamidu signals for us to rejoin his fleet. I have the ship ready for sailing. What are your orders?"

Bingham's voice broke through his captain's thoughts. Blackbane took a deep breath and nodded.

"Aye, I'll be coming back aboard. Wait for me at the jolly boat."

The captain went to the stairs, deciding to take one last journey through the silent convent. Entering the long, quiet hall, he passed a line of open cells with bedding and clothing strewn into the passage.

Still deep in thought, Blackbane almost missed the quiet groan and the creak of a wood he heard inside a room. He stopped, placing his hand on the hilt of his karabela. A deathly silence covered the area as he stealthily slid along the wall to the entrance of a room. Carefully, Blackbane went to the doorway. Glancing inside, he saw a chair and a simple table with a single candle. Then he noticed a foot move from behind the overturned bed. With practiced precision, he pulled his sword from the scabbard and rushed into the room. He went to the foot of the bed and saw a partially naked figure covered in blood on the floor. Blackbane reached down as the plump woman curled up in a fetal position. She begged for mercy.

"Get up, wench," he told her brutally. He grabbed her by her long auburn hair. "You'll serve a new master now."

Blackbane brutally pulled her to her feet. She screamed in agony, falling against the wall while desperately holding back the blood from her wound.

"Too bad you're already dead. He sliced through your liver," Blackbane coldly looked her over.

With a frown, he released her while cursing the pirate, who lost him a fair bit of gold. She stared at him for a moment; her round face twisted in a mix of terror and agony.

"Know the name of the man who raped and killed you?" he asked her. "I'll have him flogged for this. You would bring a fair price in Tunis."

"Have mercy, captain. I beg you. Don't let me die without the *viaticum*. Send for a priest to help me go to God," she pleaded.

"It's too late for that," the big man said grimly. "It wouldn't matter, anyway; damnation is your destination, just like the rest of us."

Blackbane turned away. The nun suddenly yelled at him while reaching for him. Instinctively, the captain caught her body. His reaction knocked his sword from his hand. Still holding her, he kneeled with her as she slid to the floor.

When the captain tried to rise, her bloody hands suddenly reached up and grabbed him by his coat lapels. With unbelievable strength, she pulled him close. Despite the man's struggle to force her away, the woman's face drew close. Blackbane stared into her eyes. Their unnatural glimmer revealed a resigned madness.

"Captain Blackbane, you will carry your foul sins for eternity," the nun whispered in a deathly voice that chilled him.

Again, the captain tried to push her away, a frantic feeling coming over him.

Still, she held on!

Despite the struggle, the woman used her index finger to trace a bloody symbol on his neck.

"Damn you, let go of me," he growled out as the panic grew inside of him.

With a death gasp, the woman released him, and her body fell limply to the floor. Blackbane staggered back to the corner of the room, falling into the wall. A searing pain shot through him from the spot where the nun touched his throat. The fire-like agony covered his upper body like a blanket, enveloping him in an overwhelming sense of being roasted alive. Blackbane pitched forward while he desperately grabbed at his neck with both hands. He rolled back and forth, moaning and groaning, while his body trembled uncontrollably from the scorching anguish. It seemed like hours before the agony slowly faded away. Sweat covered the captain when he finally regained his awareness.

Lying on the stone floor next to the dead woman, he rolled away from the body. Staring into the room's corner, a glint deep in the darkness of a square opening caught his eye. At first, he did not comprehend what he was looking at. Then he realized.

That's where she was trying to escape!

Barely large enough for a person to slide through, the dark square entrance revealed a shimmering flicker coming from the blackness inside. Slowly, Blackbane realized the nun must have heard him, and she was trying to hide. The sound of her opening the panel caught his attention.

Drained by the pain earlier, Blackbane slowly crawled closer.

A wooden panel lay across the floor in front of him. It hid the opening from those searching the room. Then, he recognized a faint light in the darkness, deep inside the entrance.

A candle! What in blazes is in there?

The captain picked up his sword and pushed the blade past the entrance. He could hear the scraping of the steel across the stone, and his eyes beheld a single candle at the other end of a cut stone pathway.

A hidden passageway!

No longer feeling the pain in his neck, Blackbane became entranced by the hidden passage. Scrambling through the opening, he came into a tunnel that opened up above him. He lifted himself into a crouch. The flickering candle ahead of him showed the low, vaulted ceiling of cut stones. His bearded face grimly smiled as he moved toward the candle. Reaching the end of the passage, he found steps leading down into the darkness. The captain picked up the candle, then paused.

If the nun was trying to get in here, who lit this and left it?

A shiver ran through him, but his face twisted into a deadly expression. He saw a door at the bottom of the steps.

"Someone is in for a surprise!" He thought.

Blackbane quietly followed the steps until he reached the entrance. He pulled back on the rusted handle. However, the door didn't budge. With a firm tug, the door finally gave way with a nerve-racking squeal as the rusty hinges opened.

Inching forward with the candle held out in front of him, Blackbane noticed dark shadows in the room. Then he saw something gleaming gold. Licking his lips at the thought, he stepped forward. However, the first wood step gave way, and the man fell into the murky room.

Landing on a stone floor, Blackbane grabbed his knee in pain while he heard his sword clatter across the rock several feet away. After a couple of deep breaths, the man looked around. The candle remained lit on its side next to him. A dimly lit outline of a statue came into view as the man picked up his light. He slowly rose and stared at the face of the archangel Remiel who scowled down at him.

Blackbane knew his bible well enough to recognize the angel was a fallen Watcher and one that God who led those that rose from the dead when Judgement Day arrived. The stone statue's fine detail showed him a muscular figure with wings that appeared lifelike. Dressed in armor, the angel held a sword in one hand and a staff in the other. The staff had a crystal orb at the top that looked like an eye for a moment. The eerie sensation of being watched in the flickering light caused the hairs on the back of Blackbane's neck to rise.

"Another statue to scare the children," he scoffed. "Old Captain Hornigold told me about your fairy tales."

As he looked around, he saw more statues of the archangels. Michael, Raphael, Gabriel, Uriel, Saraqael, and Raguel were standing on pedestals in a circle around him. Each angel held a weapon in their hand, and their forms had the same level of lifelike details. On the opposite side of the entrance, he briefly noticed the door to a tunnel. It explained how the statues got into the room.

However, a large object in the middle of the circle captured his attention. Covered with a dry-rotted tarp, a shimmer of golden color came through the decaying holes. Blackbane reached out a hand, then drew away at the sudden intense pain in his neck again. Still, the greed inside him won out. He tugged at the tarp, and it fell away.

Blackbane stepped back in silent awe. A giant golden cross stood over him. Elaborately engraved with Greek and Roman letters, it beckoned to Blackbane. His heart raced as he considered the treasure. There was enough gold on the cross to pay for a fleet of ships and more pirate crew.

I can create my barony somewhere!

Blackbane stared at the treasure before him. He stepped closer, blinking his eyes to ensure that the golden cross was not a mirage. The man reached out and touched the cross. He felt the cold metal as he slowly slid his fingers across the beam. Again, the fire in his neck increased, and Blackbane slowly retreated.

As he admired his find, the pirate did not hear the soft sounds behind him.

The statue of Remiel moved. Barely perceptible at first, the hard stone slowly transformed, rippling as the figure's flesh became flexible. The angel quietly took a step off its podium. Remiel walked closer to the pirate captain until he was just behind the man. The angel cocked his head as he observed Blackbane staring transfixed at the golden cross.

A moment later, the captain felt the agony of a sword blade entering his back. He looked down to see the silver blade sticking out of his belly. Blackbane fell to his knees, grabbing the cross while he slid to the floor. The captain clutched his stomach before falling to the floor. He rolled to his side in agony. He glanced at his shaking hands, but there was no blood on them. Still, the intense fire in his belly remained, along with the dizziness that filled his brain. He frantically opened his vest and ripped his shirt to expose his abdomen. There was no wound.

"How can I be dying?" he wondered aloud.

The figure of Remiel stepped next to Blackbane. He rolled the dying man over on his back using his foot. The angel's skin carried the alabaster color of the stone in the room while his face held no emotion. Remiel placed the staff, holding the eye directly in the center of Blackbane's chest.

"The man called William Marshall is dying. Your soul is damned, and your earthly body dies at the stroke of my sword."

The angel's eyes gleamed with a blazing blue-white fire.

"You've done a terrible evil against the chaste and righteous in this world. You will suffer eternal punishment. I'll let you covet this gold cross with your dying breath before I give you to the legions of Hell."

Blackbane stared up at Remiel. Then, to the surprise of the angel, the man let out a foul laugh. His voice crackled with bitterness.

"You think I'm afraid of Hell. Since my whore mother cast me into the street, I know how worthless a soul is," the dying man spat out viciously. He laughed again, then groaned as he grabbed the staff. Blackbane tried to push it away, but he didn't have the strength.

"You say that we're built in the image of God. That means everyone is a bastard for hellfire, just like me."

Remiel looked at the unrepentant human at his feet; his eyes raged with fury. The angel kicked Blackbane. The man painfully rolled away with a groan.

"Blackbane sides with the demons who recognize people are nothing more than foul vermin," the captain cried out with an agonized glee.

"Tis my happiness to see a Watcher bellowing at me. I state my case that the devil knows my black heart comes from watching self-rightcous jesters like you. I only regret not living long enough to kill and rape more. Give me that sword, and I'd happily cut down you damned messengers of God."

His lungs heaved as he gasped for the air to cough out a laugh.

Perturbed, the angel turned away. He paced back and forth. Remiel kept glancing over at the captain.

Blackbane attempted to lift himself, then fell back to the floor. He smiled with confidence at thwarting the angel who killed him.

"You son of a bitch, I fear nothing. I'll die, but I'll never cower before you wretched kneelers to a petty god of nothing." The captain smugly sighed as he felt death creep through his body.

The angel stopped his pacing at the foot of Michael's statue.

"He believes he knows much about pain and suffering. Perhaps God should reveal a bitter truth to his black heart?" After a pause, the angel nodded in agreement with the inanimate stone figure. He turned to the pirate with a foul smile.

"Mortal called Blackbane. This will not end as you foresee," Remiel said. "God has another plan for you. The merciful Lord sends you on a different path, a destiny filled with torment far beyond what you can even comprehend."

"Let's get this over with," the dying man coughed out. "Just send me to hell, so I don't have to listen to your babbling nonsense."

Blackbane let his head fall back on the hard stone. He was ready to meet the devil and give him an earful.

"Ignorant fool, you don't understand," the angel gloated. "You believe you know your fate. However, you're in for a rude surprise. In your lust for wealth and envy for power, you believe that having an inherently evil soul would achieve your goal. That is never the case. Every mortal carries a soul of grace. Now, you will learn the lessons of eternal salvation through a trial."

Remiel's hideous smile widened.

"Your earthly body will not perish on this morning."

Blackbane felt his muscles surge at the news. He looked over at Remiel with disbelief filling his face. The statue came back and kneeled by the man. The foul grin remained.

"Instead of death, you will now live as an immortal creature," the angel said. "God cursed you. But your lust for treasure will condemn you to seek treasure for Him alone. Only then can you find salvation."

"What the hell are you talking about?" Blackbane flexed his arms and eased his legs along the ground.

"You claim that I'm condemned? Next you're telling me I've got a pardon. Such righteous fools!"

He raised himself to his elbows. The area on his neck where the nun touched him still burned like fire. However, he no longer felt the suffocating lack of air in his lungs. Energy surged into his body.

He's letting me live. God is such a fool!

"The Lord is not the fool, William Marshall. You are!" Remiel exploded. "No, you don't have a pardon. You have something suitable for your bitter soul. I told you that you're cursed."

"Hell, I've been cursed from the start! God is a jester if he thinks I care about nonsense like that," the man sneered. "No wonder the devil wins all the time."

The angel backhanded the pirate.

"You have read the scriptures," Remiel reminded him. "I bring about divine visions. I foresee a future of unbearable violence and blood for William Marshall as he wonders the earth."

"You are no longer the hunter; instead, others will hunt you. Every corner where you turn will lead only to cruelty, heartbreak, and suffering for you. This is the curse of Blackbane."

"Hardly a burden," Blackbane stated confidently. "I'm still determining my fate."

"You believe so?" Remiel cocked his head as he stood.

"Your newfound immortality brings more sorrow than you can imagine. The immortality inside of you carries an energy that all demons seek. Soon, the seven deadliest demons will hunt you. The energy inside your essence will give them something they cherish. An ability to create more creatures of the night to plague mankind."

Remiel reached down and grabbed Blackbane by the collar of his coat. He picked the man up effortlessly with one arm and then poked his finger into the captain's neck. Blackbane instantly screamed out in pain. His body shuddered and convulsed while he hung in the air.

"You believe you carry no conscience. But from this day forward, you learn that your past forever haunts you. The dead will return to madden you. There is no refuge from your continuous nightmare. It is the burden you will carry until Judgement Day."

"But I'm working for God now. You said so," the man replied with disdain. "I could suddenly get religion."

"God condemned you to live until doomsday," Remiel sneered and dropped Marshall, who fell to his knees.

"Apparently, you're not intelligent enough to realize your plight. God just placed your soul between good and evil. He left you with no entry into heaven or hell. Should you give yourself up to the demons, they will rip you apart for the immortality inside of your body. Your body becomes a vessel for them to use as they please. You've seen what a spider does to a fly. That is your existence when you give yourself to one of the seven."

He smiled at the thought.

"Think about it! Conscious and aware of everything these many foul creatures do and think, yet your very soul remains part of those creatures. Your living soul will intertwine with every demon that suckles upon your immortal energy. It's such a fitting end to your existence, William Marshall."

Blackbane didn't like the way Remiel laughed at him before he walked back to the pedestal.

"Wait! You said my immorality brings demons to plague man. How can an angel do this?"

The angel stepped onto the platform and turned to address to the prone man.

"You can't get to heaven either," he ignored the question. "A few Hail Marys will not cleanse your soul. I cannot foresee that you will never purge your foul spirit, given your lust for the unattainable. Blackbane is but a ghost, fleeing creatures that want to consume them. You search for golden items that you will never keep."

Remiel's form slowly took the same position as a statue.

"The only way you get out of this curse is live until Judgement Day. You do that, and maybe God will find you a place in his kingdom." He paused and grinned at the captain.

"I wouldn't hold my breath."

With a snap of the angel's fingers, the room temperature plummeted. Dark shadows rose from the floor. The shades slowly morphed into figures of men and women, their pale faces indistinct at first. After a moment, the specters closed around the pirate captain. Instantly, he recognized them. He was looking into the faces of those people he killed.

Ghosts aren't real, just figments of my mind.

Nevertheless, Blackbane rose and slowly backed away. He hurried toward the door. Then, the beautiful face of Emma Watson pulled in front of him. The ghastly specter hovered in front of him.

No!

It was the spirit of his first love and his first murder. Her face transformed into a grinning skull. Her spectral form rushed into his body, overwhelming him with an icy chill that enveloped his insides. The frost painfully burned his belly while his lungs felt heavy. It was the agonizing sensation of falling into a vat of ice water.

This is your baptism!

Blackbane wasn't sure if it was his voice that he heard in his head. Suddenly, the black-hearted scourge of the high seas remembered the night of his first coldly calculated killing. Replaying each moment, he witnessed and felt everything as the victim of the murder. Over the next hour, he endured the entirety of Emma's tragic experiences. His body and mind endured the savage rape, followed by the agonizing death by strangulation. Blackbane tried to scream as his face turned blue. Eventually, he died only to be reborn when the woman's phantom finished with him.

Gasping for breath, Blackbane lay on the floor. He noticed the other specters watching him. He frantically crawled across the ground. A hovering figure of a boy cut off the captain's desperate escape. He Blackbane did not remember the face.

"You killed me for a shilling on the docks of Jamaica," a youthful voice reminded him.

The specter shot inside of Blackbane, and his body trembled with pain. Then, the man witnessed his escapes in the dark alley near the docks. A drunken captain demanded the child's last shilling. After he listened to the young boy's refusal, Blackbane felt the crushing pain of his arm as his shadowed grabbed him.

Then, an instant later, he looked down at the blood spreading across his belly as the shadow released him and walked away with a shilling in his hand. Blackbane held on to his stomach while he dropped into the filthy muck. The pirate experienced all the agony of the boy's death, while nearby sailors walked on, drunk and unfeeling.

The line of souls who died at the hands of Blackbane continued their slow march of vengeance and justice. Each entered his mind and body to force the arrogant one to suffer the terrible death they bore. An eternity later, the mother superior of the abbey stood in front of the curled-up pirate. No longer the ruthless pirate captain; instead, Blackbane was a man in tears and verging on madness. He begged and pleaded with the last phantom to end his life. The woman smiled, then entered his body for his next dreadful lesson.

~~~

Several weeks later, inside his stinking cell, Blackbane added another roach to his small meal. With no money and nearly all of his silver buttons gone, the former captain of the *Diano Marina* could no longer bribe the guards. Instead, he resorted to capturing whatever crawled or scurried inside his six-by-six stone room. His daily existence composed of waking to hunger and thirst while hoping his weekly ration of stale bread and foul water would arrive. Days no longer meant anything to the condemned man except the vain hope that the executioner would come.

Otherwise, Blackbane sat on the dirty stone floor of a cell buried deep inside a fortress between the sea and the lagoon of Tunis. He tried to think of a way out of his prison. The prisoner also tried to avoid sleep. As promised by Remiel, sleep only brought the reoccurring visits from his ghosts.

The men of the *Diano Marina* found Blackbane wandering the beach that morning during their search. Their captain was on his knees in the sand, bitterly crying for revenge and vengeance as he stared up into the heavens. Blackbane shouted curses at God, barely making sense. He ranted about archangels and immortality as they forced him into the boat.

Hamidu was already waiting aboard the *Diano Marina* and ordered Blackbane thrown into chains for the return trip to Tunis. When the ships arrived in port, Hamidu sent Blackbane to the court of the Beylik of Tunis.

A fat man with a long white beard and a dozen wives, the Beylik controlled most of the tribes and cities in the area.
~~~

Despite several years of successful raids that brought a fortune of gold, silver, and slaves to his lands, the ruler gave no sympathy to Blackbane. While he stood in chains before the ruler of Tunis, the Beylik condemned the former captain as an apostate. The Beylik decided Blackbane's insanity came from many lies told about the whereabouts of the gold cross in the convent. Several crewmembers of *Diano Marina* went before the court to agree with Hamidu's charges.

His mind still rattled from his experiences, Blackbane barely paid attention to the words. After the Beylik accepted Hamidu's offer of two young nuns for his harem, the ruler sent the condemned captain away.

"Be grateful that you will die from the blade of an ax when I command it," the Beyik told Blackbane with feigned sympathy. "To die behind the oar as a galley slave is not worthy of a fighter like you."

"Peki, ya siz ya da Tanrı sonuçtan şaşıracaksınız! Gördüğüm laneti hissedebiliyor musun?" Blackbane gave the ruler an excited grin when he replied in the man's language.

The outcome will surprise you or God! Can you feel the curse I know?

His hysterical laughing caused the Beyik and Hamidu to glance at each other. The looks sent Blackbane into another fit of mocking hilarity while the guards removed him from the building.

Blackbane rested his arms between the bars of his cell while he awaited his execution. Slowly, he believed in his madness. In a small way, he decided the ax would convince him of his immortality, once and for all. Then, he grew confident that everything he experienced inside the convent came from his lunacy. Even the scar on his neck was nothing but an illusion.

"Captain, I've caught a rat. I'll be eating like the Beylik today," Bingham's voice interrupted Blackbane's thoughts.

"You're a lucky dog," the man agreed gruffly in English as he shifted his uncomfortable stance.

Using their native language made it next to impossible for the guards to eavesdrop on the conversations. Because of Bingham's continued loyalty to Blackbane, the first mate ended up in the cell next to his captain.

Blackbane remained distracted as he focused on the idea of escape. The time inside the cell gave him plenty of time to think. He overheard news of war in the Baltic Sea from the guards, who relieved their boredom by spreading the latest rumors among themselves. To the pirate, the story was a godsend. Where there was war, there was an opportunity for treasure.

To hell with Remiel and his curse.

Over the days, the captain survived the maddening encounters with the phantoms of his victims. He made it through each night despite their haunting of him. The sea called him, and Blackbane needed to escape.

"I'll get what I want, then I'll tell both heaven and hell they can kiss my pratts," he said. "That damned fat Turk will never get my head!"

Blackbane openly talked to himself at times since his capture. He smiled as well to go along with his madness.

"I might help you keep your head," a sultry voice spoke from behind Blackbane.

Whipping around, he found a woman inside his cell. She stood in the corner, her bluish face slightly luminous among the dark shadows. Dressed in a long black robe, she pulled back her hood to reveal white hair, which dropped across her shoulders. Her thin face and expressive dark eyes held a stern expression, yet there appeared to be an underlying innocent sexiness to the woman.

"And who are you?" The man suddenly remembered the words of Remiel. He glanced at the bars on his cell. They remained solid, and a chill filled him.

"You may call me Naamah," she breathed. "I come to offer you a way out of your death."

"Captain, who is over there?" Bingham's voice crept into the cell. Blackbane told him to be quiet.

"Naamah is not a name, I know. Somehow, you crept into my cell. What is your purpose?" The man inquired.

Despite her attractive look, the woman's underlying darkness filled the room. She pouted at his question, but her eyes watched him like prey.

"I thought that was clear. You may escape with my help," Naamah told him as she silently stepped closer to him. She sniffed the foul air. "I smell your lust for me. It mixes with your fear."

"I fear nothing, wench. You will learn the smell of my hate for those who come to me with lies. You are the first demon to come to me unless my shattered mind deceives me," he said. "State your terms or leave me to find out whether I starve or lose my head."

The pout crossed her face again, and she drew closer.

She responded with a smooth voice, "I'm not really a demon, whatever you may think. I'm a lost soul like you. I bore the children of an archangel in an agreement. In a way, I'm condemned as you are."

"It is a sad tale, I'm sure. But I trust wandering souls even less than demons at the moment." Blackbane tried to remain in control of the conversation. He suspected something sinister lay behind the woman's demeanor.

"Yes, you enjoy what you see, but you correctly know there's a need to be cautious," Naamah told the surprised captain. "That's right; I have some ability to peer into your thoughts."

"Woman, tell me who your master is? I feel another presence behind you." Blackbane glanced over at the solid bars, vainly hoping to see an escape path.

"I have no master," she told him hotly. Then, her behavior turned innocent again.

"I heard of your plight from Asmodeus. He told me of your immortality, but he believes Remiel has laid a trap. Now, he bides his time, for he doesn't believe you will survive the ax," she explained. "Should you survive the execution, then he will come and remove your soul. Asmodeus is most unpleasant when he discovers he is wrong."

"Alright, that only tells me that Asmodeus must be your master," Blackbane observed sourly. "You have something else in mind. Get to the point, woman!"

"I stand before you for my reasons. Now, do you want to escape or not?"

"What makes you think I won't risk my head? Hell, I'm immortal. The damn ax will break," he told her with certainty. "Like your master, you want something with my soul. Otherwise, you would not come to me."

"I don't care about your soul," she told him with a sly smile while she slid next to him. Despite his wariness, Blackbane could not pull away.

"I have a question for you. Does the great Blackbane risk death on someone's word? Who is to say that Remiel was honest with you? Faith requires your complete submission to the will of God," she reminded him.

"Do you have such faith?"

She whispered the question, and he felt her hot breath on his earlobe. The temptress brushed her hand along his back.

"I'm not afraid of an ax," Blackbane declared. "Death takes me to hell. It is my path since I left Boston as a ship's boy. I need a reason for you to help me."

She smiled mysteriously. The clean air of a salty ocean breeze came to his nostrils.

"With the right help, you can live until judgment day. Isn't that what you seek? With me at your side, you can become like Samael," she said. "In return, I only require your seed. Your offspring is what I seek. It is the same exchange that Samael gave me."

Blackbane frowned, wishing he knew more about the stories from the Bible. He suddenly thought of stories about the djinn. The supernatural creatures were deceitful, offering hidden dangers.

"I don't trust you. Your request seems too small of a price to pay for your help. You are hiding something from me," he said.

"This is true," she stated. "But my secrets remain with me. Now, you have little time to decide. It will be the ax or my offer. Otherwise, you can bargain with the executioner who comes for you."

He scowled at her while he considered the idea. Blackbane knew he dared to die for treasure. He had the blood of many men stained on his hands to prove that. But relying on faith in God's word was something never really considered. Yes, the ghosts filled his nightly dreams. Somehow, he learned to handle their disturbing nightmares. And it was an angel who claimed the immortality that Blackbane held. In the end, Blackbane recognized he carried no convictions beyond his destination after death.

Do I really believe that I'm immortal in the word of an angel?

"Do we have a deal? You hear boots coming down the steps," the woman pressed him. "Are they coming for you?"

A split second later, a procession of men entered the narrow passage at the far end of the dungeon. Blackbane turned and pressed his face against the iron bars. He saw the small group of guards as they walked toward his cell. His mind raced for a decision. Finally, he relented.

"I'll take your deal, but only if Bingham comes with me," he hastily told the woman.

She smiled and took his hand.

Mating with a demon sounded better than dying, he thought, as the symbol on Blackbane's neck turned red. The burning pain in his neck grew intense. He tried to disregard the sensation.

"Follow me," she said as she led him to the stone wall. The woman walked right through the cut stone. Blackbane hesitated, then he felt her firm grip pull him forward. His eyes widened as he watched his hand disappear through the rock wall. In the blink of an eye later, Naamah and Blackbane were standing in the dungeon cell of Bingham.

Immediately, Bingham suppressed a cry while he pushed his back against the bars in terror. With his blue vest halfway over his arm, the first mate kept glancing back and forth at his captain and the woman.

"I'll explain later," Blackbane told his friend, then turned to the woman as the footsteps drew closer.

"Now what?"

Naamah sighed and grabbed both men by their arms. She pulled them with her as she walked to the inside wall of the dungeon. An instant later, the trio stood inside a dark storage room on the other side of the prisoner's cells.

"They'll have quite a time trying to understand how you escaped," she boasted. "No doubt, a few heads will roll when the Beyik doesn't like their answers."

"She's a witch!"

His long and dirty red hair partially hid the terrified first mate's round face. Bingham finally scrambled away to the other side of a barrel. However, Naamah remained between him and the door.

"He looks like a cornered baboon," Naamah groaned.

"Calm down, you damn fool. She's not a witch, and she's on our side," Blackbane said.

He glanced at her before looking back at his friend.

"Well, that's for the moment, at least. Bingham, get yourself together," Marshall commanded.

"What kind of sorcery do you call that?" The first mate's shaky voice grew high-pitched while he still sought a way to leave.

"I have power much older and more powerful than a witch," Naamah scoffed as she watched the terrified man back to the wall. "Why is he coming along? He is mortal and stinks of fear."

"Because he's loyal to me and part of the bargain," Blackbane growled back. "Enough of this bickering. We need to leave this fort and get to a ship."

The room went silent at the question as the captain looked at his companions. He rubbed his neck, feeling the scar. It remained warm to his touch.

"We have the sea on one side. I can't take you through the walls and end up in seawater," the woman told them. "We'll need to go through the main gate."

"We might just get that ax yet," Blackbane told them. "Let's find out where the door leads. Come along, my loyal friend. Let's find whether or not I'm insane!"

The Curse of Blackbane

~~~

It was dusk before the trio finally escaped from the fortress. With some coaxing, Blackbane got Bingham to join him. The two men found white robes hanging near a courtyard, which they stole and put over their clothes. They also cut away parts of another garment to fashion crude-looking turbans. The effort made them appear less conspicuous as they made their way down the passage to the gate. When they reached the entrance into the fort, the two men caught sight of guards. Quickly, the trio crouched behind the corner of the wall.

"Just be quiet," Naamah confidently told them before she rose and walked toward the two guards in their colorful, bellowing uniforms. As she drew close, they appeared uncertain about the woman in the strange attire. They made the mistake of letting Naamah come too close. Instantly, her long arms transformed into nebulous, smokey tentacles, which lifted the men from the ground. The guards grabbed for their throats as the nearly invisible strands of her shadow wrapped tightly around their throats. By the time Blackbane got to the gate; both guards were dead. Naahah's ghostly tentacles faded away. The dead men, with their tongues hanging out of open mouths, flopped to the ground

"Christ protect us," Bingham said as he automatically crossed himself. Naamah gave him an evil glare.

"Get their weapons," Blackbane ordered the first mate. He carefully approached Naamah.

"Your secrets appear in your powers as well, demon woman. Is my fate to look like these men when you finish with me?"

The question caused her to pause.

"I assume you are stronger and smarter than such pawns," she replied, as her face displayed the innocence of a young child. "I'll do far worse to you if you forget our agreement."
~~~

The woman in black turned away, swiftly walking away. Bingham stepped next to his captain and handed him a guard's belt that held a sword encased in a leather sheath.

"Captain, you've made a deal with the devil," the first mate told him under his breath. "I didn't realize you were in earnest when I overheard your conversations with her back in the cell."

"Aye, you thought me still mad. Well, everything you've heard and seen is true. There's no turning back now. Let's move!"

After they slowly closed on Naamah, the pirate leaned closer to his friend.

"It appears I'll need to learn the ways of demons quickly if I'm to survive what's coming," Blackbane whispered.

"I'm more worried about those mortals around you," Bingham quietly observed. His tone was even, but Blackbane understood his anxiety.

"I have no words of comfort, my loyal friend. I've followed a path to hell. You knew that, as well. A buccaneer searches for riches and often finds the hangman's noose. Yet you remained trustworthy even to the point of death. I would not betray you with a lie now."

Blackbane paused, debating how much to explain.

"As I've rotted in that cell, I've tried to discover another path. But my soul is too black for redemption. You've seen how demons will call me out. I have only enraging dreams, which tells me nothing. You would do well to follow another captain."

The two men went silent at the thought. Their footsteps on the hard-packed ground, along with their winded breathing, overwhelmed the distant rush of the nearby surf. The dark form of Naamah remained ahead of them. Both men glanced at each other at the lack of sound coming from the woman's footsteps. However, her pace forced them to increase their speed.

"I know you as William Marshall," Bingham finally spoke. "You remember when I joined the *Ranger*? I don't forget it was you who kept that damned Black Sam Bellamy from stringing my neck from the yardarm. While you're not fit to enter a church, you've always shown loyalty to those that follow your orders. I'll walk the path to hell or worse with you."

Blackbane nodded.

"Bingham, you're a good man. However, I'm afraid that's the path we have no option but to follow. We're dealing with creatures that carry hearts blacker than ours."

Built on battle and blood, each man held an admiration for the other. To Blackbane, it was more durable than a mere friendship.

"Let's catch up with our lady friend before she kills the crew. We'll need some of them to get us out of Tunis," the captain replied with a frown that remained partially hidden by his flowing beard.

After walking along the empty road until the moon peaked above them, Blackbane saw his ship still moored on the dock.

"Most of the crew will no longer follow you," Bingham warned him when he saw the captain's eyes staring at the dark silhouette. "They're afraid of your insanity. Seymore became the first mate under Hamidu. He told them you are a lunatic."

"After meeting that woman in black, perhaps you're a lunatic as well," the captain joked.

Bingham briefly grinned while he glanced at his friend, who kept observing the movements on the ship. Blackbane's eyelids narrowed at the sight of only a single person on deck. The watch wore the turban of a Turk.

"Still, no matter who the men of the *Diano Marina* follow, we're not going far without my maps and sextant," Blackbane decided with a growl.

~~~

Ishak bin Yaqoob, known as Hamidu to the English sailors on the ship, lay next to his latest harem acquisition. A young woman lay on her side, facing away from him. Captured during a raid of a small village in Sardinia a few months before, he allowed her to stay after properly serving her master. The one beside him was a blond beauty. Druda was her name. While an infidel, she bore noble blood. The man intended to give upon her the title of *umm walad* to his concubine when she sired his first child.

The undisputed leader of the Tunis pirates, Hamidu, always sought additional wives and concubines. Slaves were a leading commodity, and the number of wives was a symbol of status for the Muslim rulers along the Barbary Coast of North Africa. Young girls brought in by the raiders of the coasts fetched top prices in the market, and he had the gold to pay. And Hamidu had every intention of becoming a ruler over the land. His growing number of ships proved his ability.

Thinking of his next voyage, the bearded man tried to drift back into his restless sleep. Such nights always happened before he set sail on another razzia into the infidel lands. The raids into Spain and Italy meant the enslavement of Christians for the Ottoman slave trade. It was as the Prophet desired, and it also brought him fame and fortune. Eventually, his exploits would give him the title of Beylik of Tunis.

As he rolled over in bed, he heard footsteps on the deck above his cabin. The sailors on watch must be making their rounds, he decided. Only his most loyal servants remained aboard. Most of his pirate crewmembers were onshore, whoring in the taverns. The pirates were a mix of religions and backgrounds. And they remained pirates first and foremost. Their skills with sails and weapons suited Hamidu, for he knew
~~~

they would accept their new captain if treasure came into their hands after a raid. It was how he overcame his rival, Blackbane. Hamidu ensured his Muslim servants remained aboard. His servants would never betray him, like many of the pirates did for a few gold coins. Such men were valuable and temperamental, but there was little need to beat them into submission like a slave. All it took was a little extra gold.

In some ways, pirates were easier to handle than slaves.

With his rival out of the way, Hamidu vowed that his renamed ship would remain the terror of the Mediterranean. The sailing vessel with thirty guns struck fear into the slow merchant ships trading in the waters. Unlike Hamidu's galley crew, which required many slaves to man the oars, the sailing ship's crew held skills that a slave seldom carried. Plus, they were fearsome when boarding. Now, Hamidu had control of a vessel with the speed and sufficient cannon to dominate the trade routes coming through the area. As long as the infidel kings remained content to pay their ransoms, he would cut a bloody swatch across the coasts. When the sun rose in the morning, a new era would begin. A smile crossed his lips as he drifted off to sleep.

Hamidu drifted out of his pleasant thoughts when he heard footsteps outside the cabin door. The noise roused him. A moment later, there was a startled muffled cry which immediately turned into a gurgling noise. As the man grabbed his sword, which hung from the bulkhead, he pulled out his dagger as well. The door opened slowly. The dark outline of Hamidu's guard stood at the entrance. He entered the room, holding his throat. Suddenly, the guard fell to his knees as the blood spilled through his fingers. The man toppled onto the deck. A large, familiar shadow stood in the entrance with a short broadsword.

Blackbane!

Hamidu roared out curses in Turkish as he charged. The two large men met in the center of the cabin. Their swords struck together with a loud clang while the woman tried to escape from the room. Neither man noticed as they backed away a half-step. Each was looking for an advantage. Blackbane attacked, swinging his sword as he sidestepped closer to the bed. He already noticed his rapier hanging on the bulkhead. Hamidu displayed there it like a trophy.

The Turk countered his opponent's swing, stepping over the body of his guard. His dark eyes carefully followed the movements of Blackbane, recognizing his opponent was a skilled swordsman. But Hamidu had Allah on his side.

He attacked, thrusting his sword forward. Blackbane stepped aside, but the blade passed through his robe and embedded into the wood behind him. Ensnarled by the man's weapon, Blackbane swung his sword up. Hamidu expected his move. He blocked the swing with his long blade dagger. Hamidu closed in on the pirate, who tried to pull away. The sound of ripping fabric mixed with the heavy breathing of the two men.

The cloth gave way just in time as Hamidu swiped his blade at Blackbane's face. He followed up by swinging his sword at Blackbane. This time, Blackbane expected the move. Hamidu's strike missed its mark as his opponent parried the blade away. In a fluid motion, Blackbane sliced down with his right hand. The thick sword blade cut through Hamidu's arm, and he cried out as he fell back against the bulkhead. Blackbane grabbed his rapier from the hook on the wall. He continued his attack. While the Turk rolled away, he extended his arm for the fallen sword. The pirate thrust forward with the razor-sharp blade of his sword, catching his enemy in the belly.

Hamidu pulled away in pain, then stared down in disbelief at the massive opening. He reached for his entrails as they slid out with the blood from his abdomen.

His back fell against the bulkhead, and the Turk slid down. Looking looked up at Blackbane, Hamidu's eyes glazed over. His corpse toppled to the deck. Blackbane slid his sword into his scabbard, once more the master of the *Diano Marina*.

Chapter 2: Bitter Fruit

A cold fog descended across the *Diano Marina* as it moored near an island called Alderney. Off the primary route through the English Channel and hidden from the French coast, the ship's under-manned crew repaired their ship. Damaged after a series of battering storms, the sailing vessel limped into the shelter between the islands.

As Blackbane stood on the quarterdeck, he did not hear the grumbling from the tired men while they worked on the foresails. His attention focused on the sea for the sails of enemy ships. He had less than a third of his crew, who stayed with him when they left Tunis. Taking over the ship wasn't the plan, but Blackbane took advantage of the nearly empty vessel. When the pirates came back just before dawn, he gave them a choice. To his disappointment, many of his crew stayed in Tunis. Those sailors that followed him gave a rousing cheer when he told them he would find more ships to plunder in the wars of Northern Europe. Soon, they would live like the Beyik.

Months later, Blackbane recognized his men were growing anxious about the journey. For two months, the captain steered away from potential enemies. The path left them with few opportunities for plunder and they encountered only one vessel, which they captured. Unfortunately, the Dutch ship carried little cargo. Even more disastrous news came when the pirates learned that the captured ship's crew suffered from an outbreak of smallpox. Only Blackbane and a few of the hardiest pirates boarded the Dutch ship. With only a small chest of silver carried from the Dutch captain's quarters, the captain overheard his men grouse about their luck.

Then came the rumors. Bingham told him that some of the crew worried about dark shadows on the ship at night. The first mate showed that the men believed ghosts were haunting them. Both he and Blackbane immediately thought of Naamah. The captain still pictured her remaining at the dock while the ship pulled away just as the sun was about to rise. The woman's last words to him that day remained drilled into his memory.

"I'll find you again, Blackbane. I never forgive a debt."

He took it as a reminder, not a threat. However, as he thought more about her dark shadow disappearing on the dock, he wondered why she had never come aboard the vessel that morning. Yet, he had to consider that the demon might come aboard at night to monitor him.

Still, the situation remained complicated. The captain needed to achieve results soon. As a precaution, he and Bingham carried two flintlocks in their sword belts just in case they misread the crew's temper. After hugging the Spanish and French coasts, Blackbane needed to remain lucky to the Baltic Sea. He recognized that his current reputation made him and his men were dead men should an English or Spanish ship capture them inside the English Channel.

But it was a risk they had to take. Blackbane and his first mate came up with a daring plan to hide their piracy in plain sight. They decided to use the war between Sweden and Russia for their benefit. Blackbane intended to get a Letter of Marque from either king in conflict. It would permit his crew to pirate the waters of the Baltic legally for their gold and silver. He was even willing to become William Marshall again and change the name of their ship to get the backing of a king to make them wealthy.

Noticing a shift in the wind, Blackbane turned to the helmsman, who suddenly came to attention.

"Go find Bingham," he ordered the pirate. "And tell the men there's a barrel of wine for them if they finish that sail before nightfall."

The pirate enthusiastically nodded before he sped away. A few minutes later, the first mate arrived. He was holding a jewel-encrusted dagger.

"What have you got?" Blackbane asked.

"It was in a box that harem girl stole from Hamidu the night you killed him. She had it hidden under your bed," Bingham replied with a smile. "I retrieved it this morning. Pretty smart to hide it in the last place anyone would look."

Blackbane stared at the weapon as the first mate pulled the knife from its finely detailed gold scabbard. He'd nearly forgotten about the girl. The slave begged to return to her home. Blackbane agreed and allowed her to stay on board. Then he gave her to the crew as their reward for staying with him.

"Something's not right here. Why did she tell you about it?" The captain glanced at his friend, who appeared uncomfortable. "It's worth many times her value as a slave. The wench could have slipped away from our ship several times using this when we've pulled into a port. Yet, she remains aboard. Does she enjoy her time with the crew so much? What aren't you telling me?"

Blackbane noticed the flicker of fear on the first mate's face.

"Well, I should have told you before. I took the woman away from the crew. She's been in my cabin for most of the journey. Druda can't be a whore for the crew," Bingham explained as he stumbled. He never betrayed an order before.

"You see, I gave the men my share of the gold we took from Hamidu. It was something I had to do for a noblewoman."

The first mate grappled with his thoughts. He noticed the man waiting with a growing scowl on his face.

"Captain Blackbane, I want this woman to remain with me alone," he burst out forcefully.

Blackbane lifted an eyebrow in surprise at the news. Bingham had shown no interest in a wife.

"Why? Whores are in every port when a man has gold."

"Druda carries noble blood." His first mate's reaction caused the captain to glare. At times, Bingham was nearly as ruthless as Blackbane. Yet, he took the captain's gift from the crew and paid them off in gold.

"You know that taking my gift whore away from the crew presents me with a problem?" Blackbane groused while he stared at the expensive weapon.

"They took my share without hesitation," Bingham told him. "However, I should have come to you first with an explanation. For that error, I deserve the whip."

Blackbane absently nodded. His first mate's change of heart caused the captain to reflect on the situation with concern. Wives traveling with pirates were unusual, but not unheard of. But a wife could change a man's loyalty.

"Is this dagger a way to buy her from me?" His eyes narrowed with sudden suspicion.

The first mate shook his head, his long red hair flowing over his broad shoulders.

"Captain, you know me better than that. There is no disloyalty to my heart. What I'm giving you is not a bribe. Druda told me it's a holy relic." Bingham frowned, despite expecting the reaction.

"Remember, I witnessed what happened during our escape. You will need the weapon against the things which come to you. The pummel contains the blood of Saint Gennaro. The Muslims stole it from her church when Hamidu captured her and the rest of the slaves. As you can see, it's marked so in Latin on the blade."

The first mate handed him the weapon. Blackbane instantly felt the pain from the symbol on his neck, and he nearly dropped it. He grimaced, holding his hand on his neck. Then he skimmed the inscription on the small blade. He promptly took the scabbard and sheathed the knife. The pain went away. Blackbane scanned the deck to ensure that none of the crewmen were close enough to overhear the conversation.

"The blade is too small and thin for battle," Blackbane observed. His face showed his doubt in the weapon's ability.

"I don't see how it will hurt a demon."

After a moment, the captain slid the sheath into his belt.

"Still, any defense against my opponents is welcome. Bingham, you cur, you've surprised me." The man turned away and looked over the water.

"I'll accept your gift with no reservations," he promised the first mate. "As long as the woman remains loyal as you are, then she's welcome to sail with us, provided that you can find work for her."

"I've already told her she can work in the galley." The first mate grinned. "I told the cook that you'll soon boil him if he can't do better than serving that rancid leather he calls meat."

The captain gave the man a knowing look, but remained quiet.

"She'll impress you. Druda is a survivor!" His second insisted.

Blackbane stared at the water as he grunted.

"We'll see. Go forward and keep the men on their task. I promised that last barrel of Portuguese wine. That'll keep them happy for another night, and then we'll raise anchor in the morning. If we keep good weather and a fair wind, I expect we will be in Stockholm before our stores run out."

"I hope you're right." Bingham glanced back at the crew.

"We lack men needed should we come upon a ship." The first mate walked to the ladder leading down to the next deck, then he stopped.

"Marshall, thank you."

Blackbane nodded, covertly watching the first mate until he was among the crew. When he entered his cabin, the captain looked down at his new weapon.

I wish this trinket would send away my nightmares!

~~~

It was late at night. A thin, grizzled man half-dozed in a sitting position with his body leaning against the wooden wheel. An experienced pirate who came with Blackbane from Jamaica several years before, Little Mike held a half-filled mug in his hands. With the ship at anchor, he felt little need to pay attention to the dark waters around the vessel. As he dreamed of taverns and the beautiful wenches, the man failed to hear the noise of something sliding up from the water below.

A dark form skillfully crawled up the stern as tentacle suckers softly popped when they released from the wood. The demon expertly flipped across the railing, landing on the wooden deck. Two red eyes noticed the man leaning against the ship's wheel.

The drips of seawater softly raining down his head slowly got the helmsman's attention. When he looked up, Little Mike froze under Beelzebub's gaze. The man could only let out a feeble grunt when his iris and cornea immediately melted into a solid black pit. As the dead body twitched several times, Beelzebub turned his attention toward the faint outline of a lookout who was smoking his pipe on the other end of the ship.
~~~

The demon listened to the whistling for a moment before going forward. Behind the monster, the dead helmsman slowly rose to follow his master.

Although he wanted to sleep, Blackbane remained at his small desk by the foot of his bed. Focused on the navigation charts, he worked for the best route to Sweden while cursing his lack of recent maps. The shuffling of feet along the deck slowly caught his attention. The noise grew closer and sounded unnatural to him. With the calmness of the wind and closeness to the island shore, he became suspicious. Mutiny and treachery were always upon a captain's mind.

Instantly, Blackbane went to the cabin door with his pistol and rapier in hand. The golden dagger remained nestled in his belt. He slowly opened the door to see movement in the middle of his ship. Under the moonlight, he saw a large and tall figure coming up the ladder to the quarterdeck. The captain thought it was a strange shadow until he noticed the line of men visible behind it. Blackbane stepped from his cabin quietly to confront the men coming.

"Stop there, or I'll shoot the first traitor," the captain ordered.

The line of figures stopped, and the tall leader stepped closer. Blackbane turned cold, even though the creature's face remained partially hidden under the shadows of the sails above. Like the moss on the side of a pier, a green sheen of loose skin forced the captain to raise his pistol. The demon's eyes beckoned him, but the captain stared at the creature's open mouth. It drooped down into his neck like a giant grouper. Blackbane could almost imagine the lower jaw might disconnect like a python to swallow his prey. The moon's pale light momentarily strengthened to show him the creature's red robe and breeches intertwined in gold trimming.

"What are you?" Blackbane's mouth stumbled for the words when he saw the faces of his crew. Black pits for eyes and pasty faces told him they were no longer among the living. The scene reminded him of stories of ghouls in graveyards.

"Beelzebub comes for your soul, Marshall," the demon's voice warbled. "You want gold and blood? I'll give you a fleet of ships crewed by this undead to fill the seas with the blood of your enemies. You will go after the golden cross again. Once you retrieve it, you'll have enough gold to make the Beylik look like a pauper."

"What have you done to my men? Release them now," Blackbane ordered as he carefully avoided the gaze of Beelzebub.

"That's impossible, human. This crew of ghouls is no longer yours to " the fiend told him. "Their souls belong to me, for I've promised them a touch of your immortality. Step forward to accept your new role as the immortal terror of the seas."

Blackbane slowly paced while Beelzebub watched him with his black beady eyes. The captain casually placed his hand over the gold dagger in his belt.

"I see a problem in your offer," he told the demon. "You give me a soulless existence working for you. I see no humanity in those things behind you. It is not enough."

"What else can you expect? I save you an eternity of painful misery as each of my brothers and sisters come for you," the demon croaked out. "The crew behind me still lusts for the same things in life. They'll rape and kill, then eat their fill of human flesh. However, there's no pain or hardship anymore. It's the perfect life for a doomed pirate."

"Besides, I know you've had that whore, Naamah, tempt you. No doubt she's waiting at the next dock for you. This deal suits you better, man."

Beelzebub laughed when he recognized Blackbane's surprised expression at the comment.

"Yes, I saw her on the pier when your ship left. Why do you think she didn't come aboard? Seawater stops her powers," he told the captain. "If you don't understand such things, how do you expect to survive? Come to me, and you will no longer suffer uncertainty and doubt."

"My life is worth more to me than becoming a dead follower of a demon," he said. "You bargain with me like I have no choice."

"In that, you're correct," the demon told him after his lower jaw opened wide with a hideous type of smile and razor-sharp teeth. "I tell you what will happen tonight. Once you look into my eyes, the dead men will have their small prize to live forever. I'll have you lead them into glorious destruction across the seas. You will burn, loot, maim, and kill anything you want. Think of it, all the women you desire, along with holds full of gold and treasure. When you enter cities, the self-righteous fools will bow before you. You can mount the severed heads of rulers on the masts of this vessel. It will be as you dream at night."

The captain suddenly remembered those unfulfilled dreams. They came to him before his encounter with Remiel. The unsettling thought that the entire demon world knew of his ambitions struck the pirate like a bullet. He stepped back in hesitation.

"And you will still rule over me," Blackbane declared. "I'll stand before you like the dead men on the deck. There is no hope in those eyes. I'm the captain of the *Diano Marina*, not a scurvy ship rat who spends eternity bowing before you."

Beelzebub sighed as more tentacle arms suddenly appeared from behind his deformed body. The large sucker-covered hands held crude instruments of battle and torture.

"It's unfortunate you have such little wisdom. I guess I'll find another subject to lead my followers. As your men tear into your body, you will beg me to take your soul. Only then will I take away your suffering so your crew can feed in peace."

The crowd of dead pirates closed around their captain. Blackbane backed up to his cabin door, pulling his pistol. He quickly shot at Beelzebub. The bullet slammed into the chest of the demon, passing through with no effect. However, the walking dead helmsman behind fell to the deck, with half of his skull shot away. The ghouls closed in on their captain. Blackbane used the massive pistol grip to strike at the closest dead man, who grabbed his arm. The man's cheekbone shattered at the strike, leaving a deep indentation. However, the creature tried to bite Blackbane, who desperately struggled to pull away.

Behind the crowd, a shot rang out when Bingham joined the fray. His bullet shattered the skull of one dead crewman. Then, the first mate attacked the ghouls with his sword on the moonlight-covered deck. A second creature fell at Bingham's feet as Druda joined in the fray. The fair-haired woman carried a short sword in which she swung with amateurish vigor at a crewmember. She dispatched the ghoul in her bloody frenzy.

Bingham's attack helped his captain to escape the initial onslaught. Blackbane spun away from one ghoul, decapitating the former crewmate with a swing of his sword. Hurrying across the deck, the captain attacked the demon. His furious stroke at Beelzebub missed the mark. The beast moved aside with blinding speed. As Blackbane passed, he felt a fire sweep across his back. Beelzebub struck the captain with razor-sharp claws, ripping through the man's skin. Forced to endure the pain while he fended off two ghouls, Blackbane searched for an escape. The captain's vicious swings on the undead creatures only slowed them. Parts of their bodies fell, and blood flowed across the slippery deck.

A scream rose from Druda, who watched Bingham go overboard when a ghoul slammed its body into her lover. Out of the corner of his eye, Blackbane caught sight of the woman running to the rail. However, he was too busy to notice her jump overboard after the first mate.

The last of the undead crew got to Blackbane as he backed into the ship's wheel. A ghoul wrapped its massive arm around the captain's neck while another pinned his sword arm against the wheel. Blackbane felt the bite on his arm, and he yelled in agony. He smelled the rancid breath of the large crewman at his neck, struggling to get his teeth through the captain's collar. Blackbane cursed out in desperation.

"No! Leave him for me," Beelzebub suddenly ordered the two ghouls.

The dead crewmen stopped at the order.

The demon stepped into view; his foul face twisted into something akin to a triumphant smile. Beelzebub pulled a blacksmith tong from his black belt.

"I'll strip you of your flesh while you scream for mercy. Then I'll give your flesh to feed your crew," the demon roared as he stepped closer.

The two ghouls pulled the struggling Blackbane tight against the wheel. The captain's face turned red as he struggled to breathe from the pressure on his windpipe. His free hand pulled and scratched at the brawny arm of the ghoul with no effect.

Beelzebub brought the tong pincers toward the pinned arm of the captain. The creature's mouth opened and closed like a gasping fish. However, the demon failed to see Blackbane drop his free hand and begin searching on his belt. An instant later,

Beelzebub's howls filled the air. The beast backed away in fear, holding his belly. Blackbane lifted the Saint Gennaro dagger, then slammed it back next to his head. The blade penetrated the eye of the ghoul behind Blackbane. With a hideous scream, the dead crewman released the pirate captain. Blackbane yelled out, then sliced into the second ghoul who bit his arm during the fierce struggle. The creature fell away.

Finally released, Blackbane's eyes focused on Beelzebub, who continued to back away while eyeing the dagger in the pirate's hand.

"Rip him apart," the demon ordered the few remaining undead.

Aware that he had little time as the dead crew came after him, Blackbane went after the monster again. Beelzebub recognized the attack, and the creature swung at him with the tong. Blackbane sidestepped the blow and continued his advance. He slid around the demon and tried to strike at the monster's side with his dagger. However, a ghoul caught Blackbane by the leg first. The action sent the captain against the rail at the edge of the ship. Beelzebub struck his opponent's arm with the tong, sending the dagger sliding along the deck. Blackbane again launched himself at the demon, trying to push the creature away. His clumsy attempt to buy time failed when the force of his charge struck the beast.

Beelzebub and Blackbane fell over the railing into the black water together. Desperately pulling himself to the surface, Blackbane struggled in the cold water. The captain could barely swim on a smooth day. Now, he was in the water with a fearful beast who once released the powerful Abezethibou from the Red Sea. Blackbane started swimming for the side of the ship, barely outlined in the night's blackness. Just as he reached the wooden planks, the captain felt pressure immediately, followed by pain in his ankle. Blackbane couldn't even gasp as Beelzebub dragged the man under the water. As the demon descended into the depths, the captain struggled. Soon, his lungs felt like they were on fire, and the man realized he was drowning.

I'm supposed to be immortal!

It wasn't prayer; it was more of an observation. Blackbane decided the angel lied to him. He would sink into the dark depths where he would become fish food. The suffocating pressure and darkness pierced through the captain's thoughts. Then he saw a blue light that gradually filled his mind. Blackbane's lungs finally collapsed. The man heard the breaking bones, yet he felt no pain. Even the agony of his leg left when the demon released him.

The light intensified, and his vision showed him a vague outline of a person. The captain felt himself floating toward the person. Slowly, he recognized it was more than one person. His body passed through the shadowy forms, which slowly walked in a line. They walked on a grassy trail that reminded Blackbane of his past. He recognized the path lead to a familiar plot of land outside of Boston. William Marshall grew to a young lad on the farm.

That was before his mother became a whore on the docks!

Frequently, the thought of his childhood sent Blackbane into a rage. However, he felt calm, which seldom came to the pirate. As his floating form swept around the farmhouse, he wanted to stop and look into his old home, to step through the green-painted door. Somehow, he knew his father sat at the table inside while his mother served the family their typical meal of pease porridge with coarse rye bread.

However, Marshall had no control over the journey. Instead, his drifting soul came to a line of spirits. As he came upon the first one, he recognized the face: John Eliot, a missionary to the savages in New England. Marshall remembered seeing a painting of the man in the church his father took the family to each Sunday. The man, dourly dressed in black clothing, strolled along with a thick bible in his hand.

Behind Eliot, a small young woman clad in the ancient style white toga carried an open gold box. Somehow, he knew that her heart lay inside the box. She smiled at him as his vision faded. The line of men and women behind the woman disappeared. Only her angelic face remained in his sight. A voice whispered her name.

Julia of Carthage awaits you, William Marshall. I shall bring you peace with the touch of my hand.

~~~

A fresh breeze across his face woke Blackbane. His eyes stared momentarily at the flapping sail several feet above him. On the headsail above him, two men worked on the leech line. As he looked around the unfamiliar deck, the man heard a voice behind him.

"You Anglais?" Her hard-gray eyes observed him.

Blackbane glanced back to see a large woman on the wheel. Her tanned face had deep wrinkles and her dark blue coat barely contained her gigantic frame, emphasizing her large chest. Strands of her dark blonde hair escaped from under the woman's red stocking cap and flittered in the breeze.

Blackbane nodded at her question.

"No francais," he tried to explain he didn't speak French.

"I speak your language; she told him with a scowl—*Anglais* husband before he drown. I'm Jacotte, captain of the *l'Archimèdes.*"

"What of my ship?" He asked as he sat up. His leg movement halted. Looking down at the leg iron attached to the mainmast, he frowned.
~~~

"We found your ship abandonné, cassé…broken on a reef. We go for salvage. You lie with the dead. The men were missing their eyes. They looked pluck out by mouette. We took fine cloths with your…how you say… la cargaison," Jacotte told him.

"You mean my cargo?" Blackbane stated as he looked back at the barrels in the open hold. There were a few cannon lashed down the top of the deck as well. He guessed the remaining clothes and weapons went to the captain's cabin for storage.

"How did I get back?" He turned back to the woman.

Jacotte gave him an odd look, appearing not to understand.

"My boy, Gascon, recognized the symbol of God on your throat. He reached for the coat, and you coughed out seawater. You cursed out your name."

Blackbane rubbed his neck and felt the cursed sign grow hot to his touch. The boy she referred to was a large man who slid down a rope to land next to the prisoner. Gascon glared at Blackbane before Jacotte sent him away.

"Did you get my charts and instruments?" Blackbane asked the woman.

Her eyes narrowed with suspicion.

"William Marshall signed the charts. Is that you?" She asked. Blackbane nodded.

"The ship we found was the *Diano Marina*. I've heard rumors that a devil named Blackbane is the captain of such a ship."

The hard-bitten woman kept her eyes locked on his.

"While I don't believe all the tall tales about that ship, the corpses around your living body tell me you might be the devil. Maybe you might bring in a handsome reward? We shall see."

"What about my ship?" Blackbane asked.

"The *Diano Marina* sank just as we took off the last cannon that my small ship could handle. We'll do well no matter what happens with you," she replied. "However, I suspect you have interesting stories."

Jacotte gave him a smug, toothy smile

"With the cannon, weapons, and barrels of gunpowder, we'll make more than three trips filled with fish."

Blackbane held his hand up to shade his eyes from the sun. He recognized their direction.

"You must be heading to France."

"We're going to Le Havre. We'll take you to the *Intendant*. He'll decide what to do with you," she explained. "If you are Blackbane, he'll hang you. I'll get silver *livre* for your capture."

"You only have a story about dead men on a ship which sank," Blackbane suggested as he tried to stand. The low boom of the sail moved when the wind changed and forced him back to the deck. He looked at the woman.

"Perhaps we can make a bargain?"

Jacotte laughed at him.

"With no money and no ship, you have nothing, Marshall. Only the dagger my son found on you is worth something. And you no longer have that to bargain with. You cause trouble; then my men throw into the sea. Understand Anglais?"

"Yeah, it won't do you much good, but I understand," he leaned back against the mast.

~~~

The sun's red light snuck through a single opening inside the overcrowded jail of Le Havre the following day. William Marshall sat with his back against the wall. Bleary-eyed from his haunting nightmares, his head nodded. In the middle of the dark and dank room was an open cesspool. Around him were the criminals and debtors of Le Havre. His first day in the jail
~~~

showed him the top dogs who ran the area. Marshall paid attention to a large man with a pocked-mark face who kept eyeing him from one corner of the room. Understanding the language was unnecessary. It was evident that the opposite side of the cell was enemy territory. He felt the underlying menace coming from the prisoners there.

Lying near his feet was a short, fat man wearing the robes of a monk. The monk kept glancing over at Marshall the day before with his bulbous eyes that look like they would fall out of his eye sockets. While they never spoke, Marshall noticed the man intentionally took up the sleeping spot near him as the light left the room. The captain remained only mildly bothered by the man's presence. He was hardly a threat, and Marshall noticed how the jail guards kept the monk's clay mug filled with beer. No doubt, the fat man had friends. He had enough access to money to bribe the guards.

Marshall watched the ray of light slowly cross the filthy floor as other prisoners rose from their sleep. He felt the glimpses coming from a small group of prisoners. Judging by their threadbare clothes and shaggy beards, he guessed the men survived the conditions of the hellhole for the longest time. Marshal also surmised that his expensive clothes caught the prisoner's eyes. He did not like his odds. The event reminded him of one line in a song that sailors enjoyed singing while working on his ship.

We'll hang Paddy Doyle for his boots!

The ray of light crossing the floor finally reached the face of the monk, causing the man to swipe at the light beam, then grumbled out something in French. His reaction sent a brief smile to Marshall's face before the pirate went back to his thoughts.

I'm in jail with no weapons, no ship, and no crew.

True to her word, Jacotte and her son took Marshall to the office of the *Intendant*. Instead, they found the prefect's aide. A runt of a man named Jean-François looked over the captain. From the conversation, Marshall figured out that the *Intendant* was in Paris. He recognized the devious woman and little man bargained over his worth by the tone of the discussion. The captain understood the terms *l'espion* and *le contrebandier* while Jacotte pointed to Marshall. With a growing fury, he recognized her attempt to make him into a smuggler, perhaps even an English spy. The prefect's aide confirmed Marshall's suspicions. He immediately went to the door and called in two guards. As the guards hauled Marshall away, he yelled out to Jacotte.

"I'm coming back for my dagger, you hedge whore!"

"No, my friend here will ensure you hang. Jean-François agreed to my terms on *Diano Marina's* cargo."

Marshall scowled as he remembered the thieving woman's smile. He glanced over at the iron bars of the window and the barred door, looking for places to escape. However, the only opportunity appeared when the guards opened the single door. However, the jailer kept armed men standing outside the entrance. Trying to jump them was a fool's errand.

With a groan, the monk rose from the floor. His movement caught Marshall's attention. He observed the monk stumble in his thick boots toward the center of the room. The man lifted his robe and began urinating into the stinking open pit. The holy man began whistling like it was just another day.

Across the room, Marshall noticed a large man rise from his seat in the corner. Dressed in a tattered gray smock, he passed by the prisoners, who were eyeing Marshall earlier. They instantly joined him. As the group approached, Marshall stood.

Tension immediately filled the air. The big man came to a stop about a foot away from Marshall.

"Donne-moi ce manteau Anglais!"

The captain's brown eye's narrowed. He didn't understand the words, but he recognized the threat. The man across from him was a few inches taller and outweighed him. His pockmarked face twisted with a sneer, revealing his missing teeth.

"Go to hell!" Marshall readied himself for the coming fight.

The prisoner reached over to pull at Marshall's coat. Blackbane immediately punched him right between the eyes. The larger man backed away, holding his nose.

"Je vais te tuer pour ça!" the man raged in the attack.

Blackbane slid inside the swing as he countered with a knee to the man's groin. His strike sent the prisoner to the floor. However, the other prisoners jumped on Marshall before he could kick his opponent. Two men grabbed the captain's arms, holding him while another convict pummeled Marshall with blows to the face. The punches stunned the captain. As he tried to avoid the hits, Marshall felt another prison strike him in the lower back. Instantly, his knees buckled, and he dropped. The two men holding him lifted the captain back up. Then, he took more punishment. A savage blow to his belly doubled Marshall over in agony. He felt hands stripping him of his coat, and he pulled away. Marshall lashed out, and his fist caught one of his attackers in the face.

Then, the pirate captain found a large black mass suddenly join him. The monk landed a punch into the criminal, still holding on to Marshall's coat. While the prisoner dropped to the floor, Marshall stumbled away. The prisoner in the gray smock came after Marshall again. He grabbed the captain, trying to overpower him. The captain heard a scream in his ear as he broke away from the bigger man. He turned to see the monk had locked his beefy arm around his attacker's head, and his other hand gouged at the man's eyes. An instant later, an eyeball popped out of the prisoner's eye socket.

Screaming as he fell to the filthy floor, the prisoner held on to his bleeding face with the eyeball dangling from between his fingers. Those watching the fight backed away from the screaming man as the yells coming from guards grew closer. A moment later, several uniformed men carrying Charleville muskets with their bayonets extended burst into the room. The jailor followed, his red wool frock still wet from his spilled drink. He went over to the severely injured prisoner, who was now whimpering. The monk stepped by the jailer.

"You should take this dog away," he said, then repeated the suggestion in French.

The man in the red frock scanned the prisoners. He paused at each of the men with bleeding and bruised faces. Finally, he nodded.

"Oui, faites sortir le prisonnier d'ici," the jailer ordered the closest prisoner.

As the guards backed out of the room, a prisoner helped the injured man to his feet and led him out. The monk walked with the jailer to the door. Marshall couldn't hear their conversation, but it was apparent they knew each other.

The captain backed against the stone wall and slowly slid down as his fingers carefully probed his face. Blood trickled down from his nose and a split lip. As he dabbed at his wounds with the sleeve of his coat, he saw the monk approach.

"Englishman, what brings a gentleman among the savages?"

The fat man pulled a metal flask from under his robe. Uncorking it, he took a drink, licking his lips when finished.

"Your eyes deceive you, monk," Marshall grunted. He observed his defeated adversaries, who milled around on the other side of the room.

"I've never been called a gentleman. I've arrived without a shilling and plenty of blood in my past. What's your name?"

"They call me Leiras," the man in the robe said. "In here, I'm known as the Black Monk to these heathens."

He cursed at the group of ruffians staring at them.

"It is an unusual name. Do you always jump in the middle of a fight?" Marshall asked.

"Only when I want to meet someone with a burden," Leiras told him as he handed over his flask. The captain smelled the concoction inside dubiously, but he drank it. It had the taste of swamp water mixed with juniper, anise, and coriander. Leiras let out a deep laugh when he saw Blackbane's bitter expression while he swallowed the liquid.

"Aye, you're a gentleman, alright. I've seen much between rounds of drinks in my years. Let me guess? You enjoy the spirits of Portugal; I'll bet. I see the cloth of the Turks on you."

The man pulled an unfilled pipe from a bag attached to a belt around his waist. He placed the stem between his teeth as he grinned at Blackbane's suspicious expression.

"Your clothes carry the cut of a sailor from the south," Leiras explained. "I traveled with the heathens and rabble to the Holy Land. Once, a few Turks tried to enslave me on my trip back to civilization. I killed them so they would see the light. Now, my new friend, what's your name?"

"The name is Marshall. William Marshall. I take it you're not French," he observed.

The captain handed the flask back. Leiras took another drink before he placed his thick arms on his belly. He left the pipe dangling from his lips.

"No, I'm a man of the world. Once I was a grenadier from the canton of Schaffouse and learned your language during my time with the *Cent Suisses* company in Paris." There was a twinkle in his eye about his past as he spoke. His enormous head and thinning hair gave him an older appearance. The man's mischievous smile was infectious.

"Yet you wear the habit. Why?"

"Let's say that I'm a believer in the Lord," Leiras replied. "As I said, over the years, I've seen much in my travels. When I traveled back from the Holy Land, I came upon the Xeropotamou Monastery on Mount Athos. In their sanctuary among the villainous Ottomans, the monks took me in to learn their ways. Good people, but I found them intolerable with their rules. However, I find their wardrobe comfortable. It suits me to know that few men will challenge me from the status and authority of this cloth."

"Why are you here, and how do you keep yourself in drink?"

"The *Intendant* of Le Havre believes I stir up trouble against the Church with my visions. I don't kiss the ass of the damned cardinal here," he told him proudly. "But the jailer will do anything for a few francs. I've got one guard to refill my flask and bring food from his home. His wife is a fine cook." He licked his lips at the thought. "She comes by with food late at night. The other prisoners envy me for this service."

"Why not just bribe your way out if you have gold? There is no reason to remain here," Marshall reasoned. Leiras smiled at him.

"You're a thinking man, I see. Yes, normally, that would be the case." The monk lowered his voice, glancing around as he leaned closer to the pirate.

"In my travels, I've come across enough treasure to keep me happy. When I arrived here a few years ago, I kept it in one place, but now I have coins hidden in several places throughout Le Havre," he confided. "A guard might get greedy and try to take it all."

"Intelligent idea. Why didn't you take one guard in your confidence? You could bribe him to escape?"

"I thought of the same thing. Unfortunately, that contemptible *Intendant,* Auguste, is the *vicomté* of the area. Thus, his power scares those who must live here. The guards will give me a few things for francs, but to escape will take some ingenuity. I wait for the moment. It's better not to starve when one soon dies."

"You're condemned?" Blackbane asked.

"I've been renounced by the Church bishop as a heretic. Of course, the *Vicomte* bribed him. They threw me into this hellhole before I could escape the city. I'm sure Auguste intends to let me dance at the end of a rope. He'll be in for quite a surprise since I don't intend to stay around."

"Then you might have company at the gallows," the captain replied. "I believe that devil woman Jacotte arranged the same for me."

"Well, I'll drink to your good health and pray for your chance to haunt her until Judgment Day," the black monk told him with a sly grin. As he took another drink, he didn't see the foul glare on Marshall's face at the comment.

~~~

After waking from another nightmare, Marshall lay on his back. He heard, then felt a rat hurry by him. The rodent continued past him. They usually nibbled on those prisoners who were too ill and weak to resist. When the captain heard the jangle of keys, he looked over at the noise as the night watch pushed
~~~

the door open. The soft light of an oil lantern poked through the entrance. Standing in the view was the rotund figure of the Leiras, who hurried through the opening. Almost immediately, the door closed, leaving the darkness inside the large cell.

It wasn't much of an escape!

Marshall turned away. Two days before, he overheard Leiras promise the jailer of a fortune in silver to let him escape. It appeared the idea of treasure finally overcome the jailer's fear of Auguste. Marshall listened to the whispered chatter of a couple of prisoners who watched the escape with envy.

As the sun went down, the Black Monk took a spot near the door, and Marshall joined him. They found their places to sleep that night before the single ray of sunlight left the jail. Leiras told Marshall that he expected to escape that night. He whispered his promise to return to the pirate captain the next night.

Marshall did not believe it!

Aside from his knowledge that the monk carried strange beliefs, the pirate harbored no illusions about Leiras. No person risked their neck for the sake of a passing friendship. Bonds formed through battle and hardship carried weight in the violent world of piracy.

Marshall listened to the snores coming from a nearby prisoner, trying to forget the death of Bingham. When he asked about the body of his trusted friend, Jocatte told him that no other officers were aboard the ship. She explained that only dead men covered the decks. That meant that Bingham drowned, probably along with his woman.

What was her name? That's it, Druda!

He recalled her jumping into the sea after Bingham went over. As the man replayed the events in his head, he realized he had misjudged the woman. Bingham was a good man, and despite being a pirate, carried a sense of honor. The connection between his first mate and Druda caused them to defend each other to death. Some called it love, although such an idea made little sense to Marshall. Indeed, the women he knew carried little sentimentality. He'd seen enough bodies with slit throats in the alleys behind brothels. Prostitutes were as cold and bloodthirsty as pirates. A buccaneer entering the whore houses along the docks kept one hand on his moneybag while his other hand remained close to his dagger.

Marshall turned to his side, trying to forget. He desperately wanted a dreamless sleep to fall over him. Yet, the pirate grew to understand that such relief would never come. The worst dreams came from his time in the Caribbean and the only pure love of his life, Emma Watson.

Emma was the daughter of a prominent doctor in Jamaica. During his brief time visiting the island, Marshall became enamored with the fair-skinned beauty. However, his penchant for smuggling led to a deadly duel against the son of a plantation owner. Rumors reach him about soldiers looking for him. While Marshall ordered his men to prepare the ship to flee, he went to Emma to coax her to join him. However, she refused at first. Finally, on his last night on the island, she agreed to leave with him.

Then fate intervened.

Emma's father attempted to stop them. The doctor pulled a pistol on Marshall. Just as Emma's father pulled back the weapon's hammer, the smuggler used the pommel of his sword to strike the doctor down. Marshall ran to the doorway, calling for help. Emma kneeled by her father's side. When she recognized he was dead, she reached for the man's pistol.

Marshall heard Emma coming toward him. When he turned, the enraged woman pointed the flintlock pistol and pulled the trigger. The lead bullet ripped off part of his ear while the explosion of black power burned one side of Marshall's face. Marshall fell back as Emma tried to strike him with the pistol as she cursed him.

During his struggle with Emma, his fiery rage took over. He brutally struck the love of his life. After she fell to the floor, an overwhelming madness went through him. When she cursed him, he dragged her next to the body of her father, then raped her. The woman spat in his face when he finished. With a smile on his injured face, he strangled her.

Instead of receiving his just punishment at the end of a rope, William Marshall escaped the island. That was when Blackbane became his name. His knowledge of smuggling turned into piracy, and he learned from the best and cruelest captains. After overthrowing the pirate captain of the *Diano Marina*, Blackbane intended to engrave his name in infamy in the Mediterranean.

Now, Marshall lived Emma's death each night. He endured her last moments alive. Remiel's devious plan made the pirate's continued existence a living hell. He cursed the archangel aloud before he rolled over in another attempt to sleep.

The pirate restlessly dozed until the jangle of keys broke through. He didn't bother to look up. Instead, Marshall tried to get comfortable on the stinking floor. The noise of the keys drew closer, along with a beam of light. He felt a boot strike his butt.

"Come on, Captain Blackbane. It's time to leave this place." The voice of Leiras whispered.

Scrambling to his feet, Marshall joined the monk, who held an oil lantern. As they headed for the door, the other prisoners slowly woke. They recognized the Black Monk.

"Que Faites-Vous?" A nearby inmate asked.

"Je pars. Tu peux pourrir ici ou t'échapper," Leiras smiled as he reached the door.

Before the monk closed the door, he threw the keys to the prisoner.

"Come, we'll need to move fast," Leiras hurried away. "I just opened the doors to chaos."

Using the lantern to guide the way, he led Marshall along the passage to an archway that led to the dark street. On either side of the cobblestone street, the thatch and timber buildings silently waited for the coming morning. After they took several turns through the narrow alleys, Leiras finally slowed his pace.

"Knowing the type of prisoners, they will soon break into the nearby shops, looking for weapons and drink. This will allow us to escape the village without notice," he explained.

They took another turn and entered a small courtyard between two buildings. As they came to a barn, the body of the jailer lay next to the structure.

"First, we hide him," the monk ordered.

He reached down to grab one hand of the corpse. Marshall took the other side, and they dragged the body into the barn. After pulling the dead man to a corner, the monk sat down his lantern.

"Our horses are ready. My apologies, but it took a while to retrieve my sack of silver and return to the jail. It will be enough for the journey to Amsterdam. I told you and the guards that I had other bags secreted away. Of course, I lied."

Marshall noticed the jailer's eyes remained open after being strangled by Leiras. He went over and pulled the sword from the man's belt, along with the dead jailor's money bag. He quickly checked inside the leather bag to find a few silver livres.

"His pistol hangs by the wall," the monk told him.

The captain glanced over at the door, where he saw the outline of a flintlock as he slid the sword into his belt. He went to retrieve the weapon.

"Why did you kill the jailer if he was helping you escape?"

Marshall watched the short man pulling two small canvas sacks of coins from under his robe. Leiras placed them inside a leather bag, which he tied off on a saddle.

"Because he beat his wife and his boy, of course," the monk shrugged while he finished saddling a horse. "I saw it many times with my own eyes. The jailer was a foul spawn of the devil when he drank. I sent him to hell."

He glanced back at Marshall.

"Saddle the other horse so we can leave. Make sure you take the blankets hanging on the wall. The weather will grow cold soon."

The captain pushed the flintlock into his belt, then hurried around the other side of the stall, where he picked up a heavy saddle. As he worked, he kept glancing over at the monk, who began whistling at a catchy tune.

"You are concerned about something," the fat man observed.

"You called me Captain Blackbane before we left the jail. The name is William Marshall." The pirate finished saddling the mount.

"Ah, yes, it's my mistake. Marshall is a better name for travel to Amsterdam." Leiras agreed with a smile. "Denisot holds something for me. Now wait here; I'll be back soon."

Suspicion filled Marshall as he watched the fat man leave the barn. He went to the entrance and watched the monk's shadow as he crossed the yard and entered the back of the house. A candlelight suddenly came alive near the open window as a woman came into view. She was talking with the monk. After a moment, Marshall went to the back of the house. He glimpsed the woman who took the candle before climbing the stairs. Leiras followed her.

The captain went back to the horses and led them from the barn to the back gate of the courtyard. He stood there, debating his next steps. The monk knew the area and knew the path to Amsterdam. Worse, a waning moon barely lit the city, even if Marshall knew what road to take out of the town. The fat man knew the language as well.

An Anglais would not make it far before guards took him back to that foul jail.

With a sigh, he waited while soon expecting a noose around his neck. Every sound of the night caused Marshall to assume guards were nearby. He stroked the mane of his horse to comfort his nerves while telling himself it was for the animal. After what seemed like an eternity, the black monk finally returned. The jingling sound and light coming from a modified sanctuary lamp with a mirror preceded him. He blew out the fire, then hooked the unusual-looking item on the saddle. Leiras noticed Marshall staring at the object.

"Denisot liked my special lantern from Xeropotamou, so it was the first thing that the jailer stole from me. I bought it using her dead husband's silver." The monk whispered as he hoisted himself on top of his horse.

"She also told me of the best route out of town. Unlatch the gate."

Marshall hurried to open the back gate, and then he hoisted himself on the mount.

"What about the body?"

"Denisot already knows about the death of her husband. I consoled her in bed and paid her a few pieces of silver for her time. Now, keep quiet and follow me."

Leiras directed his horse through the gate, and Marshall followed while shaking his head.

This monk carries no more of a conscience than I do!

The two men took a winding path through a maze of dark alleyways. Unable to see beyond a few feet, the slow pace kept Marshall tense as he heard every sound in the night. He expected guards at every corner. Finally, they reached a narrow path near a pen holding sheep, and Leiras stopped his horse. The barks coming from a nearby dog caused Marshall's horse to rear back. The captain had trouble holding on.

"You'll learn to be a horseman by the time we get to our destination." The monk laughed as he spurred his mount away.

Fortunately for the men, the tiny house next to the pen remained dark as they followed the path out of the village. Crossing an open field, they rode in silence. Soon, the horses came upon a road near the docks. The waning night brought a red-purple haze on the horizon. Marshall saw the shadowed outline of the ship's masts, and he remembered the dagger that Jacotte stole from him.

"You're too quiet," Leiras told Marshall. "I sense you have doubts about me."

Marshall brought his horse to a stop. The monk did the same.

"Leiras, you've already done far more for me than I can repay. However, I return to retrieve my stolen items from that bitch, Jacotte. I'll meet you in Amsterdam. There's no need for you to risk your neck."

"No, I'll lead you to the docks. I have a responsibility to watch over you." The monk's good-natured smile puzzled the captain.

"Ah, I see you need to learn trust. Let me lead the way so you know all that I tell you is true."

The fat man turned his horse toward the docks.

"Your thief must live aboard the boat or above the taverns. Either way, we'll find her." He spurred his horse before Marshall could reply.

After the captain caught up with the monk, the pair rode slowly on the dark road. After a while, Marshall's thoughts spilled out.

"You killed the jailer, claiming he deserved his fate. I thought it was God who judged men? It appears you have taken on his role if I read my scriptures correctly."

"Yes, you are the learned gentleman I expected," the monk replied. "If you recall, I said that I was a believer, not a man of the cloth."

"Therefore, I execute the condemned as instructed by God. Like you, I'm cursed to follow the path laid out by our Creator."

"So, you know what men must die for their sins?" Marshall's skeptical tone caught Leiras, and he grinned.

"I do as I'm called upon," the monk told him. "Don't you believe God placed us together in that jail? What other circumstances can explain our interwoven path? You seek a path out of jail, and I do as well."

Everyone wants to escape a festering jail!

The captain remained quiet after his thought. He glanced over at the squat form outlined in the shadows next to him. Marshall barely made out the monk's gaze as the man eyed him.

"And what of the wife you left with a few silver livre? Is she to beg in the streets with the child?" The pirate finally asked.

"Blackbane, the killer of the unarmed women and children, worries about a widow in a small village?" Leiras shook his head.

"My name is Marshall," the captain growled back.

"Not to worry, my friend. You have a new life now. As for the woman, you saw Denisot is pretty. It's not the first time we met. A jailor does not make many livres. She already had plans for the death of her husband. That's how I knew the man deserved his fate."

Leiras gave a long whistle.

"Who knows what God has planned? Perhaps I gave her a child for her next husband."

The monk smiled at the thought while the perplexed sailor could only guess that a spiteful archangel put Marshall on the same path as an insane man.

Chapter 3: The Journey

When the riders reached the outskirts of the docks, they carefully followed the trail along the back of the few isolated buildings. The smell of drying fish came from the barn-like structures. An occasional oil lantern glowed from lamp posts near the boat tied along the dock. The two men pulled their horses to a stop at the end of the pier. Even in the dim light, Marshall immediately recognized the sloop of Captain Jacotte. Dark and low in the water, the boat he was looking for remained docked at the end of the pier, where Blackbane came ashore.

"I'm checking out the boat," Marshall slid off the saddle. "Stay with the horses and keep them quiet."

Before Leiras said anything, the captain stepped into the shadows and worked his way past the dark and quiet toll shack. Carefully, he walked onto the wooden platform, scowling at the loud sound of his heavy boots. When he got close to the boat, Marshall realized there was no watch on duty. It didn't surprise him, considering the lackadaisical attitude Jacotte showed as the master of her ship. As silent as possible, Marshall went aboard, heading directly to the ship's wheel. He took a binnacle lamp from behind the wheel and lit it with a fire striker. Marshall went to the door of the captain's quarters and slowly entered the dark cabin.

Inside, the pirate noticed the large lump in the only bed. Snoring lightly, Jacotte rolled over, and Marshall saw two people in the bed. He pulled his pistol as he sat the lamp on the table. A quick scan of the cabin revealed Blackbane's rapier hanging from the bulkhead. However, his jeweled dagger was not in sight.

Marshall stepped next to the chest bed with his pistol pointed at Jacotte. When he pulled back on the hammer, the noise woke the woman. The pirate aimed the weapon's barrel at her face.

"Remain quiet or die," he warned. "I'll be taking my things back, woman. Where's your chest?"

Jacotte's surprised expression turned stubborn.

"I can kill you and look for it afterward," the pirate growled out.

She nodded.

"It's in the chest under the bed." The woman's voice woke her bedmate. It was her son, Gascon, who rolled over. He sleepily looked at Marshall, and then he saw the flintlock.

"Alright, both of you out of bed," Marshall ordered as he pulled out his sword.

The odd couple stumbled out of the narrow bed. Jacotte wore a chemise. Her son had on a long woolen shirt and no breeches. Marshall forced Jacotte to lift the top of the bed while sending Gascon to stand by the corner. When the woman removed her captain's chest, she placed it on the table. She hesitated when Marshall told her to back away. He put the tip of his sword blade in her belly to make her retreat. The pirate opened the chest to find the Saint Gennaro dagger, along with a few coins. Marshall slid the holy knife into his belt and took the money with a smile on his bearded face.

"That's payment for stealing my cargo."

As he went to the bulkhead where his stolen rapier hung, Gason suddenly attacked Marshall. The captain pulled the trigger of his pistol, but it misfired. The flash didn't slow Gason, who ran into the pirate captain. His attack rammed Blackbane against the bulkhead with a heavy thud. Momentarily stunned, Marshall took another punch before he finally brought the butt of the heavy pistol down onto his attacker's head. The blow caused Gason to retreat. Immediately, Marshall embedded the blade of his sword through Gason's heart with practiced precision.

Jacotte cried out when she saw her son fall. She attacked the pirate who used his pistol to strike her across the face. The woman stumbled to the deck. Marshall kicked her in the ribs, sending her rolling onto her back. Then he held his sword blade at Jacotte's throat. For a brief instant, the man considered killing her.

"In another time, I would have taken bloody revenge upon you for what you did to me." Marshall intentionally stepped on the woman's arm. She cried out in pain as he pressed down hard with his boot.

"Open your hand," he ordered.

Jacotte only opened her fist after Marshall again pressed his foot down on her forearm. He used the sharp tip of his rapier and cut the letter R into the screaming woman's palm.

"I should have skinned you alive. Instead, I marked you as the thief that you are."

Marshall kicked her again, and she rolled over. The pirate heard her moaning and gasping for air as he took his scabbard and belt from the bulkhead. He calmly walked out of the cabin.

~~~

"My friend is too silent. You should be happy, as a new adventure waits for you." Leiras paused from his whistling. Since sunrise, the monk tried to mimic the early morning birds. Most of the time, his whistles were nowhere close to sounding like the bird's song.

"Are you upset that you didn't kill the woman?"

Marshall remained silent, barely glancing over at the question.

The cloudy sky brought in a mist that dampened the ground and his spirits. Marshall tried to sleep on the uncomfortable
~~~

saddle during the journey, but his mind kept returning to his troubles.

"We go by horseback to a city, and I have no means to get back to the ocean," the captain finally explained. "My crew and I sought the Swedish king to receive a letter of marque and reprisal. As a privateer, I could retire to find my way out of..." He paused, then glanced at his companion. "I'm a man of the sea, yet land-bound without a means to escape."

"Turning into a privateer, eh? A legitimate pirate with the backing of a king. You have brains, for sure. Your idea has merit," Leiras agreed. "What happened to your ship?

"Lost off of Alderney when the anchor gave way, my crew went over the side and drowned," the pirate lied. "Jacotte and her crew found the ship with me aboard the next day. She could have just taken the cargo and dropped me off at the dock. But the woman stole from me and let me hang while she counted her gold."

The monk suddenly laughed.

"She'd make a fine pirate, perhaps as good as Blackbane." His chubby face grew somber when he noticed Marshall's dark expression. "Ah, you don't see the irony as I do."

He sighed and pulled a leather bladder from his saddle. After taking a drink of the wine inside, Leiras handed it to his companion.

"Let us not beat around the bush. I know much about you. I've seen you sleep, man. You thrash about like a banshee, and I overheard the name you wish to hide," he told him. "If the stories I've heard about Blackbane are true, then you're as wicked as the devil himself. Many know of your evil ways."

Marshall nodded.

"Aye, that's the name I carried since the Americas. It is a name that I must lose in these lands. I wondered why you escaped and returned," he confessed. "I'm still not sure of your intentions, but I don't forget a favor."

He paused.

"Beyond what you overheard, I carry a heavy burden. A man of the habit…well, a believer such as you would not aid a man with my problems."

The wicked gleam came to the monk's eyes again.

"Bah, you have ambition and cunning. No man can survive as a buccaneer without such qualities. I've seen how you appraise each man you meet. You trust no one, yet the sound of gold and silver makes your heart race. I believe this is part of your burden."

The pirate captain went silent, thinking about his encounter with Remiel.

"That is part of my curse," he corrected Leiras. "But I'm also condemned to a path that wanders to a destination unknown. You seek Amsterdam. I seek Stockholm."

"Ah, you're weary like I am. Drink up; I've taken this road before. There's a dry place near here where we can sleep for a few hours ahead. We should be another day away from Amiens. After a rest, we can discuss our paths." The monk began whistling again.

After finding an abandoned farmhouse with half of its roof missing, the two men halted, then pulled off the saddle and blankets from their horses. They put their mounts under a relatively dry section of the tiny house before making their uncomfortable beds next to the one standing wall. A fire in the fireplace gave a partial impression of comfort. Unfortunately, their only food was a bundle of dry cheese Leiras carried in his bag. The monk pulled out a silver flask as well. He saw Marshall eyeing the gleaming metal in his hand.

"I've not seen that flask," Marshall commented.

"Oh, this trinket? Another item that Denisot held for me. It surprised me she hadn't sold it. She didn't trust me to finish our agreement about her husband." His grin looked foul in the firelight. The monk checked for a drink inside, but it was empty. He pulled the wine bladder next to him, then pulled a small knife from his belt. The captain stared at the flames for a moment as the monk got comfortable. Leiras tossed over a section of the cheese to Marshall.

"You dwell upon something. Hunger will come soon enough. Eat and then ask your question."

Leiras laughed at the scowl Marshall gave him.

"It doesn't take a wise man to notice your suspicious glances at me. You distrust my thoughts and wish for me to leave you. It's only natural."

The captain again considered his riding companion's motives.

"Distrust is something that comes from a lack of knowledge. You've shown me your ability to kill those you condemn as sinners. However, you do not know why I'm here. Neither do I." Marshall pointed out, then took a bite of the cheese.

A cold sweep of wind caught his attention. He looked up at the dilapidated roof above them. The rain came down heavier while the clouds darkened the sky.

"You're the infamous pirate who now hides his identity. William Marshall also carries a mark upon his neck. I surmise your nightmares have something to do with that." The monk leaned back. His bulbous eyes observed the man across the fire from him. "We are alike. Both of us cursed on this earth to stop the unholy. Why not share your story? Perhaps you'll find my thoughts useful?"

Marshall considered the ideas, then slowly nodded.

"Alright, if you wish to know. You're correct that I'm cursed."

He pointed at his neck.

"I killed a nun, and an archangel gave this to me. I'm damned to walk alone until the end of time. It is the fate I cannot share."

"Yet, someone already gave you guidance. I know this," Leiras assured him.

The monk smiled and threw over the wine bladder to Marshall. Leiras chewed on his cheese again. The pirate's skeptical look forced the man to smile.

"Do you believe that only you have dreams that tell the future?"

Leiras chuckled to himself, then looked up at the dripping water coming from the roof.

"I've seen much in my sleep. I've had a line of saints and believers pass me. Of course, they told me about Remiel and your curse."

The casual way the monk mentioned caused Marshall to lean forward. For an instant, he considered he didn't hear him correctly.

"Wait, you say a line of saints? How in the hell? That's what I saw…" He froze when he recalled drowning.

Leiras yawned and looked over.

"Did one of your visions offer you a path?"

"I'm not sure. But, I remember a voice speaking to me." The pirate unconsciously rubbed on his neck.

"It was like my vision," Leiras agreed. "It was after I saw a vision of a demon dragging you from a ship. I also recognized that woman who waits for you on the docks. It is a good thing that the saints have shown us the path. They're less likely to bed you than a succubus!"

Marshall suddenly stopped drinking the wine. His choking cough at the monk's comment caused Leiras to snicker.

"Like you, the dream showed me relics of the saints and believers. It also gave me an idea that can benefit us. Maybe even save your soul. Are you interested?"

Marshall cocked his head. His suspicious expression remained.

"I'm listening."

"We'll start when we arrive in Amsterdam. I have a friend named Aldert, who will know which *burgemeesters* we need to speak to. My friend is quite mad, of course. However, he carries status in the city. With encouragement, he'll provide us with the information. Perhaps he can guide us to diplomats as well."

"Why do we need such people?" The pirate's bearded face scowled at the thought.

"To be our sponsors, of course. You don't think we can travel through the lands without the support of important people? We need money and influence. We can't introduce you as Blackbane, of course. But Captain William Marshall from the Americas provides us with an opportunity to support our coming journeys. Many of these people trade with the English."

The monk motioned for Marshall to throw back his wine bladder. The captain did, while thinking about the monk's plan.

"I'm not sure. It appears you have ideas, but they might not match my own plans. I say Sweden is my destiny. I'm a captain. Ships leave from Amsterdam every day," Marshall pointed out.

"And how will you be a captain again with no ship or crew? You need silver and gold to get a crew and a ship. I don't see you signing on to a ship as the second mate to a captain."

The monk patted his belly, getting comfortable in his makeshift bed.

"You will learn to trust in time, my new partner," he assured him. "I believe our paths crossed for reasons known only to Providence, but we will learn the truth soon enough."

Leiras stretched with a mighty yawn.

"We should get some rest, for the journey ahead is long and difficult. These cursed lands have bandits and soldiers. One is never sure which side is an ally. Since the end of the war, the nobles here carry competing loyalties between France and the Dutch Republic. The towns remained controlled by the Austrians or the French. Hell, even the bishops will make deals with the devils across their border. Sometimes the peasants do not know who controls their lands."

He looked out at the torrential downpour of rain.

"If the rain continues, so much, the better. It'll keep soldiers and others from stopping to ask questions."

The monk pulled a blanket over him. Marshall watched his companion place his modified sanctuary lamp next to him.

"Why do you carry such a strange-looking lamp?"

Leiras grunted as he rolled over to look at Marshall.

"To help against demons, of course. It's filled with blessed olive oil, and the mirror is polished silver. I'm afraid I borrowed a piece of the True Cross from Xeropotamou Monastery. You see, I embedded in the mirror." He pointed to a tiny cross in the silver.

"Those from the dark hate the light of Christ."

With a loud fart, the monk turned over. Soon, he snored while Marshall continued staring at the lantern. Before his encounter with Remiel, the man carried no faith in the idea of relics and saints. He stole from churches and mosques for the gold and precious stones they held inside. He shook his head as thoughts of his past and future swirled around his tired brain.

Is retrieving these objects another part of my curse?

~~~
~~~

It took another day to reach Amiens. As the men rode the sloppy trail, Marshall learned more about Leiras. To say the monk was insane might be an understatement. Leiras provided many bloodthirsty tales of his travels. He claimed journeys through every kingdom within Europe and into the Ottoman Empire. While Marshall remained skeptical of the claims, there was something in the man which Marshall understood. Beneath the genial demeanor of Leiras, the man appeared to carry an iron will.

Marshall heard much in the man's views about life and the universe. Some of his beliefs were heretical enough to find the monk bound to a stake with a mob screaming for his burning. Yet the captain agreed with them. Still, Leiras shocked Marshall when he briefed him on his plan. The body parts of saints and martyrs meant everything to the faithful. Leiras intended to use the relics as a path of reclamation. However, Blackbane understood the irony of what the monk envisioned. The entire plan struck him as a self-serving and vainglorious way to remove a curse.

After stopping at a tavern in Amiens, the two men sat at a bench table where they drank beer and filled their bellies with black bread and a thick stew. As they talked and warmed by the effects of the alcohol, Leiras elaborated further about their new partnership.

"God wanted us to find and recover the lost relics of the many saints. And we'll become rich in the process. I swear to you that wealthy people inside and outside of the Church will pay in gold for such items," the monk insisted.

"If I'd known that, I'd stole more of them," Blackbane commented as he enjoyed the warmth of the nearby fire. The beer relaxed him, and he broke into a smile as he recalled his first profitable trip along the Spanish coast.

"I found a wooden case holding relics of some saint. I don't even remember the name. However, its value in gold and precious stones was the reason I took it back to Tunis. It was a silver box shaped like a casket with the finger bone of some saint. My share of the profit bought several whores for the night." Marshall raised his clay mug in a toast to his companion.

"And I still had some of the gold coins when I finished with them."

"For such lust, you pay now," the monk's sarcasm remained good-natured. "Nevertheless, I assure you that the macabre body parts inside those trinkets are worth far more to the right person in Europe. The heretics of the south do not know. Otherwise, they'd bring their goods here. However, we'll soon have enough for you to fill a house with whores."

"But why would a person wish for such things? As a youth, my preacher explained the wickedness of idolatry. Both Luther and Calvin spoke against relics." The pirate swirled his mug in thought. "You seem to believe in the power of such things."

"It is said that they healed many sick when Peter's shadow passed over them. Who am I to argue against the bible?" Leiras leaned forward. "Remember, there were many things left inside the house of the Pope who controls what we are told."

The monk leaned back, then glanced around the tavern.

"In my travels, I've seen many places and heard many stories. I've learned that the fool is obstinate. The first thing to know about fools is the fact that they know all things but their ignorance. I'm called by God when I've seen the dead come to me in my dreams. After your travels, can you tell me there is nothing to this shared vision? Then, you can explain why you keep the dagger in your possession when you might have sold it when we arrived in this town?"

Marshall pondered the question and unconsciously touched his neck. He took a deep breath.

"Then I toast your idea," the pirate stated. "But I remain skeptical. When we meet such people who wish to pay us for relics, then I will decide."

"That's fair enough," Leiras agreed as he lifted his mug. "Let's find more food and drink for the rest of the trip."

~~~

By the time they reached the first canals outside of Amsterdam a week later, Marshall still did not know his future path. The one change he noticed came in his dreams. While terrifying, his phantoms only occasionally came to him during his journey.

During their travel, the men noticed the overwhelming fear and suspicion as they passed those on the road. Marshall decided his manner of dressing caused the reaction. Leiras pointed out that Prussian troops traveling the lands around Amsterdam. The locals feared the Prussians, who looted and extorted to feed their bands of soldiers.

When the two men arrived in Amsterdam, their first stop was in the merchant's district, looking for the tailors and millinery shops. While they guided their mounts through the busy cobblestone streets, Leiras told him they must find a tailor.

"Fashionable gentlemen require the correct clothing. Your garments give you away as a man who sailed with Turks. You must appear as a captain of English ships. The people respect such allies since they support the House of Orange," the monk explained.

"I can sell my extra sword to help fund our needs," Marshall agreed. "Are you planning on giving up your black habit?"

"Most certainly not. The openness to the air below keeps my privates happy." Leiras paused at the idea. "Still, I remember a dashing red ferraiolo that caught my eye in Paris one time. The cardinal who wore it was an unholy sinner. We'll see if a tailor
~~~

can provide me with such a cape to enhance the air of godly authority as I walk among the sinners."

Marshall frowned.

"Tell me the truth. How long did you spend with the monks?"

Leiras winked at his companion.

"A year in a monastery showed me the error in their ways. Still, I enjoyed consoling the lonely young men at night," he said with a gleam in his eye. The monk noticed his companion's sour expression at the revelation.

"Ah, I see you don't approve. I enjoy all of life's pleasures. A learned gentleman should remember the wisdom of our Greek ancestors with their Sacred Band of Thebes. A person can learn much from Plato."

He stopped them in front of a tailor's shop.

"Now follow me to the promised land, my son."

It was near dark when they finally left the tailor. Dressed in the latest fashion, Marshall wore a short patterned red waistcoat over his linen shirt with fabric ruffles. His long gray coat and black satin breeches gave the pirate the look of a gentleman. His companion sported a new black habit," along with a bright red cape. Leiras forced them to stop by a tavern where he filled his silver flask with rum.

"You should remember this drink," the monk told him. "Stories of your escapades in the Caribbean reached us along with this fine drink."

"Aye, I recall the hangovers from that demon rum as well. Now, where is your friend?"

"He lives in the most prestigious part of the Herengracht. His neighbors are traders who may know the name of Blackbane. You must remain tight-lipped about your past travels," Leiras warned. "I suggest you remember those times before your days as a pirate."

The men climbed on their horses and spurred the mounts through the narrow streets. They reach an area that Leiras called the *Gouden Bocht*.

"It's the words for Golden Bend. Many of the most prestigious families live there," he explained. "The traders here have connections with routes to South America or the Dutch East Indies."

Leiras stopped them in front of a three-story brick townhome. The four-column façade ran up to the engraved pediment along the roofline. Leaving their horses tied to the wrought iron rails of the stairs leading to the front door. Across the canal was a similar-looking street filled with a row of more townhomes.

Marshall glanced back at the passing *trekschuit* that floated along the canal next to the street. The small barge, which was only about eight feet wide, had a rudimentary sail. However, the vessel mostly used donkeys walking alongside to carry passengers and cargo through the system of canals in the area. The watercraft vaguely reminded the pirate of a Dutch *fluyt* he captured.

A haggard-looking male servant answered the door, then allowed Leiras and Marshall inside. He left the two men in the parlor. Black ebony side chairs and table sat in the middle of the room. Elaborately carved in intricate designs, the furniture was luxurious, but showing its age and wear. A dark wood desk and bookcase contained a few volumes of leather books.

"How do you know this man?" Marshall looked longingly at the canal, which led to the sea.

"I met Aldert in Paris. He enjoyed the same whore houses as those in the *Cent Suisses*. You should disregard his strange ideas concerning those in the Vatican."

Leiras stepped close to Marshall.

"He believes in the Jewish pope Andreas," he whispered.

Marshall's eyes widened at the comment. Expression of such a belief in Catholic kingdoms led to execution.

"Still, Aldert might find our path useful in receiving payments from the Spanish consul. He has your obsession with money; however, he's lost a good bit of it over the years." The monk winked at his partner.

Soon, Aldert entered the room a few moments later. Wearing a red robe with blue trimming over woolen breeches, the man's long gray hair hung over his shoulders. Aldert smiled at Leiras, extending his hand. Rotting teeth, a narrow face, and a long nose gave their host the appearance of an angry bird.

After the monk introduced Marshall, the men walked to the table.

"The captain comes from America. He'd make a good man for your trading routes," Leiras bragged. Aldert nodded as he looked over at the pirate. Aldert pointed them to the chairs.

"It's too bad you're a year late for what I need," the merchant told them in accented English. "I've sold my ships to pay debts since the Prussians and the English make my life hell on earth. The city suffers from the chaos outside the walls. At times, one must wear an orange cockade to show their support for the patriots. I just returned from the bourse. It's like a ghost town. I'm afraid my fortunes suffer along with those of this city."

Marshall went to the window as the friends caught up on the latest news. He watched the activity outside. A boat filled with soldiers in blue uniforms paddled by the house. The pirate's attention went back to the conversation when Aldert rang for his servant.

"My friend, it's been a while. What brings you back? I see you still carry the look of a papist."

The monk laughed.

"The *Intendant* of Le Havre would find your suspicions quite comical. He considers me a Calvinist heretic. Now, my new friend and I are on a quest. Visions brought us together. We follow the path laid out before us. Of course, I had to tell you about our expedition."

Leiras continued his tale, explaining his idea of bringing religious relics back to Amsterdam. When he finished, Aldert's expression told Marshall it didn't go well. Their host scowled at the thought when his servant finally entered the room. He ordered the man to bring them tea. After the man left, Aldert turned back to his friend.

"My friend, we've had this discussion before. I realize you don't follow the teachings of Calvin, but you don't believe in such idolatry. You said that it encourages the rabble to miss the light of God. If leaders of the church in this city find out about this, they will mark us for lynching."

"What is profit without a minor risk? I told you that God guided us on this path. Are you telling me you don't believe in visions any longer?" Leiras glanced over at Marshall. There was a grin on his fat lips.

"Besides, we aren't guiding the rabble. The leaders of Amsterdam have no interest in our mission, only the Catholics will. As you said, there is chaos and uncertainty in the country. William and I think there's a nice profit in our future to find these relics."

"William, our visions were quite clear, wouldn't you say?"

Marshall grunted with a nod.

Aldert's expression softened at the thought. "A profit, you say?"

"Yes, it's an endeavor that might bring more silver than then your ships brought in a year. My idea is for the Spanish counsel to help in our endeavor. It's known that the French curry favor bringing home such items. But you have not seen such visions. It's a pity, since you're held with such esteem in the city."

Leiras rose from his chair.

"Marshall and I should go on to the tavern. We can leave in the morning." He motioned the pirate captain toward the door.

"Leiras, you and your friend mustn't leave so soon. I'll have drinks brought to us, and we can discuss your idea further." Aldert hurried to the door ahead of his visitors. "Perhaps I know of people that can provide you and your friend with support for such a journey."

"My friend, you're such an excellent host. But I'm not sure we can expose you to the ridicule or danger should others hear about our idea. We can't impose upon your hospitality." Leiras patted the gray-haired man on the shoulder. "Knowing you remain on good terms with the regents, I don't want to put your family name at risk."

Aldert laughed.

"The regents suspect me of many things since I shame the sinners. They will hardly believe such a tale. Still, the fools would rather destroy such objects rather than make money from them. Please, my friend, you are my guest." He beamed. "It does a man's heart good to help God's work. Then, we can enjoy the pleasures of life by using sinner's gold and silver."

Leiras gave his friend a sigh.

"Very well, you've convinced me."

~~~

Marshall staggered through the narrow confines of a back alley while he followed the pale light of an oil lantern he held in his hand. Trying to get his bearings amid the stench of rot and decay, his numb mind told him the sun would soon rise. He didn't care since he filled his body with rum and wine, and he felt euphoric.

Into the evening, Leiras promote his scheme, and, after initial resistance, Aldert slowly warmed to the idea. While Marshall held reservations concerning their new partner, he realized he had no cards to play. His only option was to find a
~~~

ship leaving Amsterdam. However, Marshall had no appetite to shipping out as a mate for another captain. Marshall and Aldert's conversation showed he needed contacts in the skipper's guild near the waterfront. The situation left Marshall tied to the goals of Leiras. He still struggled with the idea that a saint might save him from an angel.

I thought they worked on the same side!

A bottle of port later, the monk and the trader toasted to their future success with the pirate.

"I have a friend who's on good terms with the Catholic console," Aldert told them. "I'm confident that his help can give us financial backers."

Aldert paused, his face turned red.

"I'm afraid my funds remain limited for such an adventure."

"Then, I will purchase a bottle for us tonight," Leiras smiled.

Not long after the conversation, the monk and his friend led Marshall to a nearby tavern. The pirate noticed his partner's attention remained on profit. The very idea of selling relics at a substantial profit engulfed their thinking. For himself, Marshall kept wondering if the religious objects helped his situation. The archangel cursed the man until Doomsday. However, a dream and an insane man of the cloth guided him to this point. Marshall recognized the effect his Saint Gennaro dagger welded upon a demon. At least, the religious artifacts provided him with protection from the demons.

How will my new path help, or am I just groping for a chance to escape fate?

Finishing his drink, Marshall left. He intended to go back to Aldert's home after the trader insisted his partners would stay at his home. The monk offered directions, but the pirate shook his head.

"I'll find my way," he confidently insisted.

When Marshall stepped from the full room, he immediately enjoyed the solace of the quiet street. Fog covered the canal and drifted across the twisting, narrow streets. The captain slowly realized he had no idea how to return to the house as he walked along. Still, he held no concern. The maddening paths of Amsterdam either led back to either the docks or to the center of the city. From there, he would find his way to the Herengracht canal.

He decided the twisting, confusing path was a suitable allegory for his life. While his new partner still had enough silver to survive for a while, Marshall felt like a beggar. It reminded him of his times in Jamaica.

Then he saw the pale figure in the shadows at the same time he heard the familiar growl of hunger. The noise came from the belly of the creature. In a flash, the man's sword slid out from its leather scabbard. That was when he noticed two more of the pale figures lying in wait on the other side of the alley. Ghouls held the advantage in numbers. Marshall kept his weapon pointed at them. He backed away when he heard a footstep behind him.

"William Marshall! Or would you rather be called Blackbane? I've meant to greet you," the icy voice came from behind him.

The captain looked back to see a tall, slim figure standing at the entrance to the alley. Marshall backed up to the wall and held out the lantern. The light revealed an unfamiliar tan face with thin lips and black eyes that bore into his. The man blocking his path reminded the pirate of a creole native of Curaçao. However, his dark clothes were too delicate, even for a slave trader. His coat, waistcoat, and breeches were of the latest style. However, he wore no wig. Long black hair fell on his shoulders.

"Whoever you are, back away before these foul creatures have us both," he told the dark man, who laughed and stepped closer.

"The man who claims no fear warns me of danger," the stranger replied. "But then, I have nothing to fear. They will only eat your flesh upon my command."

Marshall glanced back at the ghouls, who stepped toward him. He recognized their black eyes had the same look as the stranger. The creatures had skeletal bodies covered in the rotting rags of their burial clothes. While they might regularly feast on corpse bodies, the flesh of a living person was a delightful treat to a ghoul. Marshall whipped his rapier around within an inch of the stranger's throat.

"Foul vermin, approach me, and they will feed on your flesh," he said.

"I fear no human," the stranger held his ground. "You are not of your namesake, are you? I know you'd run your sword through an unarmed man. You should heed the words of that Englishman Shakespeare. He wrote something about cowards die many times before their deaths. Yet, the valiant never taste of death but once? Maybe he knew of you."

Enraged, Marshall thrust forward. However, his sword went through the shadow. The stranger stepped forward, and his dark soul passed through Marshall. Instantly, Marshall felt an unbearable cold thrust through his chest like an ice blade ripping into his lungs. He staggered away and fell into the wall. Then, the ghouls jumped on him.

Despite the paralyzing freeze in his arms, Marshall turned to point his sword at the closest monster. The ghoul embedded its body into the long blade, screaming in agony as the tip went through its back. Unfortunately, the other two monsters grabbed him and took Marshall to the ground on his back. As he struggled to free himself, one ghoul bit down into his heavily muscled arm. Marshall yelled out, twisting to dislodge the ghoul's bite. The creature hung on to his arm, its teeth sinking into the man's flesh.

"Stop!" the dark stranger ordered the monster.

Marshall screamed out when he felt the ghoul's jaws cut away skin and flesh before it retreated. The creature chewed on the hunk of Marshall's meat in its hand as the stranger calmly picked the lantern from the ground. The captain quickly glanced at his bleeding wound, then looked at the dark man, who kneeled next to Marshall. He held the glowing light close to Marshall's face. The fire caused the ghouls to look away, chattering from the pain to their sensitive eyes.

"They won't feed on you if you decide to be reasonable. I've heard that you turned down one of my brothers. However, I have an offer which you should accept," he told him, his eyes locking on Marshall's.

"Alright, enough of the butter," the captain replied. "What are you offering?"

"Beelzebub offered you a fleet of ships for you to exact your vengeance upon that fat man in Tunis," the stranger said with a grim smile. "I have something much more substantial for you to consider." He paused for effect. "I'll remind you that your flesh limits you. What if I promised to stop the pain and suffering of your curse? What if I offered you salvation?"

Marshall narrowed his eyes at the term.

"Who are you to offer such a thing?"

"Mammon is at your service, and I'm quite in earnest," the fiend insisted. "I enjoy sowing injustice in the world of man. Like you, I covet the precious things in life, such as gold and silver. I'm the god of avarice. You and I are brothers."

"You talk of salvation, yet you're fallen. I see no benefit to me."

Mammon's expression turned foul.

"I see you still carry that hideous symbol on your neck. I can remove that when you give your soul to me. You seek relief from your world of suffering and misery. The past will stop, along with your nightmares. You can join me and lift the burden you carry. I'm happy to let you join me. Let me become the way to your salvation. Look into my eyes and see what can be."

As the man lay there, numb, but for the area of missing flesh from his arm, Marshall felt a strange calm overwhelm him. His mind screamed to look away; however, he stared into the dark eyes of the stranger. The captain saw an endless pool of soothing black water. It was a repulsive place to his mind, yet it felt suitably comfortable to the man. Mammon called him to join their souls together.

"Time sides with me, and it can come to you. All things coveted will embrace you for eternity."

Powerful urges overcame the man's resistance as he lay in the alley's filth. He saw his hands ripping out the heart of a fat man who tried to protect his chest of treasures. Marshall felt ecstasy as a chain made of gold and silver coins enveloped him, binding around his chest. Like a snake, the chain tightened. Even though his breathing grew difficult, Marshall smiled at the precious metal, slowly killing him.

"Away, you foul spawn of the underworld!" A loud voice screamed out from outside the pool of black. The familiar sound of echoed along with a thread of foul sailor curses.

The voice woke Marshall from his trance while an unbearable bright light filled the alley. He pulled his Saint Gennaro dagger and backed into the wall. The lantern glow caused the ghouls to cry out while retreating away. The stranger calmly stood, shielding his eyes from the glare.

"He will be mine! A drunken brother cannot stop that," the black-eyed man claimed as he held his ground. Marshall finally recognized Leiras as he drew closer. The fat man fumbled with his robe, finally pulling out his silver cross. He extended his olive oil lantern. The light coming from the lamp grew even more intense as it reflected from the silver mirror. The sound of holy prayers chanted by the monk filled the air, and the dark shadows in the alley disappeared along with the ghouls.

"Mammon, get back to your sulfurous pit," Leiras ordered before he recited the Lord's Prayer in Latin. His words slurred enough that Marshall noticed he mispronounced several of the terms. Mammon's face turned to a grimace at the prayer, and he backed away from his quarry.

"Blackbane, we'll meet again. Think hard about my offer," the demon told him. "Otherwise, I'll have the ghouls strip you of your flesh while you beg to die. Then, I'll grind your bones to powder. When I'm finished, you'll find no vessel to hold your wondering soul."

As the hideous noise of wailing souls emerged beneath the feet of the humans, the creature slowly turned into a dark mass of fog. The air stank of Sulphur and rotting flesh as the vapor sunk into the ground. Only the lantern he carried remained. It lay on the ground, the metal covered with a green patina.

In the sudden vacuum, the only sound came from the heavy breathing of the men. Marshall scrambled to his feet. Marshall went to retrieve his sword after sliding the blessed dagger into his belt. Leiras came to him.

"Are you badly wounded?" The monk used the light from the lamp to reveal Marshall's injuries.

The captain asked for the monk's flask. Leiras pulled out the silver flagon, taking a quick sip before handing it over. Marshall carefully poured the liquid on his wounded arm. The bleeding area still showed the teeth marks from the ghoul. He yelled out in pain, then he grabbed Leiras to keep from collapsing. Cleaning the next wound sent the captain into a frenzy of curses. The monk's clumsy attempts to help caused Marshall to pull away.

"Enough. Lead us to Aldert's house, and I can look over the rest of my injuries there."

The captain picked up his sword and slid it into the scabbard. Leiras scrambled to pick up his lamp and joined him. They walked out of the alley, and the monk guided them along the empty street. Before long, they found the canal leading to Aldert's home.

"I thank you for the help," Marshall told the monk. "I don't believe I could stop him."

"Probably not. Mammon has a way of looking inside a person. You're lucky I stumbled upon you. I wondered where you went in this fog."

Leiras directed them to cross the empty street as he used his lamp to light their path.

"It was strange. I normally don't get lost," the captain commented, then looked over at his companion. "By the way, how did you know his name?"

"The demons have their ways. They can look inside of you and show you a different world," Leiras ignored the question. "You see what the demon intends for you to see. That's how he guided you to the alley. You must remember to keep a trusted advisor by your side."

"And you be that person?" Marshall wondered aloud.

The monk took a sip from his flask and nodded.

"Who else carries this sacred lamp?"

~~~

The next morning, Marshall slowly crawled out of his bed. His aching body sent a wave of pain through him with every movement. He looked over to see an empty place on the other side of the bed. With only two beds in the home, Leiras shared the bed with the pirate. The monk was already up and out of the room.

In the day's light, Marshall looked over his injuries. Painfully pulling off the cloth bandages he made from one of Aldert's old linen shirts, the pirate found his wounds remained
~~~

bloody and raw. He hoped that the rum kept infection from the ghoul's bites away, but the man wasn't hopeful.

So much for immortally!

He redressed the gashes and started to dress for the day. However, his new clothes were gone. Marshall quickly put on his undershirt and left his room. Outside the door, he nearly ran into a plump little servant girl who carried a bundle of clothes. The woman's blue eyes stared up at him with momentary fear from his foul expression. Then, she said something in Dutch that he didn't understand and handed him his suit and breeches. The clothes were still damp, but the servant girl cleaned away the worst of the mud and grime. She had even sewed the tears in the fabric. Before Marshall thought to thank her, the girl was gone.

When he finished dressing, the captain found Leiras downstairs in the parlor. From the dirty dishes on the table, he'd just finished another plate of breakfast.

"I wondered if you were planning on sleeping the day away." The monk leaned back in his chair, which groaned in protest.

"I need to leave," Marshall said. "I can get a ship to Sweden. The dagger I have will get me enough silver as a passenger as a gentleman."

Leiras rubbed his belly.

"That is true. But what happened to your crew the last time you met a dark angel at sea? You understand the demons follow wherever you go. You need patience and something more than that dagger to keep them away."

"How do you know about my crew?" Marshall growled.

Leiras smiled.

"I told you that you talk when you sleep."

The suspicion remained on the pirate's face as he sat at the table. The plump girl suddenly appeared with a plate of food for him. He looked her over as she quietly left them.

"I don't have the nightmares as often," Marshall turned back to his companion.

"Besides, do you speak Swedish? Do you have contacts within the king's court? Believe me when I say a trip to Stockholm will not serve you well." Leiras reached over to pick up a delicate teacup.

As he drank, the monk's bulbous eyes watched the pirate. Marshall's expression turned darker as he considered his options again. After a moment of silence, he nodded.

"Alright, you've got me lashed to the capstan. Where's your friend, Aldert?"

"Our new partner is already at work. He's meeting with his contacts at the bourse. Aldert expects he can sell our idea to several backers who will front our travel money," the fat man said as he set down his cup. "My funds are only what's in my purse. Plus, you need your dagger."

Marshall said nothing as he picked up the dark bread on his plate.

"As long as it gets us out of this forsaken place. I don't like the idea that more demons looking for me in the city. The place closes in on me."

~~~

Two days later, Aldert brought Marshall and Leiras the first hint of good news. As they gathered around the trader's table, Aldert's excitement was contagious. It surprised the men when he mentioned meeting with the Catholic Spanish consul in secret.

"I know. It surprised me that Jordán del Río met with me. Diederik mentioned he knew the Spaniard, but I didn't believe he'd be interested." Aldert poured port wine into small cordials, which he handed to his guests.

"However, this morning, del Rio and Diederik agreed to fund a trip for us. It seems the French are already looking for a
~~~

relic." The trader's joyful expression turned somber. "However, del Rio added a provision to our agreement."

Marshall glanced over at the monk, who took a sip of the drink.

"They say God works in mysterious ways," Leiras stated. He held out his glass for more drink.

"I knew you would understand, my friend. It's a simple matter. Our sponsors already found an item for us. They wish for you to take the relic from a Frenchman who travels back to France. Maximilien Gabriel, who's the son of the 9th Duke of Sully, recovered a heart of an obscure saint to curry favor for his king. Since Gabriel is a favorite of French Marshall de La Croix, the Spanish wish to intercept this item." Aldert smiled after drinking his port.

"While I'm not privy to the workings of diplomacy, I assume such action by the Spaniards would hurt Gabriel's standing. And, since Marshall is English, I considered his support of the idea."

"I'm sure you did. But finding such a noble is difficult among the many kingdoms in Europe," the monk replied.

"More like impossible," Marshall grumbled as he turned to the window.

"Ah, we think alike, my partners. I suspected this issue as well, so I asked Diederik. He told me that the shipping guild has reliable information that the French nobleman returns from Augsburg in Bavaria. He's coming by boat along the Rhine. They expect him to arrive at the village of Ewijk on his way to Paris."

"How can he carry such confidence in the Frenchman's destination?" Marshall asked irritably.

Aldert's surprised look at the question made Leiras suppress a smile.

"It's a fair question, even with your excellent contacts."

"Yes, my friend, I hadn't thought about that," Aldert quickly agreed. "Diederik said that the Van Stepraedt family has holdings there. He knows they are staunchly Catholic. It's rumored the family brings in priests for mass. It's only natural that Gabriel will stop there."

The man told his partners about the shrine that carried the hear of Sant Julia of Corsica. His description immediately caught Marshall's attention. He went to the table, focusing his question on Leiras.

"Who was this saint? I've never heard of her."

"I don't know much about her," the monk confessed. "They martyred her in the time of the Romans. Monks took her to the Benedictine abbey at Brescia."

"According to Jordán del Río, the monks encased her relics in a gold and silver vessel. The French stole the display during the War of the League of Cambrai. This is part of the reason that Spain wishes to engage us to get it back from the French."

"How does Gabriel get a relic from monks unless they're corrupt, or he stole it?"

Marshall eyed the Dutchman.

"I'm not sure," Aldert admitted. "Does it matter?"

"Not in the least," Leiras spoke up. "However, to reach this village, we need money. What is the agreement?"

"Twenty silver rijksdaalder is for the trip. A hundred gold docats when we bring the artifact back to del Rio. You'll receive a letter from del Rio introducing you as men of good standing and in alliance with his needs. He's an investor in the Caisse d'Escompte, so getting money to Gabriel is not an issue. Just use the letter you have."

Aldert licked his lips.

"Why does Diederik agree to this? A regent would not welcome a Catholic into his home." The monk's cautious tone struck Marshall, and he looked at Aldert.

"Ah, it's good to be suspicious as I am. Diederik told del Rio that he won't object if the Spaniard takes possession outside of the city walls when you return. As you can imagine, if word gets out about such a trade, it would mean trouble for his family."

The merchant explained.

"And I suspect that Diederik already took his cut of our money," Marshall interjected. "How much?"

"Fifty docats," Aldert admitted. "I'm afraid it's the best we can do."

The pirate captain stared at him for a moment and returned to the window. Leiras patted the arm of Aldert.

"You did fine, my friend. Get us the money, and we'll leave at first light tomorrow."

Aldert shook his head.

"You misunderstand. You and Marshall must make the trip alone. I'm afraid I cannot join you on this journey. My affairs require me to remain in the city."

"I see," the monk leaned back with his drink. As he tipped the glass, Leiras glanced over at his companion by the window.

Pirates run the entire world! Marshall thought as he finished the glass of sherry.

~~~

Marshall found the servant girl in his room when he entered. She spun around with the Saint Gennaro dagger in her hand. Instantly furious, he crossed the room.

"Je zou dit niet moeten hebben!" The blue-eyed girl attempted to rush past him.

Marshall grabbed her wrist. With a pain-filled cry, the woman dropped the weapon. Flinging her to the bed, Marshall jumped on her. He slapped her, demanding answers.

"Why are you here, cursed witch? Who told you to steal my dagger?"
~~~

"Het spijt me, doe me alsjeblieft geen pijn. Ik zal het niemand vertellen!"

Fear filled her face, but he couldn't understand her frantic reply.

"She says that she won't tell anyone," Leiras spoke up as he stood by the door.

Marshall glanced back. "What do you mean? Why did she try to steal it?"

The monk asked the girl, who gave him a long answer. An amused grin crossed the fat man's face as the girl explained.

"You have another protector. Isabel claims that she's trying to shelter you. She's Catholic and recognized the Latin inscription on the blade. Isabel believes you are of the same faith and doesn't want you to sell it. I believe she's overheard some of our conversations and thinks the authorities will haul you away."

Leiras smiled, then he told the girl that she misunderstood.

"I explained that you and I are working for God. Curiously, Aldert doesn't understand that he has a heretic working for him. Well, I guess that would make three of us under his roof at this point."

Marshall looked down at the woman, who relaxed. Then he slid from the top of her. He took the dagger and put it in his belt.

"Just tell her to leave my stuff alone," he growled.

"Hij vindt je aangenaam," Leiras told the servant girl who smiled as she sat up in the bed. Her cheeks turned red as she nodded.

"We're about to leave on a long trip, and she's a cute thing." The monk closed the door.

"What's going on?"

Leiras frowned at the pirate.

"I'll let you figure it out. But she's quite taken with you."

"Trek je kleren uit vrouw en behaag hem voordat Aldert leert wat je hebt gedaan!"

The monk snapped at the servant as he closed the door.

The girl's expression changed to concern, and she immediately began disrobing. Marshall watched her for a moment before he understood. He glanced at the door.

Damn cagy monk!

He pulled off his shirt. Isabel's nervous smile forced the pirate to smirk as he took her arm

"Come closer, Isabel," Marshall said as he drew her next to him.

Chapter 4: Paying a Debt

The trip out of Amsterdam occurred as a bitter winter wind swept through the country. The trekschuit that Aldert hired for them proceeded slowly as the two-mule team walked the towpath next to the canal. While it had a sail, the calm day forced the use of the mules. Aside from Marshall and Leiras, who rode as passengers, a mixed cargo of textiles and fabrics filled the boat's middle.

Before they left, Aldert gave the travelers a bag of silver coins along with last-minute instructions. When Marshall counted out the coins, he realized the merchant took his cut of their money. He mentioned it to his partner.

"It's expected. At least we have enough," Leiras shrugged. "Our letter of introduction will provide us with a means to get in the door of most nobility, be they Spanish or French." The monk smiled when he saw the captain shivering under his heavy wool cape.

"Too bad you won't have the little servant girl with you on this trip."

Marshall nodded.

"Aye, I'll agree with that. She's sweeter than the whores a pirate finds along the docks. By the way, what did you tell her?"

Leiras grinned.

"I left her with the fear that you'd tell Aldert about her attempt to steal the dagger. After I watched her staring at you from the window, I'm confident she'll happily greet you when we return."

"I'll not stay there again," the pirate grunted.

"Too bad you've just broken another heart. You don't trust Aldert."

"No, but, then again, I trust few people," Marshall admitted. "I won't return to places where demons might wait for me."

"I can understand why." The fat man pulled a leather bag and filled his pipe. "However, you appeared extremely interested in this venture."

The pirate nodded.

"I saw it in one of my dreams."

"Then you had a vision. We're on the right path," Leiras confidently stated.

Marshall looked at the gray sky.

"We'll find out in a few days, according to the barge owner. This canal takes us to Medel, then we follow the Waal River. At least he speaks a little Anglais, as the natives call it."

The monk chuckled at the statement.

"As long as we stay away from the nasty fends who hunt you, we'll be fine. When we get to Ewijk, we'll check on the Van Stepraedt family. I've found the roadhouses know a lot about local estates. Hopefully, our prize awaits us. From there, we'll determine our next steps."

"That sounds reasonable," Marshall agreed as he hunched down in his coat.

It was late afternoon when they finally reached Ewijk. The desolate stop along the river appeared devoid of buildings. Only a single road crossed over the mule footpath and led away from the dock into the nearby flood plain. The barge owner directed the men to follow the path to the line of trees in the distance. After retrieving their bags, Marshall handed one to the monk.

"Cold and bleak," the pirate commented. "I'll bet your privates aren't happy in this winter wind. I'm yearning for the heat of the desert right now."

"Aye, that's why I bought breeches for days like this," he replied with a wink. His friend's expression went grim.

"Now keep your wits about you, my pirate friend," Leiras warned. The lands remain in turmoil. The Dutch, the Hapsburgs, and the French all control different areas.

"I'm just an Englishman, remember? That part I can do well enough." Marshall reminded him.

"It's fortunate for you to act like a follower of Luther. Where we're going, the Dutch Blue Guards remain to keep down the Catholics. We can't have those soldiers believe we're French. When we go south, we'll need to worry about the Hapsburgs and the kingdom of France. To make it worse, the Prussian soldiers wear blue as well."

"It's easier to believe that no one's our friend," the pirate wrapped himself with his cape at a gust of icy wind.

"Why can't these damn relics be in the desert?"

During the rest of their walk along the road, the men talked little. They finally came upon a whitewashed building of stone where horses and carts made it challenging to get to the entrance. The noise coming from inside broke the silence of the night as they entered the inn. A blast of heated, smokey air struck them.

A lull in the conversations occurred when the crowd looked upon the two strangers. After an uncomfortable pause, the men continued to a table, and the sound of conversations gradually filled the room again. A boy came to the table, his wide eyes looking over the monk's red clothes.

"Monseigneur, wat kan ik voor u halen?

Leiras grinned.

"Apparently, I'm moving up in the world," he told Marshall. "He thinks I'm a bishop within the Church. I'm royalty to the right people."

The monk ordered two drinks and food. The boy bowed before he hurried away.

"Well, you've got everyone's attention. It's no wonder with the outfit you're wearing." Marshall grumbled. "It's difficult to keep people from wondering what we're doing here."

"Ah, you needn't worry. After a few drinks, we'll soon know every bit of local gossip." The monk pulled his pipe and filled the bowl with the tobacco he carried. "That is the advantage we have on this trip."

Marshall remained quiet as the boy returned with mugs of beer. As he covertly scanned the room, the pirate recognized the inquisitive glances directed at them. The patrons appeared curious, not hostile.

His focus came upon a tall man dressed in a coat with a collar, waistcoat, and breeches of deep blue. His manner and style indicated wealth. As he drank, Marshall noticed the tall patron kept glancing over from the corner of the room where he sat with other fashionably dressed men. Casually, the pirate pointed out the stranger's interest in them to his comrade.

"Yes, I've seen him as well. He carries the look of a gentleman. Let's see how curious he becomes." Leiras rubbed his palms together when he noticed the boy returning with their food.

It wasn't long after the meal when the stranger approached their table. He hunched over in a stoop due to the low ceiling of the inn. He spoke in French to Leiras.

"Forgive my interruption, father. It's an honor to have someone of the cloth traveling through this unholy land. I must say you're a brave man. Many of our faith keep a low profile in these times."

"Well, I have a special relationship with some of the authorities, which provides me with protection."

The monk gestured to the seat across from him. The stranger sat next to Marshall, who nodded congenially.

The pirate didn't pick up on his friend's glib falsehood, only getting a few words. Instead, he watched the other patrons in the tavern. Fortunately, no one appeared interested in the table's conversation.

"Who do I have the pleasure of addressing?" Leiras continued.

"Johanne van Stepraedt," the stranger nodded. "My family has an estate nearby." The man glanced over at Marshall.

"My friend is from America," Leiras stated. "William Marshall knows only a few words in French."

"Ah, an Anglais!" He smiled when Marshall looked at him.

Johanne turned back to Leiras.

"I understand you arrived on a barge from Amsterdam. Are you traveling far?"

"We're traveling upriver to Karlsruhe on business," the monk replied. "My partner has a mission from a counsel in Amsterdam. I'm providing William with expertise in matters of certain relics."

Johanne's expression darkened.

"Oh, I wish you were here yesterday."

Leiras gave the man a broad smile. "And why would that be, my son?"

Johanne's eyes narrowed, and he glanced around.

"I had a friend and his wife, who stayed with us. He carried several items in his possession. Well, I'm sure he might need your expertise."

The monk quickly changed tactics. He called over the boy who served them.

"Please bring this gentleman a drink. We have much to discuss!"

The pirate gained knowledge from the French and English conversations at the table. Johanne's family hosted someone of importance recently. Leiras mentioned Johanne admitted the person who stayed with him carried something for a king. Apparently, Maximilien Gabriel left the day before on his way to France. When Marshall attempted to hurry the monk away, Leiras told him there was no hurry.

"Gabriel left by barge. He doesn't enjoy traveling by carriage with the Prussians around. We'll cut him off by getting horses and traveling directly to the city," he whispered when Johanne left the tavern to relieve himself.

When the Dutchman returned, he invited the two men to his estate.

"You and your friend must come with me. You may stay at my home and use our conventicle for mass."

With a broad smile, Leiras accepted. Marshall sighed and followed the men outside.

The moon rose over the road as Johanne's servant drove the cart, holding the three men in the back to the van Stepraedt estate. Johanne and Leiras happily sang a song, his voice out of key, while Marshall leaned against the small cask that they brought with them. Their new host enjoyed his spirits nearly as much as the monk.

As they came around the curved drive to the estate, the white buildings shone a ghostly pale under the moonlight. Johanne van Stepraedt noticed Marshall's interest in the buildings and pointed to the small castle keep.

"The Spanish occupied our home in 1585, and it burned during the Siege of Nijmegen," he told Leiras. The visitor didn't realize the monk was paying more attention to the drink in his mug. Finally, he translated the story for Marshall.

"Johanne tells me that after the fire, only the massive base walls still stood. His family began restoration when the war finally finished. Since they banned the Catholic rituals, the family made the castle vault available for other believers in the area. They secretly attend mass here. He calls it the family's personal *schuilkerken*," Leiras told him. "That's where we're going tonight. Johanne promises us excellent beds to sleep on when we're finished."

"Are you sure about this?" Marshall warned his friend.

"Of course I am. I've seen enough ceremonies to make myself the damn pope," the man replied as he ceremoniously hoisted his mug.

When they arrived at the dark estate, it didn't take van Stepradt long to gather his family and servants for a late-night mass. A hidden passage took them into a makeshift chapel filled with religious statues. Johanne told the monk he saved the items from destruction by the Protestants. Leiras enjoyed his new role as an honorable bishop, and his eyes gleamed when people genuflected as they passed him. The man went to the front of the room while Marshall remained in the back.

The pirate watched the proceedings with growing discomfort. At first, he scanned the crowd, who watched and followed along as the monk perform the Liturgy. Feeling a flash of heat fill his neck, Marshall quickly left the room. Rubbing the symbol that burned like fire on his flesh, the man left the building and walked into the courtyard.

Damn, Remiel doesn't want me around a cross!

Gradually, the chilly night refreshed the captain. As the pain in his neck went away, the captain considered the irony inside the building. What would Remiel think about a sodomite killer preaching to the people?

And God cursed me!

He wanted to scream out loud as he took a deep breath. In the courtyard's stillness, the crunch of gravel under his feet was the only sound. As he came near the barn, the sound of the mass reached him from an open window in the turret.

"I wondered when you might leave that foul ritual."

Marshall stopped. Ahead of him, Naamah leaned against the side of the barn. She wore only a dark-colored linen undergarment. Cut low to reveal her upper chest and shoulders, her loose-fitting shift fell below her knees like a dress. A belt around her middle emphasized the curves of her body. Without a gown and petticoat, the woman looked exotic and tempting.

"You show much of yourself. Why are you here?" Marshall glanced around. Nothing revealed itself in the shadows.

The woman beckoned him with her finger as she turned. She disappeared through the dark entrance.

"Come inside. I've brought us something to drink."

Marshall hesitated. He saw nothing suspicious. Still, he pulled his pistol before he carefully entered the small building. The smell of horses, hay, and manure struck him. The animals remained quiet when he passed them.

"Over here," Naamah whispered.

The light on a lantern hanging in the back of the building guided him to a small, open area filled with hay. Naamah sat on a red blanket, leaning back on the straw. She lifted a clay pot.

"Come drink with me, my lover."

Marshall went to the open window, but only the lights of the nearby keep showed. An intense feeling of a thousand eyes watching him caused the man to scan the area again.

"What are you afraid of?"

Naamah's mocking tone grated at him.

"I've seen your evil used against men before," he reminded her. The captain fingered the blessed dagger in his belt before he sat next to the woman.

"That's better." She handed the pot of wine to Marshall, who eyed it suspiciously.

"My, you're a suspicious one." Naamah laughed, then she drank from the container.

Marshall took the pot from her.

"Why are you here?"

The woman laid back on the hay.

"Isn't that obvious? It's time for you to repay your debt to me." She unbuckled her belt and pulled up her shift. She ran her hands along her legs.

"Don't I look pleasing to you?"

Marshall finished his drink and nodded. He unbuckled his sword belt and laid it next to them.

"Aye, I've not seen a woman for many a day."

The man leaned over. She pulled him down, and they kissed.

"You're a liar. You had a servant girl recently. I can smell her on you."

She grabbed him by his upper arms. With incredible strength, Naamah rolled him over on his back, coming on top to straddle him. She pulled her hands away to remove the rest of her garment. She arched her back and enticed him with her breasts over his face. The woman giggled at his expression.

"A man must pay his debt. Isn't that correct, Blackbane?"

Before he could respond, Marshall suddenly felt a pair of small hands gripping both of his forearms. When he struggled to release the grip, the captain felt more hands holding his legs. As he fought to free himself and the naked woman laughed. She brushed away the hay next to them.

Four giant black toads held him down with human-like arms and hands. Their bulbous eyes stared at him while the creature's slimy skin oozed pus. Despite the demon on top of him and her minion's powerful grips, Marshall continued to struggle.

"Don't worry, my love. My familiars won't harm you unless you fail my needs tonight."

The naked woman scooted down to his thighs before she pulled down his breeches. When she positioned herself on top of Marshall, she leaned down and softly kissed his lips.

"I'm always in full control of my human lovers!"

When Naamah finally let the toad-like creatures release her human lover, Marshall could barely move. The experience left him physically exhausted and mentally stained. Her cat-like eyes were no longer enticing. Instead, her blank expression reminded the captain of a dead person as she rose to stand above him.

The sex wasn't pleasant. Instead, it became a demeaning display of the demon's control of Marshall. But Naamah's insatiable appetite was irresistible. Somehow, the creature kept him aroused despite the pain from her scratches and bites. The marks that covered his chest and shoulders came from the creature's greedy need to inflict pain during her organisms. Several times, he bit into her flesh in a desperate attempt to make her stop. However, it only increased the woman's frenzy. Eventually, his mind became numb, aware of only pain and pleasure.

"You've seeded my womb, mortal."

He croaked out that he paid his debt. He glanced around for the woman's familiars, which had already disappeared.

"Perhaps, it's too soon to tell. Perhaps I'll return to enjoy your body again. Unless my husband finds you first."

The naked woman picked up her clothes and walked outside. With several grunts, Marshall sat up and followed her. One hand held his breeches while the other grasped his belt and sword. When he reached the courtyard, no one was there.

When Marshall finished dressing, and he returned to the house, the captain Leiras in the kitchen. A small man with a large bald spot in his long gray hair served food for the fat monk. Leiras glanced up as he took a bite. His red face still beamed at his special treatment.

"I wondered where you went." His friend's words were hard to understand with a mouth full of swan meat. "The family left us this servant to guide us after a late snack. Grab food now, for we have an early ride tomorrow."

"What have you heard?"

Leiras glanced over at the servant, who brought over a plate with turnips and black bread. He shook his head and returned to his food.

When the men finished eating and finally reached their room, the monk waited until he was sure the servant left the hallway.

"I believe our host uses his servants to spy on his guests. That servant appeared to understand English."

"Are they suspicious of you?" Marshall sat on one bed and leaned against the stone wall.

"No, but Johanne knew far too much about Gabriel's ideas to meet with King Louis of France. I remained careful. However, my inquiry was useful. I found out that Gabriel carries two caskets containing religious items, including the one we seek. According to Johanne, the Frenchman and his wife went after the relic attributed to Saint Simpert, who was a cousin of Charlemagne. Gabriel claims he found it in Augsburg. He'll take it back to France to curry favor with the king."

"Did our host tell you all of that over the beer?"

Leiras nodded.

"He enjoys an air of a gentleman among the peasants who toll the lands here. Johanne wants me to stay for a few days. I believe they expect great things from my sermons. Of course, you're invited to stay as well."

"But we're heading to Charleville."

"True," the monk agreed. "I suggest we wait for the next trekschuit upstream, then pick up a carriage to our actual destination."

Marshall shook his head.

"We'll lose several days. If any snow comes, we could miss the Frenchman. We need to leave tomorrow and get to Gabriel as soon as we can. Can you talk them out of a couple of horses instead?"

The monk's reluctance showed on his face. Marshall suspected his comrade enjoyed his new status a little too much.

"I suppose it's for the best," his friend finally agreed. "I'll talk with him in the morning." He yawned as he undressed.

It wasn't until late in the morning of the next day that Johanne van Stepradt realized the necessity for Leiras and Marshall to leave. The column of blue-coated Dutch soldiers entering the nearby village forced his hand. Johanne practically insisted his visitors take his horses and leave immediately.

After Marshall arrived inside the barn, he waited for a stable hand to finish saddling his black and white mare. The captain glanced at the corner where he and Naamah lay only a few hours before. As he stood there, the servant led a saddled horse from one bay.

"Why so lost in thought?" Leiras asked as he took the reins from the servant, who left to saddle another horse.

"Nothing," he replied too quickly.

The monk watched the pirate as he took the reins from him. Marshall's expression revealed concern, but he hid it well.

"It probably doesn't concern me," Leiras shrugged and went to observe the servant.

Marshall tied down his blanket on the back of the saddle, then led the animal from the barn. He was already on the mount when he heard the pounding of hoofs coming from the road. The gray-haired man who served them food last night rode past him at full gallop and hurriedly stopped near the house. The servant hurried inside while Leiras came out of the barn.

"We'll need to move quickly," Marshall stated as he looked down the road toward Ewijk.

The monk quickly threw a leather bag on the saddle. When the pirate heard the metallic noise, he noticed his friend's unique lantern tied to the saddle. Leiras clambered on the seat as Johanne hurried across the courtyard to them.

"Prussians in the village are asking about a man in a red robe. I'm sure they'll be coming this way soon. Godspeed you on your journey."

Leiras made a sign of the cross for the man while he quickly blessed him. Moments later, the two men rode away from the van Stepradt estate.

After riding several miles, the men finally slowed their mounts. The chill in the air left their exposed cheeks and fingers tingle from numbness. The constant clanging noise coming from inside the monk's bag finally got to Marshall.

"What do you have making all that racket?"

The fat man grinned.

"Supplies for our journey. I found several silver pieces inside their schuilkerken, mostly crosses and a few chalices."

"You stole from Johanne? What was the point?" The captain glared at him.

"For the same reason that a pirate steals. Because it's there and I wanted it. However, I have another reason. The crosses ward off evil. Besides, we can't look like relic hunters without a few items in our possession."

Marshall decided against arguing about the logic behind the monk's idea.

"Or you can get us burned at the stake for heresy," the man grumbled as he stopped near a tree. The captain ordered Leiras to come next to him. He stripped a limb of leaves and handed the monk a fistful of them.

"I'll cut another limb. Fill your bag with leaves to stop that noise. We don't need every Prussian in the area hearing us as we travel."

At a crossroads, they met a merchant on his cart. The man eyed the elaborately dressed monk before he pointed out the direction to Charleville. The smell of wood smoke slowed the men to a stop near a creek that crossed the road. Further down the road, they saw the source of the smoke. A small hamlet with a couple of visible buildings lay ahead of them.

"It's as good a spot as any for a camp," Marshall said as he led his mount off the road. "We should be far enough away not to attract attention."

"I'd prefer a bed," the monk grumbled through his clenched teeth that held his pipe. "We should check for a tavern down the road."

"Not with those robes you're wearing. You saw the look that the merchant on the cart gave you. We're in the wrong area for the clothes you're wearing. Next town, we get a black robe for you."

Leiras remained silent in grudging agreement as the two men pulled their horses behind an old hedge line. Marshall slid off his mount while the monk went into the woods to relieve himself.

It wasn't long before the pirate captain heard horses galloping from the village. Marshall couldn't see the riders when he heard them slow. He whispered to Leiras, but his companion remained out of sight. The man waited with his hand on his pistol when the horses trotted on. Marshall turned back to untying the bags from his saddle.

A few moments later, two men in blue uniforms stepped through the brush and into the clearing. They pointed flintlock muskets with the bayonets fixed at Marshall. Each grenadier wore a single-breasted coat in blue with white trousers. On their head was a leather hat called a kasket. The caps told Marshall that they were Prussian soldiers.

"Was machst du hier?"

The captain shook his head.

"I'm English, understand?"

The soldier's confused glances told him they couldn't understand him.

"I understand," another voice piped up. Out of the brush, another uniformed man joined his men. Dressed similarly to his men, the officer's bearskin hat had a brass plate in the front.

"Anglisman, why are you here?"

"I'm coming from Amsterdam and heading to Charleville on business." The captain glanced back at the two men pointing their weapons at him.

The officer nodded and stepped over to the monk's horse.

"You travel with another?"

"Yes, he's in the woods. He carries a sickness," Marshall lied.

He noticed the officer's eyes widen at the idea of someone with a disease. Then, the man lifted the heavy bag attached to the saddle of the monk's horse. The clanking noise inside made him glance suspiciously at Marshall. He pulled the bag from the seat. Facing the officer, the pirate captain kept a wary eye on the men holding the muskets while he slipped his hand to his pistol. Then they heard the noise of footsteps within the brush. The fat man in red emerged with a smile on his face.

"Gentlemen, how good to see a friendly face!"

The officer looked at the man for a moment, then he opened the bag in his hand. The Prussian pulled out an elaborately engraved chalice.

"You're coming with us," he held out the item as the monk drew closer.

Before the officer could pull his pistol, Leiras was on him. He got the man in a headlock while the two struggled for control of the weapon. The Prussian wrapped his leg around the monk's, and they fell backward on the ground.

At the same time, Marshall slid out his flintlock. He turned and fired. Black smoke filled the air as his shot struck one of the Prussians in the belly. The second soldier's shot missed the pirate, who was already on the move.

As he ran at the second soldier, Marshall pulled his rapier. The soldier swung at the pirate captain with his rifle, but Marshall sidestepped the blow. After thrusting the sword's thin blade into his enemy's chest, the pirate captain slid away. The man fell to the ground with hardly a sound as Marshall rushed forward at the injured soldier, who cried out. The pirate swung his sword across the man's neck. Blood spurted out of the wound as the dying Prussian's fixed stare remained on his killer.

When Marshall glanced back at Leiras, he and the Prussian were back on their feet. However, Leiras held the upper hand. When he released his chokehold on the officer, the dead man slid to the ground like a rag doll.

Marshall hurried to the road after picking up one of the dead men's muskets. In the growing dusk, he found the three horses of the men. He saw nothing to show the location of the other riders they heard earlier. The captain quickly led the animals back to his comrade. He found Leiras going through the clothes of the dead men.

"We need to leave now!" Marshall tied the horses to a tree.

"Yes, my friend, it's unfortunate they weren't going to listen to reason."

"Especially when they found your loot," the captain growled.

He dragged the closest body into the high grass. As he came back, the monk stripped the largest dead man of his clothing. When he finished, he helped Marshall move the other bodies out of sight.

"I'll gather the weapons, and you get their provisions," Leiras said. He gave a brief prayer as he made a sign of the cross for the dead men.

"I don't think they'll care," the captain snarled.

"Oh, that's where you're wrong. Their spirits need a path and guidance to reach heaven."

"You think they go to God?"

"Of course, it's obvious that they died as part of His plan," the monk replied. "It's your soul you need to worry about?"

Marshall shook his head at the idea.

"His plan got me into this mess in the first place. I guess I'll have their ghosts haunting my dreams. I'd like to tell God what to do with his damn plan."

As he groused, Leiras chuckled while he pulled on some of the dead man's clothes. Marshall rummaged through the Prussian's bags, transferring food and wine to into their bags.

"I'm afraid these coats won't fit me," the monk pointed out. He went over to the horses where the man draped the gray wool blanket over his shoulders. When the captain finished strapping a musket on the back of his saddle, Leiras handed him the officer's pistol.

"You should keep it," Marshall told him as he looked over the strange assemblage of clothes on his friend.

"Well, you don't stand out as a bishop anymore."

"I don't like the constrictions of these pants, but they're warmer," the monk conceded. "Let's get going. You can keep the weapon."

It was nightfall as the men rode away. They led the captured horses along the road. After the fugitives rode through the village, they released the spare horse near a trail leading away from their path. Then, the men slowly traveled on the dark trail to the Meuse River. With only the dim starlight to guide them, neither man spoke. They realized a long night lay ahead of them.

~~~

After finding an abandoned gristmill inside a rugged section of forest near the Meuse River, Leiras and Marshall settled for a few hours of sleep. When they woke, the sun was already at its midpoint. After a quick meal, the captain spent some of his time reloading his weapons. The men continued along the path
~~~

toward a village. When they spotted the blue coats of Prussian soldiers, they pulled away from the trail to enter the forest again. Eventually, the riders found the river where they found another road. A farmer gave them directions to follow the Meuse River south, where they would reach Givet. The town was their gateway to France.

It was nearly evening when the two men found a place to stop for the night. The road to the town remained busy throughout the day, and they found the locals to be friendly. Many spoke French. Even better, the travelers found no soldiers on the road. A Frenchman they met along the way told them about the bridge of the river into Givet. He told them it was already too late to get across the river since the path was closed after dark.

"Then, we have another night of sleeping on the ground," Leiras complained after the traveler left them.

"Well, there looks to be an old house ahead. We can stop there to get a fire going. It'll be turning cold overnight." Marshall pointed out.

Pulling their horses off the nearly deserted road, the men found an open patch of grass near a massive walnut tree. Leiras came to a stop and looked closer at the figure of someone standing under the tree. He looked closer and saw a beautiful black-haired woman.

"Welcome, gentlemen," the woman said in French as she stepped out from the shadows.

Marshall turned his horse at the sound of the voice. He glanced around the area suspiciously, pulling his pistol.

"A fair lass who appears far from home," the monk replied with a smile. "The heavens brought us great fortune."

Dressed in a bright white silk dress with a low-cut front to expose her cleavage. She wore no overdress or hat, which made her appear underdressed. The heavy gold chain necklace around her neck looked out of fashion. However, the men recognized the immense value of her jewelry, which made the woman an easy target on a lonely road. Leiras glanced over at his partner, who continued to scan the area.

"You honor me, fair monk. I'm on my way home." she stared at Marshall as she spoke in English. "I'm glad I finally got off this road. It's dangerous for me to travel at night. However, my home is not far. Escort me, and I'll provide you with accommodations. The chill of the air is already on us. Such illustrious men seldom come our way, and I would be a poor host without offering you a place to stay."

"I'll bet you tempt many a traveler in such fine clothes," the monk slid off his mount. He tapped out the ash from his pipe on the heel of his boot.

"I don't see a farm near here." A hint of suspicion carried in the monk's voice.

Marshall nodded agreement as he glanced back at the ramshackle hut. He noticed nothing unusual in the growing darkness.

"She appears overdressed for a farm wife," he pointed out.

"Oh, I'm not married, and my home is deeper in the forest. Follow me, and I promise you a fine meal." The woman replied in English with a smile. "It's not far."

The woman turned and hastened away.

"Hopefully, she's a wonderful cook," Leiras led his horse off the road. Marshall looked around the dark shadows that were overcoming the remaining bit of twilight. He slid off his mount and led the animal along the narrow trail.

As they followed the woman into the darkening woods, the two men noticed the surrounding silence. Their mounts grew restless, snorting and shaking their heads. Marshall stroked the neck of his animal, feeling the same trepidation. The encompassing blackness weighed him down. When they reached a small house in a clearing, the men stopped while the woman went to the entrance.

Bright light exited from the structure's open windows. Yet, the only noise they heard inside the home were whispers, combined with sounds of groaning and panting. The woman waited at the door. Her face lit up at the visitor's expressions of bewilderment and suspicion.

"Are you afraid to enter, my bold travelers?" Her voice teased them.

"Bring your lantern," Marshall quietly advised the monk as he stepped by him.

Something about sounds inside the house bothered the captain. However, he stuffed his flintlock into his belt. Leiras joined him with his lantern jingling in his hand.

A light blasted him as the woman opened the front door. The men held up their hands to shield their eyes from the blinding glare.

"Step forward, my travelers. You must be weary from your trip."

As they passed through the golden doorway, the men's found a massive vaulted room. Instantly, both men recognized that the place was bigger than the building's exterior. The many golden ornaments and statues covering the side tables immediately caught Marshall's attention. Along the painted walls, murals bore images of naked Greek and Roman gods and demigods in various positions of intercourse.

However, their attention soon focused on the corner of the room, where partially dressed maidens and boys lay on the richly woven carpets and pillows. It was impossible to avoid watching the group while they moaned and grunted while masturbating. They paid no attention to the visitors.

Slowly, Marshall recognized the reason. Each person in the small group had their eyelids sewn shut. As he stood there in utter disbelief, Marshall felt Leiras place a hand on his shoulder.

"We've entered the domain of your foul friends, and we're cut off from the outside now."

Marshall glanced back to see the door was no longer there. He placed his hand on the dagger in his belt.

"Is this a kind of hell for them?" Marshall asked aloud when he turned to the woman. The woman said nothing. Instead, she summoned someone from behind a column.

A naked man stepped toward them. He was an identical twin of the woman, and he swayed to the sounds of the lust in the air. In his hand, the man carried a silver goblet. When he came to a stop in front of Leiras, the monk looked the man over with approval. The naked twin gave him the cup.

"Drink up. It's gin for us to enjoy before the festivities."

The monk absently took the drink, his eyes staring at the twin male who joined his sister.

"What are you doing? We have no escape." The captain glanced around for the windows that were no longer present.

"Escape comes from meeting the demon who lives here," the monk stated. "I believe these are his servants. It's not unexpected to deal with such creatures."

"You might mention that before we entered this damn place," Marshall growled to his friend.

"My gentlemen, it's time for my master to speak with you." The woman unhooked the clasps that held her dress. She slid off her dress with practiced ease. As she stood next to her sibling, she gave Marshall a perfect smile to go along with her enticing body.

"Don't be afraid. We can fill all the desires you carry."

"I fear nothing here," Marshall sneered at her.

"Of course," she replied. "Please follow us."

The woman led the way to an arched doorway, where steps descended into a dark tunnel that smelled of musty dirt. As they followed the stairs down, the group passed by torches held by skeletal hands that jutted out from the damp walls.

"We're passing into the realm of the dead," the monk whispered.

"Now would be the right time to think of a way out of this," the pirate hastily replied.

The men followed the woman into another massive underground room, where an overpowering stench struck them. The room reeked of sewage. Then, they realize the reason. Captives hung along the walls, urinating and defecating from their chained positions. Sewn eyelids on the victims caught Marshall's attention and he mentioned the hideous sight to the monk.

To both men's amazement, the victims appeared almost joyful. Hung by their cuffed wrists, instead of the expected pain and agony, prisoners smiled with delight, some moaned and quivered with pleasure.

Marshall noticed the doorway behind them was no longer there. Only a stone wall stood where the door once existed. Two sets of cuffs hung from the wall.

"Come closer, Blackbane. I wish to discuss your future!"

The muscular naked creature with a massive bull's head and a human body sat at a candle-lit table. Marshall focused his attention on the gold card table, where the demon flipped a playing card from the top of the deck. Each time he put the card down, pulled a few of the captives would groan and tremble in an orgasm.

The pirate glanced over at the monk, who laughed at something the naked man whispered in his ear.

"Alright, which demon are you?" Marshall turned back to his host. "And what is your offer?"

The demon remained in his place, looking down at his cards. The woman placed her hand on his arm, and Marshall felt his thoughts grow cloudy.

"Come closer to the master," she insisted.

Marshall's mind screamed no. However, the man felt his will fade when he looked at the woman. He followed her toward the table.

"Asmodeus is the name used by mortals who fear me," the bull-head demon flipped over another card. Instantly, several captives called out in ecstasy as they shook in their chains. The clatter of metal against the stone wall echoed in the chamber. Marshall saw the image of a chest of silver on the card.

"My spy told me you followed a trail to Givet. I brought you to my world for your end."

Marshall immediately thought of Naamah, the wife of the demon. She must have told Asmodeus of his journey.

There's no telling what the creature learned from me that night!

As if the demon read his mind, he continued.

"My wife said you're a man who lives for gold and earthly pleasure. I believe that you'll find my offer in this realm far more engaging for a man of your passion."

Blackbane glanced over at a fat woman who screamed out during her orgasm. Her shackles pounded against the cut-stone wall while she enjoyed herself.

"Living in a stinking world of piss and excrement carries no interest to me," the man scowled at the sight.

The bullhead finally looked up at Marshall, casting its head at an angle to view him with one moist, dark eye. He slid his legs out to reveal his bull-sized shaft and testicles hanging down between his legs.

"These wretched things on the wall smell nothing but the scent of an aphrodisiac high. People thrive on the perceived pleasures I give them. Like laudanum addiction, they adore the satisfaction that I dole out. If I quit doing this, they would suffer agony. Lust is an addiction that they will never give up."

"Why are their eyelids sewn shut?" The pirate's skin tingled when the woman brushed his neck with her fingers.

"It is part of the agreement. No distractions from an eternity of pleasure. Once the body dies, their souls enter our domain. That is the bargain for this world's paradise."

"Hardly paradise," scoffed Leiras. He pushed away from the naked man, who had his arm around his shoulders. He looked at Marshall.

"Asmodeus, the demon of lust, lures unfortunates into these traps with promises of carnal and other desires for eternity. Whatever the person wishes for, they receive. Then, he plays a game of chance with the other demons for rights to their souls. Once the soul leaves the body, they no longer feel the pleasures offered in the agreement. Instead, the being finds only the torment of endless want, an unfilled thirst along with the never-ending fire of desire that is never met."

The monk turned back to the demon.

"I thought Raphael exiled you to Egypt."

The creature with the bull's head leaned back in his golden chair. Casually, the demon flipped another card. This time, the game piece showed the image of a whip and a wooden paddle. Screams of ecstasy filled the chamber as a dying body of an older man thrashed in his chains.

"Sariel, your angelic friends might trap me, but only for a short time. I take it you've not met my Cambions before. Atsais is an incubus who wants your fat body for his pleasure."

The male escort tackled Leiras from behind and sent him sprawling on the floor. The monk's lantern tumbled across the floor, coming to a rest at Marshall's feet. He watched the woman back away from the device while the incubus slammed Leiras's head into the stone floor, stunning him. When Marshall tried to move, the pirate captain felt one side of his body go numb when the woman's hand came down on his shoulder. Marshall nearly toppled before he fell to one knee.

Marshall looked over at the grinning incubus as he stripped off the clothes from Leiras. The creature threw the garments over the Xeropotamou lantern. Then, the incubus kneeled behind the angel to mount him.

"My offspring are very effective in dealing with humans and angels," the bull-head creature stated. They watched Atsais rape the overpowered Leiras.

"Sariel, you should know better than to enter my world. You'll find the painful pleasures from an incubus mating with you nearly as fun as his ideas for young monks."

Marshall turned away from the scene.

"Blackbane, you witnessed pirates' rape and pillage before. What makes you look away now?"

The woman's commanded him to look back at his friend's rape.

"Blackbane, I forgot to introduce your succubus, Siasta. She and her brother know of your eternal nature. I've given them permission to feed upon your soul. You'll learn pleasure and pain beyond your comprehension as they use your body."

A wave of agony suddenly swept through Marshall when the woman touched him. The pain refocused his thoughts and made him angry.

"Why do you call Leiras by another name?" Marshall forced himself to look at the bull-headed demon.

"You don't know of your guardian angel?"

Asmodeus shook his head in amusement.

"It seems you can't trust anyone. This creature was once an intermediary between God and humans, at least before the days of Jared. Unlike those of us who fell from Heaven, Sariel still yearns for acceptance among the other angels. He made the mistake of enjoying his human form. Angels must avoid the human's sinful nature or remain in his sorry state."

Stunned at the idea, Marshall looked over at the two men pressed together.

"I thought angels were immortal."

"When they take the form of man, they carry similar weaknesses and frailties. As God's creation, we cannot die, only transform. Just like I've taken on a form suitable to my realm."

The beast rose from his chair. As he drew closer, the succubus came up behind the man and wrapped her arms around his neck. Marshall felt pain flood through him while his mind went foggy again.

"Which leads me to your immortal nature. Blackbane, I've heard of your ability to escape my brothers. That's why I used the lust in your heart to trap you in my world. You saw the gold on Siasta's neck along with the cleavage. I knew it was enough to entice you inside the house."

"Then you're not offering anything, only taking!" The captain grunted out.

The demon nodded as he held his enormous shaft as a display.

"I've decided to use you and your curse to my benefit. We'll start with your subjection and humiliation. Your repeated rapes begin the process of taking your immortal essence. The succubus and incubus will use your seed for breeding and creating more creatures like them. You will help my kingdom to grow while you wither away."

"I told you that you have nothing to fear, my lover. The master enjoys breaking the will of his guests," Siasta whispered in Marshall's ear. "Soon you'll hang as a display on the walls like the rest of our trophies."

He felt her breasts pressed against his back. Despite his mind rebelling at his coming fate, the man noticed the anticipation running through his veins as he grew hard. The thoughts of sex with the creatures sickened his mind. But, the image of Naamah came back to him. He recognized he was falling into the demon's control. Yet, the darkness overwhelming him remained alluring and overpowering.

The succubus loosened her grip to pull open his jacket. Her nails dug deep into his shirt as she ripped the cloth open. Atsais finished with his assault of Leiras and rose to his feet. The monk lay face down on the floor, apparently unable to move.

"Look at his eyes dilate. The human wants our attention," the incubus went to the side of his sister.

His mocking tone ripped into the pirate captain. A thought came through the fog, and Marshall laid his hand touched his blessed Saint Gennaro dagger. Immediately, the angry man felt his mind clear, and the pain stopped. His fingers wrapped around the handle. When Atsais pulled back on the captain's jacket, Marshall jabbed the blade into the incubus.

A roar escaped from the evil creature as he fell back. In his pain, the incubus kicked the covered lamp away from the clothes as he fell to the floor. Marshall swung around with his elbow, striking his sister in the face. The force of the blow forced the creature back but barely fazed her. The woman's eyes turned black as night and her incisor fangs extended outside of her lips.

"You're mine!"

Asmodeus quickly grabbed the captain by the head with his large hand. Fingers gripped into the man's hair, painfully pulling him away from the succubus. The captain drew his pistol while he sliced at Asmodeus with his knife. He caught the demon in its muscular forearm with the blade. An inhuman growl erupted from Asmodeus when it released Marshall.

Suddenly, the succubus was on the man's back. Her fangs dug down into his shoulder. He yelled out in pain while swinging her around. The captain propelled himself back into the stone wall. Her body shuddered from the force of their combined weight when they hit the wall. Seeking his advantage, Marshall slammed his head into the creature's face. Still, she held on to his arm and he could not strike out with the Saint Gennaro dagger.

Atsais, holding a hand over his injury, came after the human. Marshall ignored the fangs in him as he pulled out his pistol. He pointed it just as the male demon swung a clawed hand at Marshall's chest. The explosion from the flintlock filled the room. Atsais fell back from the force of the impact when the lead bullet pierced his chest. The demon looked down at the wound, which poured black blood. Then, the incubus turned back to Marshall with a smile.

"I'm going to enjoy ripping you apart!" Atsais told him.

Siasta dug her fangs into Marshall again after she pinned his arms behind him. The creature slurped his blood with increasing frenzy while her twin placed his black, blood-covered claws on the man's neck. Marshall stiffened, ready for the monster to rip out his throat.

"Don't bother to bleed him. He can't die, you fool. Take him to the table and bend him over. You can suck him dry while I enjoy him!" Asmodeus snorted.

The incubus dug his fangs into the captain's other shoulder. Marshall nearly collapsed from the pain, and he dropped the pistol. However, the man desperately hung on to his dagger.

The creatures sensed their triumph as they pulled their fangs from their victim. They dragged Marshall away from the wall to give to their bull-head master. With a gloating laugh, Asmodeus turned back to the table.

Then, the demon stopped!

Standing by the table was a naked Leiras. Blood flowed from his forehead injury, but he had a smirk on his face. He'd just finish lighting his Xeropotamou lantern using a candle from the table. The monk turned the light reflected from the mirror toward the demons.

Asmodeus fell back while throwing up his arms to shield himself from the holy fire blasting him. His massive body slammed into the Cambions and their prisoner, who they released. The prince of demons tried to push forward at the monk. However, the lantern's light peeled off the foul creature's skin. Asmodeus raged and bellowed in frustration and agony from the relic's power.

With renewed energy, Marshall swung around and embedded the dagger into Siasta's side. As the creature screamed, her twin came at the human. Atsais reached out and grabbed Marshall by his ripped coat. However, the demon's arm turned black from the holy light. As the incubus shrieked, Marshall slammed his blade into the demon's neck. Warm black blood shot across the man as he stabbed again and again. Atsais fell to the floor, gurgling, while the blood flowed from the massive gashes. His sister fell to her knees next to him, trying to staunch the flow as the Cambion twisted in pain and disbelief.

"Release us now, foul demon of hell!" Leiras yelled over the ominous and loud growls coming from Asmodeus.

The monk stepped forward while Marshall grabbed his pistol and hurried to his side. An overpowering stench of burning sulfur and rancid flesh filled the air. Still caught in the grips of the holy illumination, Asmodeus roared as the beast's skin bubbled and burned. Finally, a staircase appeared behind the two prisoners. It was the exit from the underworld. Without a second thought, the captain headed to the doorway. Keeping his lantern focused upon Asmodeus, Leiras backed toward the door. He swept up his red cloak. He grimly smiled as Siasta screeched for revenge. Her demon brother lay dead in her arms.

The men scrambled up the stairs as an increasing rumble trailed behind them. Using the light coming from the monk's lamp, Marshall hurried up the steps that appeared to keep going. Finally, he stepped into the chill of the night air. The noise behind him suddenly stopped when Leiras joined him.

The monk whirled around with his light, but a house no longer stood in the small clearing. Instead, they were in the middle of knee-high grass, their panting breath showing in the night's chill air. Marshall sheathed the bloody dagger as he listened to the frightened whiney of their horse as the creatures rode off into the dark forest. The man turned to his partner as Leiras wrapped himself to ward off the chilly night.

"Let's get a fire going. You and I have a lot to discuss!"

Chapter 5: Charleville

"I'm afraid I've done you a disservice," Leiras admitted as he drank wine from a bladder, shivering from the cold. "Of course, I should have told you everything."

He went silent, glancing at Marshall. The pirate remained silent while he continued to build a fire.

"In my defense, it's difficult for people to believe that I once carried a power against such creatures."

Finally, the small flame spread across the tinder and slowly developed into a fire. The captain leaned back against his saddle while an uncomfortable silence fell over them. After escaping the clutches of the demon and his minions, the two men spent part of the night tracking down their horses. They remained far from the road. But they had their supplies.

Marshall turned to his wounds. He hoped the twins' fangs didn't have poison in them. Reaching around awkwardly, he dabbed at the wounds with a rag soaked in gin from the flask that Lciras gave him.

"The Cambions aren't known to have poison," the monk spoke as if he read Marshall's thoughts.

The man sucked in his breath at the sting from his wounds.

"Well, as long as those damned creatures remain in hell. It's a hard lesson we've learned, angel. Lust let my guard down. Damn Remiel and his curse." Marshall glanced over at the angel.

"If we remain as partners, from now on, we tell the whole truth."

Leiras nodded his head after another drink.

"I'm afraid your blessed dagger killed only one of them. However, I enjoyed watching Atsais suffer as he died. As an angel, I once had the power to melt such a vile creature into nothing." He paused for more drink.

"Unfortunately, your dagger can't destroy a creature like Asmodeus. Certainly, my lamp cannot kill them. It only drives them away. We could drive a stake made from the blessed cross through the heart of Asmodeus, and it wouldn't kill him. Only the Lord can destroy them."

Leiras wondered if the man was listening to him.

"You know that they'll still hunt you."

Marshall stopped his work and shivered from the evaporation on his wounds. He looked at the monk. For the first time, his comrade appeared tired and lackluster.

"So, do I call you Sariel now?"

The angel shook his head.

"That's the name of an angel. I wouldn't recognize it."

"Alright, then I want to know why you have no power to fight demons," the captain stated.

The monk tightened his tattered red robe around him as he looked into the flames. He sighed lightly.

"I once held enough power to keep them away. I was a principatus, as the mortal priests call our species. We are the educators and guardians of people. That means we influence through a dream or a whisper."

"That explains how you know so much about my visions," Marshall replied.

"Yes, that's true. While I never had the tremendous power of an archangel, I had enough to stop demons from despoiling me like tonight."

He growled out the last sentence and went quiet for a moment. Marshall's thoughts turned to his own predicament when Asmodeus and the offspring raped him. It chilled him to the core with his reaction.

"My role helped to guide the chaste and holy away from the path of evil," Leiras finally spoke. "It got so I could smell a demon a league away. Avoiding the traps set by the dwellers of the underworld helps a mortal remain on the righteous path."

"I wish I knew this earlier. I had my suspicions, but I kept thinking of the gold chain around that woman's neck. Asmodeus recognized your human weaknesses as well. The damned creature took advantage of both of us," Marshall grumbled.

Leiras picked up a stick and started poking the burning wood. His face expressed concern.

"It puzzles me. I didn't pick up the demon's scent until we entered his domain. I think the debauchery blinded me inside that home. Perhaps it was a test for both of us," the angel shrugged.

"Since I was a messenger and promoter of the divine, I floated with the winds. I've traveled the world since the time of the Enoch. We use reason and foresight to guide those people deemed worthy. That's how I can snatch bits and pieces of your dreams. I guess it's a reminder of how I once showed people the way."

"What happened?" The pirate asked while he pulled dried meat from one of the Prussian's bags.

"I found a body," Leiras replied. A smile came to his lips when he saw Marshall's reaction to the news.

"Yes, this body, once firm and muscular, carried a sort of divinity when I first found it. The young man had eyes of blue and black hair." The angel looked down at his belly and laughed. "I know it's hard to believe women and men flocked to me at one time."

He leaned back against his saddle.

"I knew a mother would lose her son that day. He stepped into the path of a horse. I saw the soul leaving and took the body for my purposes. It was a temporary plan to relieve a widow of her grief and bring her into the light of God. She was important to the faith."

Marshall leaned over and handed him a piece of the meat to his comrade.

"Did it work?"

Leiras nodded as he leaned back. He chewed thoughtfully.

"St. Mary of Egypt is the name you might know. Hard to believe that it was nearly fourteen hundred years ago."

Marshall shook his head. Despite the things they went through so recently, it was nearly impossible to believe. The angel recognized the expression on the man's face.

"Oh, I know what I tell you is difficult to understand. But this explains why angels rarely enter a human body for long. It's too easy for us to remain. I'm living proof that the body ages slowly once we're trapped inside. You hear about alchemists who live forever. They're really just spirits trapped like me."

"What about the mother?" The captain decided against trying to rationalize what he heard for the moment. "How can you bring the light to a grieving mother?"

"Yes, a lovely lady," Leiras smiled with the pleasure of the memory. "At the time, she was a prostitute following a pilgrimage to Jerusalem for her trade. Once she saw her son rise from death, the woman fainted. It's a natural reaction. It didn't take long for her to become a believer. After that, I took her by the hand and became her guardian of sorts."

A knowing grin from Marshall caught the angel's notice.

"No!" A furious glare filled his face.

"Such a thought is blasphemy, then, as it is now. I wasn't the corrupt thing you see sitting before you. I led the woman into the desert after she made her vow to the Virgin Mary to become a hermit. She lived out her days in solitary prayer and work."

The angel drifted into silence as he remembered the woman. After a moment, he returned to the present.

"Still, she was a bewitching woman. I would not stop such sinful actions now in my present unholy form. The wretched creature before you came from the generations of people I've followed and the debaucheries I've added to my collection. My youth gave me battles against the heathens, where I waded in blood and gore. Fat and happy came from the feasts after my victories, along with the copulating of males and females."

The monk sighed as he thumped his belly.

"Rich food and drink helped to drown the occasional regret. I suppose some wish for such immorality." he glanced at Marshall. "However, it's not good for the soul. Still, I see the demons who walk among us. That is part of the reason I decided you needed a guardian angel. I knew you sought guidance. It is my specialty."

The angel sighed.

"I guess I can understand your weariness of immortality. I'm seeing the pitfalls."

The captain thought about his encounter with Remiel.

"Over the years, I recall each bitter result of my errors every night. Once I celebrated my foul ways. Now… Well, it makes a guy wonder about his place in the world," Marshall conceded.

"Aye, you're correct about that. The future is easy when you have full control of your past." Leiras gave a brief smile. "That's my bit of wisdom."

The pirate grunted, then took a drink from the flask.

"Then what's your stake in this game? I'm not sure what you get out of helping me."

Leiras let out a deep breath.

"Once you retrieve the relic, I'm convinced Remiel will return to you. The angels will not stand idle while the saints come to you."

"Yeah, to gloat about my curse," Marshall stated.

"Perhaps, but I wish to speak with him anyway," the angel went silent.

Marshall listened to the sound of the night creatures in the woods around them for a moment.

"Is this a vision or a hope that Remiel returns?"

"Maybe both," the monk shrugged. Then he frowned.

"Since we're letting our secrets out, tell me why I smelled a demon with your scent when you returned to Johanne's home?"

The fat man took another bite of his meal while watching the captain. Marshall's cheeks flushed, and he tugged at his beard. Finally, he confided in the angel.

"I owed a debt to Naamah. She got me out of a Tunisian prison, along with my first mate. She's enticing, and I didn't mind. Or I least I didn't until it was too late."

Leiras grimaced at the news.

"The harlot of angels seduced you. An immortal sinner mating with a demon. She's looking to bring another Cambion into the world. What were you thinking?"

Marshall glared at him. "When the ax man comes for your head, you make a deal."

The angel shook his head. He reached over for the bladder of wine.

"You're immortal, but you have no faith."

"Exactly," Marshall agreed, as he tipped back another drink of gin.

~~~

The rest of their journey into Charleville went without a problem. The sun came out and warmed them as the two men rode. Their spirits lifted as they drew closer to the city. Marshall mentioned the need for clothing. Leiras looked over his ripped and torn clothing as he nodded in agreement.

"Yes, I'll need something to replace my robe."

"As long as you don't wear something that gets the authorities' attention again. They might hang us," Marshall grumbled. "You need to remember we can't stick out too much."
~~~

The monk grinned briefly.

"I'll see what I can do. Now, to the problem of Maximilien Gabriel. From what we've heard, the heart of the saint is inside a container of gold and silver. Since it's delicate, we must insist on seeing the item first. Also, we cannot let the Frenchman know our true purpose for retrieving the relic."

"Aye, if it's valuable, then we can expect he'll have guards as well. Plus, a nobleman trying to gain favor from a king was unlikely to sell us the artifact that we seek. It leaves us only one option," Marshall replied. The man scowled as he thought about it.

"In the past, I would kill the Frenchman and just take it," he continued. "A fast ship will get a man and his crew out of trouble. However, I don't like the idea of becoming a wanted murderer of a French aristocrat inside France. The authorities know our names from our escape back in Le Havre. We're not under the protection of a king. Somehow, we must persuade him of the fortune he'll make by selling it."

The pirate wondered if it was just another part of his devious curse.

"Something else bothers you," Leiras puffed away on his pipe.

"We don't really know what these visions mean. How am I supposed to stop this curse when I must break the commandments to do it?" Marshall tried to explain. "It's bad enough that I have demons after me. Stealing a reliquary with no plan carries little appeal without knowing my destination."

The angel remained silent as he smoked.

"It's a dilemma," Leiras finally agreed. "Perhaps when we get the Heart of Saint Julia, she'll guide us. There's a reason we say that God works in mysterious ways."

The angel chuckled as he pulled his pipe from his lips.

"Perhaps Maximilien Gabriel de Béthune is a demon."

The captain glanced over.

"That's not helping."

~~~

When the men finally arrived at the massive fortifications guarding the city, they followed the bridge across the. Inside the island city that split the river, they found streets filled with activity. As they wound their way into the main square, Leiras insisted upon finding a tailor.

"I'm going to purchase two robes with a coat. These breeches bind you." He saw the frown on Marshall's face.

"We must look like men of property. After our last encounter, we're lucky to have the letter of introduction that Aldert sent with us," the angel reminded him.

By the end of the evening, the two men had new clothes and a room above a tavern. The area was close to the sizeable gothic cathedral known as the *Basilique Notre-Dame*. They went to the *Place Ducale* where the aristocrats had their homes. A trip to the dock after the tailor determined their quarry remained a few days away. Snow and ice slowed most of the river traffic.

While the visitors wandered through the streets of the city, Leiras led the way in his black cape, which he wore over a purple robe, topped with a black hat. Marshall hoped his companion might tone the style down more. However, the tailor convinced them that men of their status needed such colorful clothing. Besides, it was available within a few hours.

When they stopped in front of a store, the pirate captain glanced over at his reflection. Although he'd never admit it, he enjoyed the cut of his blue overcoat with gold embroidery, along with his blue tri-corner hat. Even more, the deep pockets inside allowed him to hold his flintlock easily. According to the tailor, the noble who intended to buy the coat died from typhoid earlier that week. A visibly concerned Marshall forced the man to handle the clothing before they purchased the garment.
~~~

"You forgot you're immortal," Leiras snickered as they left the building.

"Maybe, but I've seen too many good men die from tainted water and clothes."

In the streets, officers in their colorful uniforms mixed with merchants and vendors in the small shops along the streets. The angel explained they stationed the French military men at the nearby engineering school. He also told Marshall some of the other things that he learned as he listened in on the various conversations. The pirate had to admit his comrade carried a natural talent for getting tidbits of information from strangers. While he wasn't sure if his ability came from being an angel, the knowledge they gleaned might help them.

One of the first bit of useful information that they learned concerned the Duke of Sully and his habits. Known as a fashionable and ambitious aristocrat who continually owed money, Gabriel had a new wife who enjoyed the limelight. In celebration of the news, the men found a place to eat and drink.

After their dinner, the two men remained at their table, drinking the cheapest liquor they had. Marshall grimaced at the gin they served. Leiras remained unaffected by the taste, but he grinned at the pirate captain's reaction.

"I thought sailors of His Majesty's navy enjoyed gin?"

"You'll have to ask one of them. I learned my trade on merchant ships running between pirates and blockades throughout the Caribbean. I miss the rum," Marshall complained. "Give me a barrel of that over this smelly stuff."

Still, he ordered another round using his rudimentary command of the language. He enjoyed the warmth the drink gave him. The weather turned cold and dreary again. Outside their windows, the merchants were closing their shops while the night watchman lit his lamp to begin his rounds.

"You are a traveler, but you never told me how you got to the Mediterranean." Leiras glanced out the same window that Marshall gazed out in thought.

The captain leaned back in his seat, his eyes narrowed as he recalled his past.

"The British Navy blasted our ports in the Caribbean. My crew and I headed to Africa. We captured a couple of slavers off the Western Africa coast. Then, we put into Casablanca, where we sold the slaves back to the Turks. After a few more raids along the Spanish coast, we found Tunis to our liking. The Beylik gave us a fair price, and we found the port sheltered us from the French and the British navies."

Marshall took another drink.

"It was a thousand years ago. Still, I hunt for treasure, but demons are after me, not the British." He forced a grin. "Still, you discovered interesting news about Gabriel's need for money. It might make our job easier."

"Here's a toast to that," Leiras raised his glass in a toast. "I hope we find him as pleasant as this tavern."

The monk leaned back in his hard chair while he stared at the mug. After a moment, he asked his question.

"Tell me, William Marshall. Does Emma still haunt you?"

The man looked at Leiras. He wasn't surprised that the monk knew her name. Marshall probably yelled it out in his sleep a hundred times.

"Almost nightly," he confessed. His eyes focused on the street outside. "I relive what I did to my victims from their experience. I'm just getting better at hiding the terror and pain that I feel."

"Remiel is a devious bastard, alright," Leiras stated, then sighed. "There's not a lot of difference between them and the fallen ones at times. A murder is a difficult thing to recall, then to be cursed to live through the experience repeatedly."

He shook his head in sympathy.

"How about the others? You mentioned them occasionally."

"The other ghosts come less often. I think they know that I'm being punished by the demons hunting me. They approve, of course, but I don't feel their need to hate me as much."

The captain looked down at his drink.

"That's the first time I've ever discussed them."

Leiras stared at Marshall.

"That's one reason for confessions. It's good for the soul and your character."

The captain glared at him after a curse.

"I'm not a damn rum gagger! Suffering is a sailor's life. I'd sooner touch Saint Elmo's fire, then confess."

The angel kept his gaze on Marshall.

"Believe it or not, I still pray to the almighty who gives us freewill and penance at the same time. Human have not tainted everything passed down in the scriptures. You're not the only one tormented by the visions of a bloody and sinful past."

"Do you remember your first killing? Was she gasping for air while all you had to do was release her neck?"

He stopped and took a deep breath.

"She looked into my eyes, and they were pleading for my help." The pirate dropped his head as he placed his cup on the table.

"Aye, I've had too many of these."

Silence filled the air around the table. Only the steady hum of nearby conversations and scraping boots on the wood floor came to the men.

"The young lad had the brownest eyes. Like those of a cow going to slaughter," the angel finally spoke while he looked into his cup.

"My sword gutted him. The boy had no armor to speak of; hell, he was archer. Still, I watched those eyes begging me to do something. Instead, I stared while he struggled to put his intestines back inside."

Leiras went quiet, then looked at Marshall.

"When he died, I watched his soul leave the body. It was the last time I saw such a miracle."

He took another drink.

"It's a wretched thing to grow old with such memories."

The monk slammed his cup down on the table and called over the barmaid for more drink.

~~~

On the third morning in Charleville, Leiras awoke to find Marshall already gone from the other small bed in the room. As the man lay back in their new accommodations, he listened to the bells clanging above them. The little townhouse owned by the Church sat next door to the cathedral. Their host, a religious scholar, carried a profound interest in the monk's travels in the Holy Land.

Leiras met Charles Dryden at the tavern during the night of heavy drinking with Marshall. The two visitors accepted the scholar's offer to stay with him until they completed their business. In the last two days, Leiras spent most of his time regaling their host with his tales of adventures among the Ottomans. Marshall pointed out their new host was probably looking for another patron. The angel used some of their money to purchase food and wine for Dryden. He considered it a way to keep the man interested in his tales until the Duke of Sully arrived.

After struggling to get out of the sagging bed, Leiras put on his robe before heading downstairs. He found the pirate captain standing at the parlor window. Marshall remained quiet and stared at the light snow coming down outside.

Dryden was in the room as well. At his desk, the short, pudgy man wore simple black clothes. His hook-like nose
~~~

wrinkled absently as he wrote in his leather journal. A precarious stack of papers shook next to him. Along the wall, shelves held his impressive array of books. When Leiras first arrived, Dryden proudly went through his display of bound writings by Church scholars.

Dryden studied and stayed in France, and his sponsor, the bishop, employed him as an archivist. However, his goal of becoming a philosopher at a university remained out of reach. The man complained to Leiras that his services mostly focused upon English translations of the great Catholic stories. When Leiras asked the reason, the man smiled.

"My bishop still hopes that the English crown will return to the Church. It's a quite mad idea, of course. But he lets me work on my rebuttal to Jean-Pierre de Crousaz's wretched *Treatise on Beauty*."

Leiras went to the kitchen where the old woman who worked as the housekeeper and cook sighed. The gray-haired lady then pulled a plate from a shelf. The angel rubbed his palms together as he watched the woman fill his plate.

Just after Leiras finished his breakfast, a young boy wearing little more than rags arrived at the front door. He excitedly informed the lodgers that Maximilien Gabriel's trekschuit had just landed. After receiving several copper deniers from Leiras, the skinny lad hurried away.

Dryden offered to introduce the men to Gabriel.

"You honor us, and we gladly accept," Marshall stated from a worn chair. He noticed the excitement in their host's offer.

"It's time to get dressed and prepare to introduce ourselves to the duke," the monk smiled. He watched Dryden hurry to the stairs.

"It appears our host is looking for a sponsor." The captain nodded.

"Plus, it gives us a chance to watch their servants who'll unload the baggage at the house."

"I believe you have a plan that you've not spoken about," Leiras started up the stairs.

"No, just working on an idea should we not persuade Gabriel to sell the relic."

As the three men stood near the large townhome, Dryden gave them the history of the homes on the busy street. A three-story building hovered over the road, made of locally quarried stone and fronted by iron gratings under the windows.

According to Dryden, Wolfgang Guillaume Joseph Léonard Vital owned the home. The prince of Arches and Charleville seldom stayed there; instead, he and his wife lived on a nearby estate.

Outside the front door, a fashionable carriage stood empty while servants unloaded several enormous trunks from the back. After the men carried the last heavy box inside the home, the trio of men walked across the street.

The huffing servant who handled the trunks opened the door. Dryden introduced himself while Marshall noticed the bottom of a dress at the top of the stairs. After a quick explanation, the servant led the men into a library just off the main hall. As they walked inside, Marshall glanced up to see a beautiful brunette woman looking down at them. Dressed in a flowing cream silk dress and a close-fitting blue bodice that covered her upper body. The woman still had on her feathered hat. She turned away while Marshall looked up again. He went to Leiras, taking him aside.

"I shouldn't be here. I recognized the woman at the top of the stairs, but I cannot place where I've seen her before."

The angel followed the servant into the hall. When the man looked back, Leiras gave an embarrassed smile, then returned to the room. The servant closed the white doors behind the monk.

"I didn't see her, but I'm sure it means nothing," the angel shrugged. "Just keep by the window and see if you can remember where you know her."

Duke Maximilien Gabriel arrived a few minutes later with his wife. They did not impress Marshall. Heavy powered makeup and white linen breeches and vest covered the man, along with an elaborate wig. Gabriel gave the captain an image of an overeager inbred fool.

A blunderbuss!

It was the term sailors gave such a man. When Marshall bowed to the duke, he caught to the cloying smell of Gabriel's perfume.

On the other hand, when the aristocrat introduced his wife, the captain couldn't keep his eyes from her.

Elisabeth Anne Magon di Villafranca had a charming smile and cat-like green eyes. She casually looked over at the men as Dryden introduced them. Marshall wasn't sure, but Elisabeth's full lips pursed slightly when the scholar told her his name in French. He saw the hint of recognition in her eyes when their eyes met again. He hastened to the front window, trying to avoid staring at the duchess.

Where the Hell do I know her from?

The woman quickly spoke to her husband before leaving the room. The duke nodded absently as his focus went to a tall male servant who held the door for his wife. Leiras immediately started his conversation with the nobleman. While Marshall didn't understand much of the discussion, he nodded when the monk pointed at him. The captain noticed Gabriel's expression was initially suspicious. However, the duke grew interested as the conversation continued. Dryden interjected frequently in apparent support for Leiras and Marshall. From what the pirate could make out, the scholar saw an opportunity to bring the bishop's authority to their side. Marshall noticed Leiras' glance at him over the unexpected obstacle in their planning.

The damn scholar will force us to keep the reliquary in the cathedral here!

While Marshall turned to look out the window in growing frustration, Gabriel whispered to his servant. After the man finished pouring drinks for everyone. Marshall watched the servant leave. The noise outside the door a few minutes later caught his attention. The captain placed his hand on the handle of his pistol in his pocket. Then, the doors to the room opened, and two servants carried in two wooden chests.

They're enthusiastic host went to the chests. Gabriel pulled a key as the three men joined him. Leiras nodded to Marshall while explaining in English about the honor of the duke in our interest.

"He says that we are the first gentlemen in France to see such unique relics of saints."

The first item pulled for the guest's viewing was a thick silver cross about the size of his hand. Latin inscriptions embossed with gold covered the edges and the front of the silver piece. A narrow glass vial ran inside the long part cross. When Gabriel held the item to the light, they saw the dark substance inside the glass.

"That is the blood of Saint Simpert. The monks in Augsburg assured me of its miracles." Leiras translated the words of Gabriel for Marshall. "Various thieves stole it from the Basilica di Santa Croce throughout its history."

The pirate drew close, his eyes fixated upon the item. Each end of the cross had sharpened ends with barbs. The piece almost looked like a weapon.

"What do you think?"

The angel shrugged.

"I feel a power in there, could be a saint," He turned back to their host, inquiring where he got the artifact.

Marshall noticed the Frenchman pause, then stammer out a nervous reply. The captain smiled.

"Tell Gabriel that he's got an expert eye for such treasures."

Leiras frowned, wondering about his partner's approach. He carried out the instructions. Gabriel immediately beamed as he let loose with an elaborate description of his journey from Augsburg.

The second reliquary out of the silk pillowed case showed a slightly larger artifact. Thick glass set inside four columns of solid gold barely displayed the unidentified brown rust-colored lump inside. Gabriel held the small but weighty display in the palm of his hand as he explained his trip to retrieve the heart of Saint Julia of Corsica.

Marshall grabbed the edge of the table to steady himself when vertigo suddenly struck him. Leiras asked the cause, but the captain shook his head.

"Too many drinks," he replied. "It's time to negotiate."

It took another couple of hours as Leiras and Dryden listened and interrupted the tales of the duke's journey, who continued to drink. At one point, the monk leaned over to Marshall.

"Did you see his eyes light up at our first offer? I believe more wine will make his stunning tales about his trip unbelievable. Right now, it makes the journey of Marco Polo nothing more than a ride through a daisy field."

The captain suppressed a snort.

"Do you think he'll come around to your idea?"

Leiras nodded.

"I believe he didn't realize how much money he could make. Our host is a man who can focus on only one thing at a time," the angel grinned. "I pointed out how additional francs can pave the way inside the court of King Louis XVI if we get Saint Julia.”

When the men finally left the home of Duke Gabriel, Leiras was upbeat in their prospects. He praised Dryden for his assistance in persuading the Frenchman to consider giving up one relic. The angel winked at Marshall as Dryden turned toward the cathedral.

“I’m afraid our scholar friend is in for a disappointment when the heart of the saint quietly leaves the city in the middle of the night,” Leiras told Marshall.

~~~

The next morning, Marshall stood by the front parlor window when he noticed a golden carriage stop in front of Dryden’s home. He watched as the driver slid down and opened the door. Elisabeth Anne stepped out in a green silk dress, carrying a parasol. She was alone.

Marshall went over and opened the door as she reached for the knocker.

“I take it you have no servant,” she told him in perfect English.

The captain’s surprise brought a smile to her lips.

“Our resident scholar is a pious and poor man,” Marshall finally stated. “But the house is clean. If you’re looking for Dryden, I’m afraid he’s out for a while.”

Elisabeth laughed as she handed him her silk shawl. Curiosity built in the man as Marshall led her to the study. Leiras stood when she walked in. He offered her a seat, then looked at Marshall, who shrugged. The monk went to the table and brought over a decanter with several goblets on a wooden tray.

“To what do we owe this honor, Duchess Gabriel di Villafranca?” the angel asked in French.
~~~

"I see you remember my title," she replied in English. "I thought I should come by about your conversation with my husband yesterday."

Marshall handed the glass to the woman.

"Thank you, Captain Blackbane. Your manner has improved." Her amused smile bothered him.

He hesitated, then shook his head.

"I'm afraid that you're mistaken. My name is William Marshall from Amsterdam."

Elisabeth ran the tip of her index finger around the rim of the glass, then looked up at him.

"A woman doesn't forget a pirate who boards her ship returning from Rome. I recognized those cruel eyes and your stance when you entered my home. You make quite an impression when you kill my personal escort in front of me. His blood remained on my dress during the trip to Tunis."

Marshall remained quiet, looking at the drink in his hand. The pirate took a sip of the absinthe, which he didn't taste.

"Perhaps you don't remember that day." She turned to Leiras. The monk silently watched her from the chair opposite.

"I supposed a bloody killer can't remember every murder. However, I can recall every detail. A sunny Mediterranean day with fine weather. Our ship, the *Sibilla,* sailed from Naples, and we were only one day out of port when the *Diano Marina* attacked."

"It was over after our cannon fired across your bow," Marshall interrupted. "Your captain struck his colors, and we boarded. Your ship's manifest stated the cargo was seventy chests of silk, pepper, and cinnamon heading to Marseille. I placed the passengers in irons after the crew moved the chests to the *Diano Marina.* I had my first mate, Bingham, along with part of my crew, to sail your ship with us back to Tunis."

He smirked at her shocked expression.

"Now, for the rest of the story. You, the prisoners, and your cargo brought in fifty-eight thousand shillings from the Beylik of Tunis. I split this amount among the crew after making our payments outfitting the ship. A few of my men returned to their homes in England and America to make a new start. The rest drank and whored away the money or buried it before leaving on a ship for their next raid. True to my terrible ways, I paid off my personal debts to avoid enforcers coming for me, then spent much of the rest in the brothels. It's the lot of a buccaneer."

Marshall went to the decanter and poured more liqueur for himself.

"Now, let's return to your history. As I recall, a noblewoman like yourself who cannot pay the ransom is sold as a slave. Obviously, you didn't remain as one of the many wives of the ruler. Therefore, you never became a slave or a wife."

"Yet you still don't remember my name." Her bitter tone forced him to look at her.

"The faces I always remember!" He snapped back, then downed his drink before coming closer.

"You wore a blue dress of silk. Rather foolishly overdressed for someone trying to escape while in the middle of a battle. Your vain and self-important expression wasn't that different from what you show me now. The old man who was your escort was a fool. He attempted to protect your virtue when there was no need. I ordered my men not to molest the passengers. He died for his stupidity."

His eyes darkened as he recalled the events.

"As for your name, I've never asked for the names. That arrangement came from the Ottoman rulers after they paid me. They took the ransom or bought noblewomen for their harems. The fact that you're here, married to a nobleman, means your family paid a hefty ransom to get you out of Tunis."

"All they had," her voice rose with suppressed rage. "When my husband died last year, I had his title and nothing else. No place to call home or a family for support."

Marshall stared at her as she looked at her glass. From the angle, the woman reminded him of Emma Watson.

I must be crazy. She carries the same features!

Even her manner reminded him of the woman he killed.

"Mrs. Gabriel, you've landed on your feet in France. You can't hold such grudges now. You've got a loving husband," Leiras interjected. "Soon, your children will…" Her laughter made him stop.

"I thought you were paying attention." She took a sip of her drink. "You're not an idiot, but you missed the obvious. My husband is a noble who needed a wife with a title. Children are not in the mix for a sodomite."

She leaned back.

"You can't plant a garden without the seed."

After a deep breath, the woman looked at Marshall again.

"Let me proceed with the business at hand. Your interest in my husband's grisly prizes intrigued me. I'd like to know the reason for your attempt to purchase one of them."

Marshall glanced over at Leiras, who leaned forward in his chair.

"I'm afraid the nature of our client's position makes it impossible to explain," Leiras stated. "But I can assure you that the relics carry the power of life and death of some people."

"Ah yes, that's a political answer, dear monk. Blackbane, your appearance so many miles from the sea forced me to consider your motives. My guess is you plan on melting down the gold. That's more suitable for a pirate."

"Men have reasons for doing something beyond the need for gold." He growled as he finished his absinthe. He placed the glass on the table with a scowl.

Elizebeth Anne laughed. It wasn't friendly.

"We have access to men who will pay a substantial sum for the item," the monk offered. "Your husband's debts and ambition make this offer an opportunity for you."

"I'm afraid that I've already found someone who can help with my husband's debt problem. While you might require the relics, I'm afraid that my need is greater. You won't get them. On this point, I can guarantee it."

"Then why are you here?" Leiras asked as he poured more of the liquor. "Your husband already informed us about your trip to Paris tomorrow morning. Are you here on his behalf?"

"When my husband showed you those items, I saw the same look in Captain Blackbane's eyes when his men hauled away the cargo on our ship."

Marshall's eyes narrowed.

"So, are you here for spite or for your husband's interests?

Her callous smile gave him his answer.

"I'm here for my business. The irony in this endeavor is quite delicious. Blackbane taught me how cruel men rule this world. I've stopped my husband from going any further with your offer. With my help, he's destined for the court of King Louis. While it's apparent that you've checked on us, I've left a note to the bishop concerning to unscrupulous men attempting to extort my husband."

Elisabeth Anne raised her glass for Leiras to refill.

"Then you've lied to him for us to be arrested." The pirate glanced over at the angel. Leiras picked up the decanter and stood next to their visitor.

"I've done more than that. You might not realize that there is a small garrison of French soldiers in this city. That's a result of France's royal armaments factory that's at the edge of the river. Chevalier du Challar, the *Capitaine* of the troop, graciously offered to help me in my hour of need. His family will provide a loan to my poor, deluded husband. Once we're in the court, Chevalier will eventually take over my husband's affairs. I've already informed him of your interest and your real identity."

"Entrez s'il vous plait," she suddenly called out.

The door opening behind them caused the men to turn. A tall man with a pistol in his hand stood at the door. A scar ran across his face, along his lips. His dark blue coat with red trim and white vest along with a pelt hat over his white-hair wig identified him as a French officer.

Marshall dropped his hand from his coat when the Frenchman pointed his pistol at the pirate's head. With a scowl, he turned, then bowed to Elisabeth.

"Madam, it appears that you've taken to pirate ways. Your scarred friend will take over for the eunuch that you married."

The woman's eyes danced with delight as she nodded in agreement.

"Too bad you won't live to see it. I suspect the bishop will insist you and your friend must burn at the stake for heresy."

Elisabeth smugly nodded to the officer.

"Je vous ai couvert, vous allez maintenant m'accompagner au poste de garde."

The Frenchman waved his pistol, showing the prisoners to head toward the door.

"I believe Chevalier wishes for us to accompany him to the guards." The monk explained to Marshall as he leaned over to pour the woman's drink. The pirate captain came around the sofa with his hands held up since the officer's cocked weapon remained pointed at Marshall's head.

"Puis-je vous offrir un verre?" Leiras suddenly asked. The officer shook his head at the offer of a drink.

Leiras shrugged, then dropped the decanter in the woman's lap. Her cry was the distraction Marshall needed. He immediately tackled the officer. In their tussle on the floor, the pirate wrapped his hand around the pistol's firing mechanism. The Frenchman let go of the weapon, then he reached for his sword. Marshall slammed his forehead into the Chevalier's nose. His action stunned the officer. Marshall slammed the barrel of the pistol into the man's head and saw the officer's eyes roll back. The pirate got to his feet, breathing heavily from the sudden fight.

"Get something to tie him in the chair," Marshall ordered Leiras.

While he pulled out his other pistol from his coat, the pirate watched as the Frenchman recovered. He waved the stunned man to the chair while the monk cut cords from the drapes for make-shift rope.

"I haven't forgotten you, madame. Just remain quiet," Marshall glanced over at Elisabeth Anne, who hadn't moved.

To his surprise, the duchess focused on dabbing a handkerchief at the green absinthe covering part of her dress. She only watched the fight with passing interest. Even more puzzling was her lack of curiosity about the outcome. After the woman finished, she leaned back with a self-assured look.

"I'll remind you that you're in France. There's no escape," she smirked. "The authorities will come after you. As of this morning, all of France will know that the infamous Blackbane traveled here."

"Then you won't mind if I try to avoid your trap," Marshall growled. He backed to the front window and looked out at the quiet street. The driver on the carriage nodded with his hat over his eyes.

Leiras finished tying the officer to the chair as the pirate captain stepped behind the woman on the sofa. He placed the barrel of his pistol against the back of her head. In the mirror across from them, he saw her eyes widen with fear.

"You say that you remember me," Marshall contemplated his next moves. "Unfortunately, you forgot you can't leave a ruthless man with such limited options. You should expect that I'll just splatter your brains across your boyfriend there. It is just another in my long line of killings. Not your wisest move."

Marshall smiled grimly as he pulled her shawl from the back of the couch. He stared at her reflection. Her eyes revealed growing concern. He slid the garment over her shoulder, and the man noticed the prickling flesh of her skin.

"I find it strange for you to even bother with such an elaborate scheme. Obviously, you only needed to convince your husband to ignore us or send word to have the bishop arrest us. Instead, you wanted to watch me cower in fear. Bitch, I'm long past that point. You do not know the fear and pain that awaits in the shadows for me every night."

The pirate cocked his head.

"You have the looks and a brain to get ahead in the world. Unfortunately, you're consumed by an act of petty revenge against someone who cares nothing about your problems."

He roughly pushed her over on the sofa and tied her wrists together. The bindings caused her to cry out in pain. The captain ripped off part of her dress, shoving it into her mouth. He saw the fear in her eyes when he rolled her over.

"Duchess, the pirate Blackbane won't even bother to rape and kill you. You're not worth my time. I'm sure Dryden will return home in a few hours to release you and your boyfriend. Enjoy your trivial life among petty nobles, you worthless whore."

~~~

The two men hurried out the back door of Dryden's house on their way to the stables for their mounts. After a delay in getting their horses saddled, the men finally left the city. Each rider kept expecting French troops to stop them as they passed
~~~

small clusters of uniformed men. Eventually, they traveled into the countryside, where the line of carts and horses diminished. When they only came across an occasional farmer and merchant passing by them, they could relax. With only a few hours of daylight left, Leiras grew concerned about the path Marshall led them. They were going south to Paris.

"Are you trying to test your immortality? You're leading us into the mouth of the lion."

"No, but a plan came to me as we waited on our horses," the captain explained as he pulled his mount to a stop. Leiras stopped his mount next to him.

"Since we're now wanted men, I started thinking like a highwayman. This is the main road to Paris. As we've seen, it's not well patrolled. We could return to Amsterdam with nothing, or we could just take what Gabriel stole. I think we should ambush them in the morning when they come through here."

The monk pulled out his pipe and stuffed it with tobacco. He scowled at the idea.

"It's dangerous to rob a noble. Even this close to the border." Leiras looked over the area. "Why are you so sure that they'll come this way in the morning?"

Marshall held a sly grin.

"You heard Elisabeth Anne. She relishes the idea of getting to the court of the king. Her husband is a way to achieve that. I'm sure that the French captain will send the troops after us, assuming we're heading the other way to escape. He'll believe that we're running for our lives back across the river."

He pointed down the nearly empty road.

"That means our quarry will never expect us to be waiting for their carriage. I'm pretty confident that Gabriel will head to Paris. Elisabeth will insist."

"How can you be sure?" Leiras looked down the quiet road.

"I can't, but we've seen the Duke's carriage with his crest. It'll be easy to spot. We can wait for them from a nearby treeline. Once we grab the relics, we just need a couple of days at the most to get around the city and out of France. I have an idea which provides our devious Duchess of Sully an opportunity to assist us in this as well."

"They'll have guards with them," Leiras warned him. "The nobles don't travel alone."

Marshall smiled.

"As I recall, they have a weakness because the guards always follow the carriage. The nobles won't stay behind their escort because of the dust kicked up by the horses. A little sailor ingenuity should help us eliminate our biggest problem."

~~~

By mid-afternoon of the next, the two would-be highwaymen still had no prize. After creating an improvised trap of sorts with a length of line that they made from several pieces of knotted rope, Marshall positioned himself under the bridge. Leiras acted as a lookout on higher ground while the pirate waited.

As the day progressed, Marshall had several occasions when hoofbeats drew close only to see his partner signal it wasn't the carriage. A gnawing uncertainty grew as each cart passed above him.

The damn Frenchman wasn't coming!

Marshall pulled his rapier and began sharpening the blade while he waited. The chill of the air crept through his woolen clothes while he remained in the bridge's shade. Finally, he heard a whistle. Leiras waved excitedly. The captain laid his sword aside, then stood next to the rope coming down from above. Attached to the opposite bridge support, the line lay across the road at the end of a bridge. At his feet was a boulder that the rope wrapped around. The rock perched precariously
~~~

above a drop of several feet into the water. The man placed a long limb he cut earlier to use as a lever at the foot of the boulder. He heard the increasing noise of hoofs and wheels on the hard-packed road. Marshall waited while watching for the carriage's silhouette in the morning sunlight.

Just as Gabriel's carriage passed, Marshall sent the boulder over the ledge. The rope sprang up with barely a noise. A few seconds later, the two riders plowed headlong into the line that stretched across their path. Toppling off their horses, the guards landed hard on the wood planks.

Already Leiras headed to the bridge with Marshall's mount in tow. He quickly reached the pirate captain. By the time the stunned guards struggled to their feet, Marshall was on his horse and scattering the enemies' mounts. A moment later, the men were galloping after the golden carriage.

When the two bandits drew close, Leiras hurried along the side where the driver finally noticed his pistol pointing at him. Immediately, the driver slowed the carriage to a stop.

Marshall came up alongside the wagon just as Gabriel's servant looked out of the carriage. He grabbed the servant by the collar and pitched him into the ground. Marshall slid off his horse and opened the carriage door wide. He smiled at the duke and his wife inside as he pointed his flintlock pistol at them.

"I guess you weren't expecting to see me again," he calmly told them. "Out of the carriage."

On the other side, Leiras waved the driver down from his perch. After Leiras slid off his horse, he forced the man to help the injured servant get off the ground.

"I'm taking both of the reliquaries," the captain grinned at the furious Elisabeth Anne.

Gabriel sputtered out oaths and curse in French.

"He says you'll hang for this outrage," Leiras translated.

"Yes, I get that threat many times," the captain replied. He turned to the woman. "Alright, Elisabeth, tell them we're going to the trees over there. Don't resist, or someone will die. You understand?"

"Go to hell," she scoffed.

"That means I'll have to shoot your husband for no reason," he growled at her. He pointed his pistol at the man's nose. "Do you really want to test my patience?"

With a glare, Elisabeth Anne translated his orders. As the group went to the nearby treeline, the duchess explained to her husband.

"She's telling him you're a notorious pirate who'll kill them," Leiras explained. "We're stealing the relics for money."

"Well, the duchess is correct about us killing them. Bring us rope from the back of the carriage," Marshall pushed his gun into the duke's back.

When Leiras returned, the captain's hand squeezed into the Duke's shoulder as he forced the man to face a tree. Leiras gave the servant the rope, forcing the man to tie his master and the carriage driver's wrists together on either side of the tree. In French, he told the man to hurry, or the madman Englishman would cut off his head. When the harried servant finished, the monk inspected the work, then ordered Elisabeth Anne to the next tree.

"No, the woman comes with us to provide us protection," Marshall grabbed her by the arm.

Elisabeth protested, and the captain flung her to the ground. Gabriel's curses continued while Leiras tied the servant to a nearby tree. When he finished, Marshall grabbed Elisabeth by her shoulder, forcing her to stand.

"Alright, woman, it's time for some payback. You can tell your husband that it was you who caused this robbery. We were quite willing to pay you a fair sum. Now, your husband gets nothing. We'll release you when we're safely away."

When she refused, the captain flung her to the ground in a growing rage. Leiris interceded.

"No, we don't have time," he told Marshall.

The angel quickly translated the instructions to Gabriel. He advised the duke not to bother searching for them, or they would find the woman dead. When he finished, Marshall roughly grabbed the woman by the arm, then hauled her to the carriage. Leiras climbed to the driver's seat after tying the reins of their horses to the back of the wagon. As he flicked the long leads, the monk urged the lead horses forward. Marshall waved at the tied-up victims as he entered the carriage.

"We'll need to discuss your future during the ride. I'm growing tired of your presence, and there's really no need for me to let you live."

The captain leaned back in the comfortable seat across from the visibly nervous woman.

Chapter 6: A Friendly Gesture

When the carriage finally stopped behind a thick hedgerow, the moon showed brightly. Several miles before their stopping place, Leiras pulled off the main road and turned the coach onto a rough path that led around Charleville. The light of the moon showed enough of the way for Leiras to reach the area near to the river. The day before, the monk spoke with a local farmer to get directions for bypassing the city.

When the angel slid to the ground, he wondered what Marshall planned on doing with the duchess. It surprised him the woman appeared unmolested as the captain pushed her out of the cab.

"Stand over there," Marshall ordered her.

The men transferred reliquaries to the back of each horse. Leiras retrieved a bottle of wine from the carriage, then clumsily got on his mount. He watched with amusement as Marshall led the silent woman to his horse.

"You surprise me. I thought you would kill her from the rage I saw in your face."

The captain unhooked the reins from the carriage.

"The duchess stayed quiet enough."

He glanced back.

"Besides, I'm not Blackbane any longer."

"Why not leave her?" Leiras nodded. "She can't do much from the carriage."

Marshall paused, looking over at the woman.

"It's a thought. However, there's always the chance that those guards might be pretty close behind us. Let's just get out of France first. Get on the horse, woman."

She ignored his offer of assistance and climbed on the saddle. The captain pulled up behind her with the reins still in his hand.

"Since you've not asked, I'll tell you now. I'll abide by my promise. Once we're out of France, we'll drop you off at the first village. Then you can shout to the heavens about your adventures with the terrible Blackbane."

"You flatter yourself. I'll make sure that I'm in the audience when they hang you." She replied.

"The result will surprise you," Marshall growled, then dug his heels into the horse.

~~~

By mid-afternoon the next day, the riders finally crossed a bridge to enter the Principality of Liège. Marshall and Elisabeth bypassed one village, letting Leiras to go in alone to determine their location. When the monk returned, he led them to the main road back to Amsterdam. It was on a different route.

"We'll stay on this road and drop off our passenger at the next village," he told Marshall. "Then you can return to your life."

The monk's attempt to get a response went nowhere. The duchess only turned her head.

Snow started falling as they crossed the bridge. Heavy, wet flakes landed on the riders. Elisabeth complained of her discomfort, but Marshall just snarled at her. However, he stopped in a quiet area next to a creek to water the mounts. The riders went to the nearby trees to relieve themselves. When Elisabeth returned, Marshall gave her an unrolled blanket from the back of his saddle. Leiras took the time to light his pipe.

The angel puffed on the tobacco while they continued on the road. Along the way, the two men shared the rest of the wine. Elisabeth refused their offer of a drink. Leiras shrugged his shoulders, then tossed the glass.

They exchanged barely any words with the steady snow and daylight steadily waning. Despite Marshall's dislike of the woman in front of him, he enjoyed the warmth that her body
~~~

gave off in the cold. Her perfume scent struck him occasionally, forcing him to recount their first encounter on his ship. As he considered her need for revenge, the thought struck him that Elisabeth had carried a short temper. Like him, the anger led her into situations that made her life worse.

You're a fool. She's nothing like you. Just a petty noblewoman who blames others for her fate.

The travelers only met one cart in the last several hours as they rode along. When the snowfall extinguished the monk's lit pipe, he began complaining. Finally, the exhausted riders came to a stop at a burned-out chapel inside the dense forest.

"I don't think we'll find other accommodations tonight. And the horses need rest," Marshall told them.

"Along with their riders," Leiras reminded him. The monk looked over the area. Ancient tombstones by the building gave him an uneasy feeling.

"I don't like this place," the angel stated. "I smell death when soldiers looted the place."

The captain looked around, then slid off the saddle. He stretched, stomping the ground with his boots.

"We need rest," Marshall told him again. He reached up to pull off the blanket that Elisabeth held over her shoulders to shield herself from the snow.

"Get down," he ordered. "We can get a fire going and warm ourselves."

The woman glared at him, refusing to get off the horse until he stared at her for a moment. Finally, she slid down. Marshall handed her a sack of dried food along with their bladder of wine.

"Under the tree," the man nodded toward an evergreen tree near the remains of the cemetery gate. He tied off the horse.

The duchess went to the tree, where she kicked away the pine needles covering some of the ground. Marshall followed her with the blanket. Leiras pulled off the relic display from his horse and joined them. While the pirate captain started a fire, the angel pulled a wool blanket and supplies from his horse.

After kicking away the snow from a spot by the tree, Leiras settled down with the surrounding blanket. He leaned against the case holding the saint's remains after picking up the food.

"Here, have some," the monk offered Elisabeth the bag.

She knocked it to the ground.

Marshall witnessed her reaction as he rose from coaxing a small fire. He pitched in several more broken branches into the gathering flames. The man scooped up the bag from the ground and pulled a hunk of dried meat to chew on.

"Morning will come early. You should have something," he suggested to Elisabeth.

"You cursed dog. Don't pretend to care about my welfare." She slapped away the offered food.

"Listen, you worthless bitch. I don't expect your gratitude, but I could have left your carcass to the vultures. You're still alive for the moment. You can eat your food or go hungry. Just keep your damn mouth shut unless you want a broken jaw."

Marshall stomped away, cursing the woman using every demeaning sailor word he could think of. The duchess watched him with a note of triumph in her expression. Leiras picked up the canvas bag and rummaged through for a bigger slice of beef.

"He's a foul man, but he's learning!" he told her in French.

"Don't bother to defend him. You're worse than a pirate. You're slandering the church by wearing those robes and that cross around your fat neck. No doubt, you're a pathetic heretic! If they don't hang you, they should burn you at the stake."

Leiras laughed so hard his belly shook.

"Madam, please spare me your vacuous anger. We came to your house as honest brokers, yet you seek to judge me after you betray your husband's best interests."

His frosty smile hardened as he leaned forward, his bulbous eyes turned mean.

"Madam, you dress like a lady with the tongue of a serpent. At one time, I'd shut you up by forcing you to use that wicked tongue on my pole until I filled your mouth with my seed."

He leaned back again.

"When we left France the first time, God called upon me to remove a husband who beat his wife and child. I wonder what he thinks of your sinful relationship with that French officer. I surmise it's not your first adultery, nor will it be your last. When the Lord judges you, don't think he'll overlook your transgressions. Perhaps he'll order me to rape and kill you before dawn."

The monk watched as the woman glanced over at Marshall, who worked to remove the saddles from the horses. Neither was sure if the man was listening.

"He probably won't mind whatever I do with you," the impersonal voice of Leiras brought her attention back to him.

"So if you live until dawn, we'll free you. Then, you can return to your eunuch. Live out your days while you order the unfortunate rabble to toil and to serve you. The irony is that your memories will always return to the few times where her heart raced when you experienced this perilous adventure. Then, you can die an old woman to be judged for your sins."

He pulled his silver flagon, then took a drink. The monk licked his lips.

"I wouldn't gloat when we free you. I predict you fear the reaper. Our judgment is in place. I would say the same goes for you. However, my friend and I don't fear the reaper any longer."

Leira's comments infuriated Elisabeth. However, she looked away, choosing to remain silent. She saw the insane look in his eyes. On top of that, the man's words struck too close for comfort.

~~~

Elisabeth Ann kept nodding off as she covertly watched Leiras. She lay on her side, facing the campfire. The few remaining flames barely gave enough light to see the tombstones. The man in the monk's robes leaned against the tree trunk. His enormous head nodded, and his eyes were closed. Now that the snow stopped falling, the woman decided her guard would soon go to sleep. She glanced over at Blackbane, who slept with his back to her. He snored lightly.

While she waited for Leiras, Elisabeth kept going back over her planned escape. She might not know the territory, but the woman was confident in her horsemanship. Once she got to a horse, Elisabeth intended to find help. With only one mount between them, a band of armed men would soon capture the thieves. The bonus was the death of the two men and her return to France with the reliquaries. She smiled at the idea.

The monk's movement caught her attention as his nodding head jerked back. Then he adjusted his position. His eyes remained closed. She glanced over at Marshall, who didn't move.

The duchess remembered Blackbane when he appeared on the main deck as her armed escort tried to help her escape. When Blackbane stepped in front of the man, her bodyguard demanded that he give his word not to sell the women on the ship.

"The ship you captured is valuable enough. These are noblewomen coming back from a pilgrimage. Put us on a boat for the shore."

"We'll hang first," Blackbane barked. "You're not in the Caribbean. The Turks pay for slaves and wives. This ship's cargo isn't enough. As Captain, I'm allotted six portions to the ordinary seamen. My men and I won't lose a fortune to save a woman's hide."
~~~

As the pirates around Elisabeth shouted their agreement with their captain, Blackbane turned away. Elisabeth's bodyguard cursed him. The old man struggled to pull his pistol from his belt. In a flash, Blackbane spun around with his sword. The woman observed the pirate captain's callous smile. Blackbane knew her escort would never get the pistol out soon enough. Still, the man killed him. He enjoyed it!

The man's body fell at her feet, his blood splattered across her beautiful dress. Elisabeth stood in shock as Blackbane casually walked away. The cruel pirate never looked back as he continued to issue orders to his men.

After arriving in Tunis, Elisabeth remained in chains with the other nobles held captive. When she went before the Beylik, she saw how the fat man eyed her. Still, the Beylik lived up to his promise of her release once her ransom came. As she waited, the woman prayed for a most horrible death to strike Blackbane each night. Those months in Tunis changed Elisabeth. She watched those who worked for the Turk leader. The woman decided she would not be a pawn for those with more power. Elisabeth learned how to use her beauty to her advantage.

The world for those who know how to control people!

The continued silence but for the crackle of the fire pulled Elisabeth from her past. She carefully looked up at Leiras, who was asleep. After another glance at Blackbane, the woman carefully lifted herself. Elisabeth stood, holding the blanket in her hand. She heard a noise behind her. The duchess noticed movement in the graveyard. Just out of the light, she saw shadows moving low on the ground. Accompanying sounds of rustling and groans came with the things Elisabeth had witnessed. A growing fear filled her as the shadows became defined and stood.

As her eyes surveyed the darkness, Elisabeth watched the tall, slim, well-dressed man coming into the area. For a moment, she considered rushing to him for help. Then she saw his black eyes as the man stepped into the light. He glanced at the woman while the shadowed things emerged out of the darkness.

The creatures she saw were skeletal with dark, mummified skin and dressed in tattered rags. Their faces were nearly gone, showing only the gray-white bone. The ghouls came close and surrounded her when Elisabeth finally screamed.

Instantly, Marshall is on his feet with his sword in hand. He hurried next to the woman. When he faced the demon, the pirate pulled his pistol.

"I've been waiting for our rematch," Mammon's ominous voice filled the air as he pulled a sword from his belt.

"You should have accepted my offer!" With a nearly imperceptible nod, the demon directed the corpses to attack.

Marshall rushed towards a ghoul, and he swung his rapier. A ghoul's head flipped into the darkness. Not far away, another foul creature reached Elisabeth. As she backed away, Marshall fired his pistol, which stuck the beast. The exploding head of the corpse splattered pieces across the duchess.

While his partner fought, Leiras had his Xeropotamou lantern by the embers, trying to light his weapon against demons. He didn't see a ghoul attack him from behind until the last minute. The fat man pulled away in time, but the creature fell on top of the campfire flames. An overwhelming stench came from the burning flesh when the ghoul's flesh extinguish the fire. It thrashed around while Leiras backed away. Another creature stepped in front of the angel and slashed his fat belly. The man cried out, but he got his powerful arm around the ghoul's neck. While he fell, Leiras twisted the corpse's skull off the body. He struggled to his feet to witness Mammon heading toward Marshall.

In the middle of the angel's fight, Elisabeth tried to pull away from a ghoul. It bit down on her shoulder before she could get away from its clutches. Standing nearby, Marshall hurried over. He used the pistol as a club to smash the ghoul's head. Elisabeth pulled away.

She watched in disbelief as Mammon suddenly appeared behind the pirate. The demon impaled the captain with his sword. As the blade came through Blackbane's chest, blood flowed down the front of the captain's chest. Marshall's eyes locked on to the woman's as the demon pulled out his sword. While the captain fell to the knees, holding his hand over his painful wound, Mammon stood over the pirate in triumph.

"Now, I'll let my ghouls eat you alive," he declared. "Your soul is mine."

Leiras stumbled several paces at the demon, who turned at the noise. The angel slammed his sanctuary lamp against the demon's head. Mammon fell back, his howling filled the air as the power of the cross inside pushed the unholy beast away.

Leiras nearly fell over as he dropped the lantern. However, he helped the pirate to his feet. The two men stumbled to the tree. They stared at the remaining ghouls and their master, who slowly came toward them. Marshall kept thinking about the remains of Saint Julia while spitting up blood. He glanced over at Elisabeth when she came next to him. She's held the rapier that Marshall dropped. The blade shook from her fright.

"You'll have help with your revenge on me tonight. That's Mammon!" He whispered, surprised that the woman remained with them.

The woman's eyes widened at the name. She glanced at him, seeing Marshall's blood pouring through his hand that he held over the wound. The man grimaced as he pulled the jewel-encrusted dagger from his belt.

"When they attack, you get the hell out of here!" He ordered her. "Get to the horses and escape back for your life."

The woman remained a statue for a moment. Her mind could not accept what she had witnessed around her. Then she glanced over to Leiras, who clutched his torn belly. To her shock, the man winked at her and nodded in agreement.

"Leiras, get the relic! I'll keep them off of you." Marshall stepped toward the demon and his dead minions.

It's time to see how our new package helps us or not.

The monk groaned as he bent down and removed the box from a canvas bag. His bloody hands slipped while hurriedly trying to open the latch.

Mammon stepped into the full view of the remaining campfire light. The skin on the side of his face was gone. White maggots wiggled among the dark, bloody muscles along his jaw and cheek.

"You can't stop me," the demon cackled as his evil creatures attacked.

Screeching, the fiends came at Marshall. He swung his pistol, shattering the corpse's skull while slashing another with the dagger. The last of the ghouls landed on Marshall. He called out for Leiras to hurry, but skeletal hands savagely pulling his beard turned into his words into a yell.

In the confusing fight, Elisabeth hacked at a creature. It screamed as it fell at her feet. The ghoul grabbed the hem of her dress. She felt the tug, and the woman scrambled away in a panic. The bottom part of her dress ripped apart, still held in the corpse's hand, while Elisabeth hurried over to the monk.

"Let me help.

"Get out of here," the monk ordered as he finally got the case opened.

Elisabeth glanced over at Mammon. The demon stepped close to the visibly weakening pirate, daring him to fight. The ghouls bit into the man's flesh and tried to drag him down. Blood covered the pirate captain.

Seeing the desperate last stand of the men, Elisabeth saved herself. She headed for the horses that whinnied as they struggled to pull free from their reins.

"I'll see you in Hell with me!" Marshall roared.

The duchess looked back and saw Marshall's desperate lunge. He embedded the dagger blade into the demon's leg. As Mammon howled in agony, Leiras turned with Saint Julia's display. A howling whirlwind suddenly swept over the area. Leiras staggered forward with the relic in his hands. A growing light erupted from the man's hands, causing the remaining ghouls to release Marshall. Trying to shield their eyes while in pain, an intense white light that shot out from the golden dome. The beam hit the creatures, followed instantly with shrieks of the damned. Suddenly, the overwhelming noise and hurricane winds stopped, leaving an eerie silence.

As Leiras looked over the scene, it appeared only the bodies of the dead remained around Marshall. The angel fell to his knees, praying aloud his gratitude to Saint Julia. Blood on his hands landed upon the relic, sending up whispers of burning smoke. Finally, the monk fell over on his side. His last view was the pale face of Marshall, whose open eyes stared at the night sky.

~~~

"I just don't understand. How is he still alive?" Elisabeth's shocked tone carried to Marshall through the still air. "For that matter, how did you survive?"

Leiras glanced over at the captain, who barely moved. He shook his head.

"Marshall had an encounter with an archangel named Remiel."

"What's that supposed to mean?"
~~~

"It means William Marshall is no longer Blackbane," Leiras told her. "It also means that you need to ask him to explain. We all have our secrets, don't we?"

The woman glared at him, but the angel focused on his injuries. Deep gashes in his belly still bled. He ripped more pieces of his garment and poured gin from his flask on the cloth. His fat belly shook in pain when the man placed the rags on his wounds.

"Neither of you should be breathing," Elisabeth repeated. It was the third time she told Leiras that since she returned from the horses. She watched him with morbid fascination.

"How did you destroy that thing from Hell?"

"We didn't! We drove him away. The holy blood in Captain Marshall's dagger, and the power of Saint Julia's heart saved us. You should consider yourself lucky. Few people survive Mammon without help."

"I still don't understand what happened. Where did those dead things come from?"

The monk's expression contorted as he moved his body.

"The undead awaken to assist their master, but they're just many of the creatures from Hell who lift the corpses walk again. They are not human, just tools used by the demon."

"You know that's not what I meant," she replied.

"I know," the monk agreed. "However, it's a long story. You'll think us mad."

The woman's laugh briefly tittered on hysterical.

"Are you joking? After what I've witnessed. I've got bite marks from corpses that rose from the ground. You and Blackbane rise from certain death," Elisabeth paused, gathering herself.

"Maybe I'm already mad?"

Marshall listened to the conversation. At first, the sound remained far away, like a barely understood discussion across the room. Gradually, the words broke through the haze that filled his mind. He recognized the voices as well.

Marshall's groan when he rolled to his side broke up the conversation. The captain got to his knees. Sweat dripped from his forehead. Then he threw up the blood he swallowed from his injury.

Elisabeth remained sitting by the monk, visibly torn by her inclination to help him and her remaining hate.

The captain crawled over to join them. Leiras handed him the flask of gin when Marshall slid between them. The man took a drink, tasting the blood. He groaned again.

"Ah, that burns going down."

"What do you expect? You've had a sword go through you. Maybe the alcohol will keep the infection down. You still bleed, so we must find a doctor to sew the skin together." Leiras went back to work on his injuries.

The pirate looked down at his wound. He opened the rest of his shirt front to expose more of his hairy chest. Then Marshall ripped the cloth from his shirt sleeve and stuffed it into the wound with a grimace.

"How is your belly?" Marshall glanced over at the deep gashes.

"The body will survive with some thread to bind the gash. I do believe it'll take an executioner's ax to remove my head before losing this body."

The captain glanced at Elisabeth, who watched them. Her expression was hard to read. Marshall leaned against the tree.

"It's a hell of a way to make some damn saints happy." He held the make-shift bandage on his chest, then he picked up the case holding Saint Simpert's relic. The man pulled out the silver cross and placed it on his wound. He groaned as he felt a spark shoot through him. Marshall paid no attention to the stares of his companions as he silently prayed. He put the blood-covered relic in a money bag that hung from his belt.

"We'll see if the saints can help the flesh heal," he told Leiras, then turned back to the woman. Elisabeth's surprised reaction made him grunt out a painful chuckle.

"Still trying to understand the world. Well, so am I. Now, why did you come back?"

The duchess glanced away.

"Where was I to go? I don't even know where I am," Elisabeth finally told him.

"Well, that's an answer." Marshall rested his head on the rough bark of the trunk. "I'll admit that you surprised me. Few women I've met before would hold their ground against such creatures."

"I've met worse," she shot back. "They're called pirates!"

The captain snorted, then suppressed a groan at the effort.

"Aye, we've eaten people alive," Marshall growled sarcastically. "It's too bad that a ghoul didn't bite off that wicked tongue of yours," he pitched the silver flask into her lap.

"Here! It won't help your disposition, but use it on your wounds. I don't want you to die on us before we return you to your husband."

~~~

After a few hours of rest to recover, the ragged and bloody trio finally left and rode out of the woods at dawn. They pulled into the village of Grognaux at dusk. The trio said little as they tried to ignore the pain of their injuries. Even the talkative Leiras showed little interest in a conversation.

Marshall noticed Elisabeth's continued glances as they rode. She remained hostile to him, yet, her actions showed she would fight beside him. It didn't make sense. The man found a sense of irony in the fact he didn't really remember Elisabeth
~~~

beyond the dress and her pretty face. She was nothing more than the value of the gold she brought.

It's pretty much the same now. She's just a way to escape from the French.

He told her the truth about remembering those he killed. His nightmares kept their images fresh in his mind. Still, it surprised him he failed to account for Elisabeth's inner drive. He always fancied himself a judge of character. Yet he missed her need for revenge. Elisabeth's determination threw off his plans. He guessed Remiel guided the woman as a foil against him.

Well, I've made many enemies over the years!

His fight against the demons convinced Marshall he might be on the correct path. Saint Julia provided him guidance from beyond the grave. Still, he and Leiras continued their wicked ways of pursuing a saint's artifact. Yet, human curses and sin were far different from the pure malevolence he witnessed from his enemies. He wondered if Julia understood the heavy burden of sins weighing on Marshall's soul.

Maybe she recognized his inherent disadvantage against those who cursed him or pursued him.

As Leiras guided their group toward the tavern, the few people on the street cast suspicious looks when the group passed. Elisabeth sagged in the saddle in front of Marshall. He leaned over occasionally, pulling back her blanket to find that she wasn't sleeping. Instead, she stared ahead. She appeared oblivious to his question and remained silent. Unless he misjudged her return to their camp, the captain believed the duchess fought an internal battle as much as he did.

Perhaps she's carried similar questions about good and evil?

Leiras hailed the first man who stepped from the tavern. He discovered they were near the village of Dinant, in the land controlled by an influential Bishop, named de Hoensbroeck.

"You should wait for the rector to return," the man told Leiras after the monk explained their bloody appearance came from bandits. "As the judicial vicar, he'll organize a force to send out after such outlaws."

"As they should, however, we must reach Amsterdam. You can tell the rector of our troubles when he returns." The monk's frown at the name of de Velbruck was caught by Marshall while he watched the conversation from on his horse. The captain credited himself for understanding more of the language. Elisabeth moved slightly as she leaned against his back. While the pressure of her upper body on his wound hurt him, the man let the dozing woman sleep.

The shopkeeper's eyes narrowed when Leiras asked about a Dutch doctor. He explained that the closest was in the town of Namur, where the Dutch controlled the citadel. Leiras thanked him, and he hurried his companions along the street.

"We need to leave here and go to Namur," the angel whispered as passed by the few stone buildings. "I know the bishop pays for spies throughout the lands of Liege. He carries a love of executions. They don't call him *bourreau roux* for nothing."

"You can leave me here," Elisabeth spoke up. "You may fear the Red Executioner, but not I. The bishop is a well-known nobleman, and as a Catholic, he will return me to France."

"Madam, I don't think that's wise. Even among the devout, he's not a man known for his tolerance and compassion," Leiras warned.

"There's a church, we can drop Elisabeth off," Marshall suddenly agreed to the duchess's idea.

"She wants to return to her class. No harm will come to her inside a church. The priest will provide her with food and a bed. She can get back to France on her own."

Leiras shrugged his shoulders, and they stopped in front of the dark church. After the woman slid off the back of the horse, she didn't look back as she hurried to the doors.

The two men watched for a moment, then Marshall spurred his horse.

"Let's go find that doctor," he stated.

~~~

When Elisabeth pulled open the doors, the darkness inside surprised her. Even stranger was the fact that no crosses or religious statues showed as she walked by a wall. The displays looked ripped off the walls, leaving only broken holders. She took several steps into the silent building and was about to leave when she noticed a figure in a white robe.

"Can you help me, Father? I'm trying to return to Charleville." The woman spoke in French as she came closer.

Silence filled the room as the figure remained on their knees, praying at the empty table filled with lit candles. The altarpieces of art above the table were gone, ripped away at some point in time.

Elisabeth drew closer, her nerves on edge when the figure stood, then turned around. The robe fell away, and the naked tall man stood before her. It's wings spread wide to reveal his true nature as an angel. His face revealed no expression, but his gold irises stared down at her.

Elisabeth dropped to her knees and bowed to him.

"You can rise, Elisabeth. I've been waiting." The angel used flawless Eastern Lombard, the language she understood from childhood.

"What are you here for?" She stammered out, avoiding his eyes with her own. The woman crossed herself, and he frowned.

"I expected your kidnappers to come inside with you. The kidnappers delayed you. Given the condition of your dress and your injuries, I surmise that the ride to this village was more
~~~

difficult than expected. I'm surprised that your companions left you to fend for yourself."

The woman looked at her torn dress and nodded.

"I told them to leave me here so I can return to France. They were hurrying to the next town. Their injuries need a doctor's help."

A sly grin came to the creature's lips.

"That's what they told you? They were more interested in dropping you off and getting their payment for the relic."

She looked at him, her dirty face showed her surprise.

"That's correct, they have a religious artifact taken from my carriage. You must stop them. Blackbane is a malicious criminal, and the crazy man who rides with him blasphemes and mocks the very word of the Lord."

"No, my child. It is not I who will stop them. Saint Julia of Corsica guides them. I won't interfere with a saint."

"That can't be. Blackbane is evil, I tell you," Elisabeth insisted.

"Oh, the man is as wicked and foul as I've seen in many years. You realize that he's been cursed for his sins. How else could a man live when he shouldn't?"

He saw by her reaction she understood.

"That's correct. Blackbane seeks atonement by gathering relics. It appears his lust still remains since he's seeking redemption while collecting a price on the relic. He's quite the character."

The angel took a seat in the pew. He looked down and patted the seat next to him.

"Please sit. We must discuss our common opponent."

The woman's hands shook as she carefully sat next to him. The winged creature took a deep breath as she passed.

"It's lovely here in the silence. This building still hasn't recovered from the war. It's so peaceful. You can almost hear the dead in the catacombs under our feet."

"Who are you?" She stared at the beautiful face.

"You may call me Remiel." the angel adjusted his wings to lean back on the dusty bench.

"Then the monk was telling the truth about Blackbane." Her voice quivered in shock and disbelief.

"This is true. However, I'm afraid that your monk is not as he seems." The angel cocked his head in thought. "However, I'm curious about Sariel's motives."

Then he waved his hand dismissively, then turned back to the woman. He ignored her puzzled expression at the name.

"Blackbane is the target."

"But why aren't you stopping them?" The woman stared into the angel's hypnotic eyes.

"I'm afraid that the saints are interested in this man. While I can't speak for them, one could say that they gave him this mission. Should he pass, I believe they'll give him more visions.

"Are you saying that Blackbane could continue to benefit by stealing relics? That makes no sense. Stealing is a sin. How can the blessed saints tolerate such things?"

"While stealing is a sin, in the case of the heart of Julia, we both know that the crime isn't Blackbane's, is it?

Elisabeth averted her eyes.

"I'm not sure what you mean."

The angel smiled.

"Come now, your husband paid men to break into the monastery. It was your idea to steal it since the monks resisted your husband's offer. You value the idea of a king's court over your soul. In his way, Blackbane is righting a wrong."

The woman's face went pale.

"I'm afraid that in the eyes of the Lord, your greed and ambition are like Blackbane's. It's rather ironic given the hate you feel for the man. I suppose you still feel he owes you for your time among the Turks."

She went quiet while a sly smile came across the lips of the creature next to her.

"However, I have an idea which might interest you. It benefits both of us."

"What is it?" Her voice trembled at the idea. Elisabeth hated how the angel understood everything about her feelings and emotions.

"I believe someone should become a competitor. That person will interfere with Blackbane's plans. I need someone to intercept the relic and return it to France."

She looked at the angel with a scowl.

"You have all the power of Heaven. You could wipe them out with a flood and spirit the heart back to my home."

The angel smiled.

"I'm afraid you're overdramatic. My involvement would be…well a bit unseemly. I'm looking for an intermediary of sorts. As a noble, you agree we do better by using others for our bidding. And you fit the need. Plus, you're here."

"But I must return to my husband," she stammered. "I cannot help your plan."

The angel frowned, and his expression hardened.

"Foul creature, I can read into your thoughts and your soul. Your husband can wait. You made that point to your lovers since you've married. As for your ability, I know you like to bend men to your way using your beauty and sex. You also carry a bag of gold hidden in your corset."

Elisabeth clutched at the side of your inner dress, touching the bag.

"You'll use those coins to travel to Namur. The last house at the end of the road will provide you with an escort. A blacksmith named Peeters has a son. Ask for the boy to provide you escort. He's a good sturdy lad who's fiercely loyal, but his father despises him. A few coins to the father will give you a safe escort on the road."

The angel looked her over as she battled her emotions. The creature reached over and delicately ran his fingertips over her exposed shoulder. She shivered under the icy touch.

"After a bath and treatment of your wounds, you'll go to St Aubin's. Talk with Jean Ménart. He'll provide you with everything you need. You will go to Blackbane and offer him gold for the relic."

"I can't do that; he knows how much I hate him. He knows the Duke of Sully is broke."

"His lust for wealth will overcome his concerns about you," the angel scoffed. He paused, then cocked his head as if he read her thoughts. His smug grin made her angry.

"Interesting! I believe you carry a dilemma now. You owe a pirate for your life."

The angel stood.

"Nevertheless, you will go to Blackbane. I suggest you use your abilities to secure a deal. You must return to France with your relics. It's written that you must follow your heart's ambitions. To achieve such things, Elisabeth, you must learn obedience to me."

He slid past the woman, who shook her head.

"Don't you mean obedience to God? Why are you doing this to me?"

The angel's unpleasant smile froze her heart.

"Like Blackbane, your actions give you a direction for this life. Your heart grew bitter from your experiences as a prisoner. You find the commandments of the Lord an inconvenience to your ambition. I'm giving you an opportunity. Another turn will lead you into the arms of demons."

The winged creature walked toward the altar as Elisabeth stood. Her face turned red with anger.

"I won't do it!"

The angel stopped.

"You can make that choice. Free will allows such action. However, your road travels through me. Follow my directions or face your decision in the afterlife."

"I'm not like him," she cried. "How can you do this? You're not God!"

"No, I'm not." The angel agreed with a grin as he glanced back.

"I'll remind you that Hell takes all sinners."

Then he disappeared.

Elisabeth waited in the dim light, half expecting the angel to return. Finally, she went to the table and fell to her knees. In tears, the woman silently prayed. When she finished, the woman rose and left the church.

Walking out to the road, the darkness enveloped her, and she shivered. The light coming out of the window of a nearby tavern caught her eye. Elisabeth started toward the building, then she stopped.

She looked back the other way. Elisabeth sighed and turn around to follow the road to the edge of the village.

The woman heard the sharp beating noise of iron and iron as she came to a small shack along with an open hut next to the road. A stable stood on the edge of the light coming from the forge. Inside the structure, a massive bald man pounded on glowing metal with a hammer. He stood behind an anvil while another burly person worked the nearby bellows. Next to them, a nearly white fire burned in a circular fire pit. It took a moment for the two men to notice the woman standing at the edge of the hut.

When the man caught sight of Elisabeth, he stopped.

"You want something?"

"I'm Mrs. Magon di Villafranca, the Duchess of Sully," she told him with an air of superiority. "I'm told I could hire your son to escort me to Namur."

The blacksmith looked at her, then his son rose from his spot by the bellows. They looked like identical twins at first. Then the large boy whispered to his father. Elisabeth noticed his excitement. His father nodded and turned back to her.

"The name's Peeters," he stated. When the man sat his hammer on the anvil, he glanced back at her. "Come into the light."

Elisabeth slowly came closer while she pulled her ripped corset higher over her breasts. She didn't like the man's unmistakable leer.

"It'll cost you ten ducats. Do you have the money?" His expression turned to suspicion when he got a good view of her clothes. She nodded.

"Of course!"

Peeters scowled at her. For a moment, she thought he might turn her away.

"The boy said a man stopped by and told him that a noblewoman would come for his help. I don't pay much attention, I only heard part of the conversation. I guess he got this one right."

The man saw her staring at the boy, who vacantly stared at her.

"He goes by little Peeters. My wife died bearing him." The blacksmith explained. "Pay no attention to him. He's got no mind.

He turned to his boy, ordering him to get water.

"You'll need a place to stay since you can't leave until morning. There's a tub inside if you want to clean yourself and your clothes. My boy will heat the water for you."

She smiled, but her discomfort remained.

"You can go up to the tavern if you want," he told her. Then, the big man walked toward the house. "Doubt there's room there, but you can try."

After a glance down the dark road, Elisabeth frowned. She shivered from the chilling night air, then followed Peeters inside.

The sparely furnished three-room building held a table, a stove, and two beds. There were no doors inside, just curtains to cover the entrances. The blacksmith showed her a food storage room with a small tub in the corner.

She noticed him staring at her clothes, and she grew embarrassed.

"Hopefully, I can clean off the stains."

"I might have some clothes my wife used to wear. There's a bench there to sleep on," he grumbled.

"Do you have a clean blanket?"

"Don't you worry, duchess. I'll take good care of you. We don't get aristocrats staying in our home."

He turned away and laughed at his sarcastic joke. Elisabeth wondered why he didn't question her about the blood.

It took a while for the little Peeters to get hot water, but Elisabeth felt refreshed when she finally finished her bath. His father brought her a simple dress and a robe from his dead wife. The cloth was rough and too large for her, but she thanked the man. Elisabeth pulled the simple dress over her undergarments. She stopped, and her eyes glanced around the dim room. The feeling of being watched still bothered her.

Just outside the house, she heard Peeters roar as he started cursing at his son. The smack of flesh on flesh followed, then a sound of whimpering. Elisabeth frowned at the thought of remaining among the common folk while she finished dressing. Going to the blanket that hung down from the room entrance, she verified no one was inside the house. Elisabeth pulled out a bag of coins that she had hidden away in her bloody clothing. She tied the bag inside her new clothes before leaving the room.

~~~

The next morning, Elisabeth woke early after a restless night. She barely slept on the hard bench, and every sound made her edgy. Her host's continued stares bothered her, and the woman kept expecting to find the massive man looming over her. However, when she woke, neither the father nor his son was inside. Elisabeth pulled the woolen cloak over her shoulders and went into the chill of the morning air.

The woman found Peeters at his forge. His son wasn't around.

"You sure don't look like a lady now," the blacksmith told her. "You'd fit right in as a farmer's wife."

"Hardly," she frostily told him. "Where's my horse and your son to guide me?"

"The priest came by looking for help. The boy went with him. You'll have to wait for your trip to Namur. Don't worry, I won't change the price," he grumbled when he saw her annoyed expression.

"I need to leave now. I can go alone," the duchess suggested.

"No, I'm not selling you my only horse." He looked at her for a moment. When he saw her hesitate, the man shrugged and turned back to his anvil.

"Why don't you take me?" Elisabeth suggested. "I'll pay you extra to do it."

"How much?" He didn't glance back.

"I'll double it," the duchess smugly assured him. "I'll see that you won't lose any money today."

Finally, he nodded.
~~~

"I'll make sure of it. Wait while I saddle the horse," Peeters agreed.

"Can we get something to eat?"

Peeters turned to the stable.

"I've got salted meat. I'll bring it along," the man continued to walk away.

While Elisabeth waited impatiently, she kept looking along the road. Even if the odds were against it, she hoped a carriage might come by while she waited. Then the duchess realized her peasant attire would not get her passage.

Peeters rode out on an old brown and white mare. He stopped next to her and offered a hand. The woman looked uncomfortable at the riding arrangement before she took hold of his rough hand and climbed behind him.

"There now, duchess. You just relax and enjoy the ride." He spurred the horse onto the road.

As they rode along, she enjoyed the warmth of the rising sun on her back. However, the stench coming from the man in front of her made it difficult to concentrate.

Why do all commoners smell so bad?

On the ship among the sailors and in Tunis, she carried scented oils in a vial to sniff when she walked among the masses. As a titled woman, Elisabeth expected deference and kept away from such foul-smelling people. Now, dressed as a peasant woman, an angel expected her to be part of the rabble of society. The shame was nearly unbearable. All of her suffering because of one man who changed her life.

Blackbane!

Seeing the man hanging from a scaffold would finally put her family's humiliation to rest. Her kidnapping and ransom led to the di Villafranca fortunes falling apart after her first marriage.

Distantly related to the Grand Prince of Tuscany, her father died while collecting the sum needed to ransom her back from

Tunis. His debt forced the woman into a hastily arranged marriage with the Duke of Sully. However, the obligation still hung over her head since her husband gave her little in return beyond the title. It was the duke's ambition to become a favorite of the king, which gave Elisabeth an opportunity. Once inside the court of the King of France, she could use her skill and charms to achieve even more. Then Blackbane stepped in to thwart her opportunity once again.

Elisabeth shook her head, suddenly remembering that Peeters called her a duchess that morning and the night before. Something bothered her about the man's knowledge.

"You said a man came by and told your boy that I would come to your home last night. What did he look like?"

The man shrugged.

"Can't rightly say with his black clothes and hat hung down low. I guess he was a gentleman. Just told the boy that you'd come for an escort to Namur."

He finished the conversation by drinking more gin from an animal bladder. His foul breath reached the woman, and she went silent again.

When mid-day arrived, they reached a small stream. Peeters turned the horse down a path into the woods until they came to an isolated clearing. He brought the mount to a halt.

"Need a break," he told her. "You can use them woods over there."

As the blacksmith helped her from the horse, he got down and went behind a tree. The woman stretched, then went behind a nearby tree to relieve herself as well. When she finished, Elisabeth leaned against the tree and began putting on her petticoat.

"No need to bother!" Peeters came around the tree. Before she could react, the man grabbed her arm and swung her to the ground. Elisabeth fell on her belly.

"Get away from me!"

She cried out for help as the man used one hand pressed down on the back of the neck, keeping her head pinned to the ground. She felt her dress lift, exposing her backside. The woman then screamed for help when he ripped her petticoat and underwear away.

"Quite your struggling, my noble bitch. I've been feeling them breasts in my back all morning. Now, I'm getting my payment early."

Despite her cries and struggles, the duchess quickly lost the fight. His calloused hand gripped her wrist behind her back while his other hand lifted her by the hips. Then, the brute slapped the back of her head until she quit resisting. When he thrust into her, the duchess cried out. She went silent while trying to bite back her involuntary grunt with each painful thrust. As rage and humiliation filled her, the woman refused to cry.

"Come on, my noble bitch. I want you to scream," Peeters mumbled out while he forced her face into the ground.

Elisabeth tasted the dirt and grass in her opened mouth, but she refused to cry out. Finally, the blacksmith groaned and trembled when he finished. The man released the duchess with a grunt, forcing the woman to her belly. The rapist rose from his knees while he buttoned his pants.

"Never had me a duchess before. I wondered what all the fuss was about. It weren't much," he scoffed. "I've had whores who'll do a guy better."

With a sudden afterthought, the blacksmith kneeled by her and pulled the folds of her dress away. He took the bag of coins hidden among the petticoat. Elisabeth struggled with him, grabbing the pouch.

"Give me that," she cried as he ripped the bag away from her.

Peeters laughed after he savagely slapped her. Elisabeth fell back, glaring at him. She rubbed her stinging cheek while the brute rose, looking at the gold pieces inside.

"It's amazing what I discovered by looking through the cracks of the wall. I couldn't have my fun last night since people might know you stopped at my place. But nobody knows a noble lady left with me this morning." Peeters gloated. Then he looked over her half-naked body.

"I've seen you arrogant bitches ride by in your expensive carriages, with men kissing your rear. But now you're just another peasant. Nobody will believe you're a noblewoman. I knew when I got you to swap out of your fancy clothes, things would work out. Up ahead on this road, there's a quiet place where we'll stop for the night."

His evil smile broadened.

"I want to see how well you do when your life is on the line. After all, I never promised when you'd get to Namur."

With a bellowing laugh, he turned around and went to the tree, where he bent down to retrieve his bladder of gin. He began singing a tune.

Elisabeth mechanically crawled to her knees while she watched him. Swelling anger came from her humiliation at the man standing near her. Her hand brushed a chunk of rock. She looked down at the object. Fury filled her as she quickly rose and stepped closer to the brute.

Hearing the woman's footsteps, the man started to turn. The duchess slammed the rock into the side of her rapist's head. Peeters fell to his knees. As he shook his head, the woman swung with all her might. The rock shattered the back of his skull. Elizabeth kneeled as Peeters lay face down on the ground. Then she continued to rain blows on the blacksmith's head. Finally, the duchess stopped. The only sound came from her gasping for air.

When she finally stood, Elizabeth dropped the stone next to the unrecognizable pulp that once was her attacker's head. In a trance-like state, the blood-covered woman stepped into the freezing creek. Elisabeth splashed herself between the legs with an increased frenzy to remove the foul residue left by the dead man. Eventually, the shivering, drenched woman stepped out of the stream, barely able to feel her hands, legs, and feet.

Then, Elisabeth Anne Magon di Villafranca, the Duchess of Sully, broke down.

Chapter 7: Namur

In the middle of the day, Marshall and Leiras finally came to a stop. They were the outside gates of the citadel, which overlooked the Meuse River and the town of Namur below. Both men paid little attention to the view, worn out from their injuries and travel. Fortunately, no one appeared interested in their travel to the town. The Prussian soldiers only demanded a fee at certain checkpoints.

As Marshall assessed the ramparts above, he recognized uniforms of the Dutch soldiers manning walls. Yet across the street, there were Prussians in uniform who controlled the town.

"Why don't you use your skill in Dutch to find us a doctor," he stiffly turned to Leiras. The pale-faced monk nodded, then he rode over to talk with a nearby guard. After a quick conversation, he returned and led them down the street.

"The Dutch have an enclave for themselves," Leiras explained as they rode around the fort. "We must remain vigilant here. The Hapsburgs control the town through Bishop de Hoensbroeck. He's not a friend of my ways."

"Which means you've had a run-in with him," Marshall sighed. His lightheadedness returned, and he was still spitting up blood.

"When I met him, he was just a priest," the angel nodded thoughtfully. "Velbrück is quite knowledgeable about the scriptures. However, his passion for understanding necromancy must remain hidden among those who control the Church. I once told Velbrück that he played with fire. Of course, he grew upset when I tried to burn his books. His priests ran me out of town."

"You have a way of making people angry, don't you?" The captain shook his head.

"Only when I'm correct. Now, don't make me laugh! My belly hurts too much." Leiras steered them toward the whitewashed home.

They saw a plump older woman with graying hair standing at the bright green door. Her initial smile showed missing teeth. The woman's friendly expression immediately changed as they came close enough for her to see their ragged, bloody clothing.

"Joseph, kom hier en help deze mannen," she called back inside the building.

The woman held the door open while the two men got off their mounts. They unhooked the boxes containing the relics from the saddles, then the men followed her inside.

A short man stood by his desk. He pointed them to a bench along the wall. As Marshall sat, the woman took his hat, and he thanked her. He half-listened to Leiras while the monk tried to explain about their wounds to the doctor.

The man stepped close to Leiras and looked over his wounds before going to the captain. Marshall scrutinized him.

"It's alright, English. I'm a physician."

After pulling back the makeshift bandage on Marshall's chest, the man's drab expression changed to interest.

"Come, both of you," he ordered them into another room that contained a single bed.

The doctor told Marshall to lie down and then had the monk take a chair.

"You give me interesting cases," he stated with an air of anticipation.

~~~

The evening sun settled in the west as Elisabeth rode into Namur. She stopped at the stables where the woman cautiously eyed a bearded blacksmith who paid her no attention. A young man hurried over, and the woman asked directions to St Aubin's cathedral.
~~~

"It's across the river," he replied in French while he pointed to the sphere in the distance. "I can go with you and bring your horseback. We're the best in town."

Elisabeth shook her head, still observing the man several paces away. She spurred the horse into the cobblestone street and continued toward the cathedral.

When the duchess reached St Aubin's, she stared at the large white stone building for a while. The design reminded her of home with the Ticinese style and Corinthian columns. Inside, the ornate structure held a massive and elaborately carved pulpit showing cherubs and saints. She went to the priest standing there. Elisabeth identified herself, then she asked for Jean Ménart. The man told her to wait, and a few minutes later, he returned.

"A messenger left this note for you," he told her.

Perplexed, the woman read the cursive lines, which told her to meet Ménart at a vender's stand behind the church. She went around the building and found the spot. When she reached the shadowed area, the duchess saw a tall man dressed in the robes of a priest waiting.

Ménart leaned over on his cane as he watched her approach. His surprisingly young but pockmarked face had a hooked nose. The man's brown eyes carried an unnerving intensity. Without bothering to ask the reason for her visit, he waved her to follow him to a nearby bench.

"You come for my help, my child. I know of your needs, and I've already engaged several colleagues to help you."

"How can you know what I need?" Her suspicious tone crept through. "Does Bishop de Hoensbroeck know I'm here?"

"One higher than the bishop came to me. The winged one told me you wish to recover an artifact and avenge your past. Do you waste our time?" the priest inquired.

"No," she hesitated. "Did the angel tell you more about my journey here?"

"Such creatures tell us only things we must know, my child," his voice calmly explained. "You're here to achieve our goal. Let's plan for the future."

The man noticed her pained expression.

"Come now, this English pirate is your quarry, is it not? The winged one stated your heart burned with the fire of revenge and justice."

Elisabeth nodded slowly.

"Now, my lady, I have arranged accommodations for you while my colleagues search for this Blackbane. Suitable attire that befits your status is already on the bed. I'm sure you'll feel better when you bathe and dress. As for this pirate you seek, I believe they'll go to the fortress for protection."

"They're injured," she pointed out.

"That narrows our search." His callous smile remained partially hidden by his hood. "The Dutch don't like the Prussians who control the town, so I'll send a servant to guide you to the area in the morning."

Elisabeth nodded absently, her thoughts wandering. Finally, she sighed.

"I must inform my husband of this delay. He does not know of my whereabouts since they kidnapped me."

"Of course," Ménart agreed. "I've already sent word of your stay under the protection of Bishop de Hoensbroeck. I'm sure he'll be relieved at your safe arrival. Now, go to the front steps, and a carriage will come for you. I'll send you a note when my men learn of the pirate's location."

~~~

"You know, Englishman, you should not recover from such a wound? Now you sit up in bed with a hunger in the belly and
~~~

a desire to leave. Some priests would send you to a stake to burn for such witchcraft."

Joseph Sax went to the window and pulled back the curtain. The mid-day light filled the tiny room. He turned around and beamed a smile at Marshall.

"However, I don't believe in magic. The sword blade that went through you missed the most vital organs. You're young and strong, so you recover quicker than others."

The pirate captain leaned back against the thin pillow and oak headboard as he looked down at the stitches.

"Well, they say God works in mysterious ways," Marshall replied steadily.

"Yes, they do. However, my work had something to do with God's ways," the physician confidently stated as he came back to the bed. His hands were behind his back as he hunched over his patient.

"Still, the massive bruising and bit marks I don't normally see except in tavern brawls." His blue eyes flickered.

Marshall remained stone-faced while letting the doctor believe that he caught his guests in a lie. The conversation stopped when the door opened.

Leiras stepped into the room.

"Ah, my other interesting case. Please join us," the doctor waved him closer. "My wife went for tobacco for you."

"Monsieur Sax, you're a man of true sophistication." The angel grimaced while closing the door. He shuffled closer.

"My fighting monk intrigues me as well," Sax continued. "I thought at first that he carried the marks of a creature's claws cutting his abdomen. Fortunately, I've seen such wounds come from the sharpened edges of a partisan. Again, the evidence points to a brawl with armed men, probably with intoxication."

Sax puffed up with pride while he gave them his incorrect deductions. Leiras smiled, then patted the man on the shoulder.

"You're an intelligent gentleman worthy of a much greater post. You should come with us to Amsterdam."

The doctor beamed, then grew serious.

"You must not show those injuries to one of your priests. Your brothers might think you suffered at the hands of a *varulv*. Then that would cause you a real problem, eh?"

"What's that?" Marshall looked up from inspecting his wound.

"The peasants think a man can transform into a wolf," Sax scoffed. His face turned somber. "I've seen the craziness that comes from such thinking when they kill people in a frenzy. It's good that we live in a rational age."

"Aye, that's for sure," the monk winked at the captain, who couldn't help but smile.

Leiras went to the table where the trunk holding the relic sat. He filled his pipe, then left the room to find a flame to light it. Sax continued to regale Marshall concerning his boredom in dealing with frequent boils, infections, and broken bones.

The doctor pointed at the shattered lantern that Leiras gingerly sat next to the containers holding Saint Julia's heart.

"I suspect you used that lamp on those brawlers who attacked you wished to steal that trunk you carry. You carry something valuable," he surmised.

Leiras glanced up at their host.

"Let us say we carry an important item to Amsterdam," the monk stated. "There are some who wish to take it away from us."

Sax smiled; his eyes twinkled at the thought of adventure.

"Oh, hush, hush. Perhaps I can impose for you to take a letter to my cousin there? Otherwise, it'll take a month if it ever arrives." The short man fondled the leather on Marshall's sword belt, which hung on a peg extending from the wall.

"Of course, it's the least we can do," the pirate replied as he stared out of the window. "We'll need to settle up with you and get on the road. We've imposed on you and your wife long enough."

"You are a true gentleman. I'm curious why a monk accompanies you?"

"He's a friend, kind of grows on you," the pirate stated. "You go write your letter, and we'll deliver it. Our duties force us to leave soon."

With a longing glance at the sword, the doctor left the room.

The aroma soon filled the small room as Leiras pulled apart his broken sanctuary lamp. He complained at the cost of getting glass made to replace the broken panes. Then he glanced back at the silent captain.

"At least I can use this lamp without the glass. We must leave tomorrow. Your dreams last night almost gave us away," the monk told Marshall.

"I can make it. It appears the pain I receive comes with the curse," the captain agreed.

Leiras nodded absently as he picked up the Saint Simpert cross. He disguised it by turning the relic into a necklace.

"There, one less need for a box. Your curse is a pain for both of us, my friend," the angel grunted. "I hoped I could get this lantern fixed before we go. Too many…" He paused when he heard movement at the door. He turned his head to see a familiar woman standing there.

"You have too many enemies following you. I agree," Elisabeth stated with a broad smile. "The doctor told me he's never seen a person survive such a wound."

The duchess glanced at the shirtless bearded man, who stared in shock at her presence. His ragged stitches sticking out from his skin in the middle of his chest made her flesh crawl.

She looked over at the fake monk when she walked into the room.

"You appear disappointed!"

Leiras grimaced and nearly dropped his pipe as he stood.

"You shouldn't be here, my lady."

Joseph Sax entered the room as Marshall wobbly stood.

"No, you must rest," the doctor said as he rushed to the bed.

"I'm alright," the captain growled.

"Monsieur Sax, apparently, you've already met Madame Elisabeth Anne Magon di Villafranca." Leiras stepped next to the woman, his eyes boring into hers.

"For her safety, Captain Marshall and I left Elisabeth in Grognaux. She was supposed to get a carriage back to France. Wasn't that correct?"

While she hesitated, the woman nodded, then she continued her charade.

"Yes, I'm afraid I had no other option. The only safe choice was coming to Namur."

"Ah, it's understandable with the tensions in the area. Grognaux has a reputation for unsavory characters, I'm afraid," Sax sighed in agreement. "I'm glad you had no problems reaching Namur."

The men noticed the woman's unpleasant expression before she glanced away. Elisabeth nodded in agreement after gathering herself.

"If you don't mind, we need to speak to Elisabeth alone concerning our cargo. Perhaps you can have someone find us a bottle of good French wine to celebrate this evening?" Leiras suggested as he handed the man a few coins. Sax happily agreed to the idea. Soon, they heard the front door open, then close.

Marshall sent to the bedroom door, then closed it. He noticed a well-dressed servant posted at the front entrance. The pirate stepped closer to the woman. His fingers slid along her sleeve as he assessed her new clothes. Her eyes expressed a curious mix of anger and panic at his action.

"Alright, duchess, let's cut through the lies. Those new clothes tell me you found help. You're up to something. How did you find us?"

"It wasn't hard to follow an injured fake monk and a gentleman who looks like he's nearly dead," she replied smoothly. "I wasn't lying when I said I had to come to Namur. That church was empty."

"Who brought you?" The pirate's skepticism remained.

"I came alone," her quick response caught the monk's notice.

"You must have stopped someplace along the way," Leiras commented.

"I don't tell kidnappers like you I carry gold coins in my petticoats," her voice rose. "I stopped at a tavern along the way. Now, would you like to see my horse? It's at the stables."

"And you're adept at lying. There's a servant at the door. Should we expect more company with you, like the last time?"

Marshall went over to the bed, where he pulled his sheathed rapier. Feeling the effects of his exertions, the man sat on the mattress with a grimace. As she watched him, Elisabeth remained quiet.

"We both know of your hatred of Blackbane." Leiras finally broke the tension. "This conversation cannot continue without some explanation."

With a sigh, Elisabeth took a seat by the door.

"Alright, I have an obligation to both of you for my escape from death. I expected you to just throw me into those dead things to allow for your escape. Yet you were willing to die while I ran away." She looked at both men as she spoke. "When I got to Namur last night, I met with a priest who advised me during my hour of need."

She glanced at the small window while she kept clasping her hand together.

"You told him about the attack from Mammon?" The angel's skeptical tone made her laugh.

"Of course not! Who would believe something like that?" Elisabeth paused, looking at her hands. "I can barely believe it was real."

Finally, she shrugged.

"I decided on a way that I can repay you. Plus, I can help myself return to France," the duchess looked at the container holding the saint's heart. "I wish to purchase that from you."

Both men glanced at each other.

"I'm in earnest. I've already arranged a loan to pay you. A priest who works for Bishop de Hoensbroeck gave me enough. I'm giving you double what those in Amsterdam have offered."

"You took money from the bishop? Does he know we are here?" Leiras stopped smoking his pipe.

"I don't think so," Elisabeth grew curious. "Otherwise, he'd be here to claim that prize himself."

"Yes, I suppose that's correct," the angel relaxed slightly. "However, it doesn't explain why he would lend you money."

"I lied to the priest. I told them you were carrying my jewelry, which you stole."

"And now you wish to purchase something that we took from you and your husband."

The woman pulled out a bag of coins from a leather satchel she carried over her shoulder. She tossed them to the pirate.

"Take a look. You're selling the saint's heart, aren't you? There's more than enough there. After all, the relic means nothing to you. You don't care who gets it!"

The captain rose with the bag in his hand. He took several steps, then he took her hand. The man twisted her hand, causing the duchess to wince. Marshall slapped the bag in her palm.

"You understand nothing. Now, leave here!"

He went back to the bed and rifled through his now cleaned clothes. Gingerly, he pulled his linen shirt on.

Astonished by his reaction, Elisabeth looked at Leiras for support. He shook his head.

"I'm afraid that you don't understand, despite your time with us. The relic is more than gold coins to him." He went to the door and opened it while she rose. "Choosing the bishop as your ally was not a smart choice on your part. I advise you to go back to France."

A wounded expression filled her face.

"You won't sell it to me because you're evil," she said bitterly. "You'd rather have heretics turn it into a personal display."

When Elisabeth left the room, Leiras watched while she hurried past the servant to exit the house. He turned back to Marshall, who placed his new necklace inside his money bag.

"If she's working for Bishop de Velbruck, we need to leave now!"

~~~

Elisabeth arrived back at the home of Ménart after taking her carriage across the river. The duchess walked inside; her expression was livid. She couldn't believe her dismissal by a killer. The woman pushed by the servant, who led her to a large room. Inside, her host rose from his desk.

"I take it from your appearance. The conversation didn't go well."

"No, that bastard gave me back the money and threw me out." Elisabeth stopped by the desk. She picked up and threw the first thing in her reach. The goblet of wine splattered on the fireplace.

"He's not interested in the gold. There's something more behind why he's doing this. The monk that goes with him
~~~

warned me about the bishop that you work for. They told me to go back to France."

"You damn fool, you told them you work for the bishop," Ménart told her in her native Eastern Lombard. "Leiras knows much more than he's told you."

"You know my language?"

The man ignored her, then called out for his servant. The man immediately entered the room.

"Send a man to the guards and watch the Sax's house. I want the Prussians to arrest this pirate and the monk before they leave the city."

He walked with the servant to the entrance while Elisabeth went to the wine cellar near the shelves. While she poured a drink, the woman glanced at a few of the titles. Volumes of *Picatrix* and the *Corpus Hermeticum* stood out among the others. She frowned when she recalled her tutor, who claimed only a necromancer would own such works.

Ménart stepped in front of a map hanging on the wall on the other side of the room. He glanced back at Elisabeth.

"I'll require your presence when we capture Blackbane, so you'll go with me. Once you retrieve the relic, the master wishes to see you."

"That's not part of the bargain. I've done as I've asked," the duchess sat her drink on the desk. "This is a wasted effort, so I'm going home. My husband will find other relics to enhance his status in court."

As she stepped by Ménart, he grabbed her by the arm.

"Foul woman, you'll do as I tell you." For a moment, his face appeared like a vulture.

"No, I won't!"

The priest slapped her. Elisabeth backed away, then reached for the new weapon she now carried in her waistband. The duchess held out the blacksmith's knife.

"I'll kill the next man that touches me without my permission!"

Ménart laughed at her as his eyes ominously flashed.

"Madam, this is not France, and your title means nothing to me. You'll rue the day that you threaten me."

With astonishing quickness and strength, the priest grabbed her wrist. With one arm, he lifted her off the ground. She cried out, and he slapped her again. Elisabeth stared at his predator's face. He grinned as he slowly and painfully forced her to release the weapon. It clattered on the floor.

Ménart leaned close to her neck, and she felt his hot breath. His mouth opened, taking in her scent like an animal.

"Don't worry, I won't hurt you. I wait for my master's permission. However, I can enjoy your delicious fear. It's intoxicating. Your blood pounding through your arteries so close to me."

The woman looked away. With a frown, the creature in the robes of the priest released her, and she fell on the floor.

"What are you?" Elizabeth stared up at him.

"It's enough for you to know that I'll kill you slowly if you disobey me. Since you want to act as an outlaw, we'll dress you more appropriately."

He kneeled and picked up her knife. He expertly flipped the weapon onto the desktop. Then, he went to the door where his servant waited.

"Get the duchess into riding clothes and have our horses readied. Send a man to watch the house of the pirate as well."

Ménart turned to Elisabeth.

"Be outside when the horses are ready. You won't enjoy my punishment if you're late!"

~~~

Marshall and Leiras were out of the city by the time their enemies involved the Prussians. Galloping along the road, both
~~~

men suffered as their sore bodies took the punishing ride. When they finally slowed, it was to avoid a group of uniformed men that Marshall noticed ahead of them. The riders pulled off the road and entered a nearby field filled with grazing sheep. They remained behind a line of hedges while the Prussian soldiers continued down the road. After crossing several fields, the men rested their mounts and themselves when they came to a stream.

"I think we just keep avoiding those troops riding through. We must remain vigilant. This is the area of the *Bokkenrijders*," Leiras advised when they came to a stop.

"The Demer River shouldn't be too far ahead. We can find a barge; then, we'll float down to Antwerp. From there, it's only a short trek to Amsterdam."

"Not with our luck," Marshall growled as he slid off the horse. "Isn't Antwerp still part of the Hapsburg lands?"

"Yes, but it's easier for us to get lost in the city, and I know the place. We'll find a way to Amsterdam by ship," Leiras spoke with confidence.

"Maybe, then again, someone will find out about the relic we carry and burn us as heretics," the pirate captain groused.

"Oh, ye of little faith," the angel shot back with a grin.

Marshall replied with a harrumph as he gingerly walked around, stretching his legs and sore muscles.

"Do you think she'll follow?" Marshall finally asked his partner. The question kept grating on him since they left.

"I'm not sure." Leiras pulled a piece of dried meat from his bag. "I'm confident that she lied to us. The bishop I knew briefly seldom parted with gold easily. Plus, he'd just arrest us for taking the relics we carry. There was no need to go through her."

"Someone else is her silent partner," the pirate decided. "Perhaps it's the priest she spoke about. Still, I sensed something deeper was bothering her. I know she's trying to understand where the demons come into this whole mess."

"That's certainly possible. It's strange, but I found almost a hint of warning in Elisabeth's presence. I agree that there's something deeper going on."

He handed the captain some of the meat from the bag.

"Assuming I'm correct about Bishop de Velbruck, then we need to consider a supernatural enemy joined Elisabeth. You have many enemies, human and demon."

"Yeah, don't remind me. Given Elisabeth's need for revenge, I expect she's been praying for demons to get me."

"No, she's confused and angry, not evil," Leiras insisted. "It means she's a perfect target. Demons will use such emotions to invade your thoughts and make you do things you would not normally attempt."

"I used to think I could figure out people, but she doesn't make any sense to me," Marshall leaned against a tree and chewed thoughtfully. "One minute, the duchess wants me to hang; the next minute, the woman is fighting next to me."

"I didn't say anything, but she lied about returning to the camp. There was no reason for her to come back. I'm not sure the woman really knows the truth in her heart," the angel decided.

"Yeah, unlike the two of us!" Marshall glanced over at Leiras, who nodded. "Are you sure of our path?"

"No more than you're sure of yours," Leiras smirked before growing serious.

"I'm not familiar with the road we're on, but we're going in the right direction. We can't be far from the land of the Dutch and their allies. Once we get to the city of Diest, we'll be safe. Prince of Orange and the Dutch troops control the city."

"Then, let's keep moving," the pirate sighed, then got on his horse.

As they drew closer to the Demer River, the sunlight slowly disappeared. The two riders came around a bend in the road where they reached a lonely crossroads. They could barely make out the weathered wooden sign that pointed them toward the next village. As Marshall turned his horse, he heard the distant sound of galloping horses. Looking back, he saw men riding fast.

Fearing the riders were bandits, the captain spurred his horse while he warned Leiras. The two men hurried along the road, heading for a bridge over the river. Following another bend in the way, Leiras came alongside Marshall and motioned toward a grove of trees. The two riders turned down the narrow trail, then pulled behind vegetation. The four riders continued along the main road and soon disappeared.

"I wish we knew the roads!" The monk grimaced while trying to catch his breath. "We can't keep going across fields. The farmers and shepherds will spread the word about us going through their lands."

"Let's wait a while, then we can work our way down the road. That should bypass those riders if they camp ahead." Marshall took the wine bag from his mount and drank deeply. His chest injury hurt from the long ride. He handed it to Leiras, took the offered bladder.

"It's needed today, my friend. I suspect where close to the river with the flatness of the land." He rubbed his back. "Getting on a boat would help my disposition."

Marshall grinned.

"Aye, the road is no way to travel. I'd give my last coin to put myself back on a ship."

The monk's expression turned somber.

"Perhaps you'll find a ship soon."

The travelers finally entered the town of Diest along the river after dark. They found stables once they passed the city gates, where they hitched their horses.

The wiry old man who owned the stable looked them over suspiciously. After making sure they paid, he pulled back a gate where they led their horses. While the tired men unstrapped their precious cargo, Leiras noticed the old man talking to a boy.

"How about a placed to get food and a place to sleep?" The monk inquired.

"I's just tellin' the boy that he'd lead you there."

"No need, just give us direction," Leiras told him as he pulled off the bags from the back of the saddle.

The stable owner frowned, then sent the child away. He came over to the men and gave them directions to an inn down a few blocks.

"The owner will take care of you," the man promised.

Sliding his bags painfully over his shoulder, Marshall led them out of the stable. The two men followed the street, walking in the middle to avoid the open sewers on either side of the narrow main road. The heavy shadows hid many of the small houses and shops along the way. Most of the windows were dark as well. At the end of the block, a single lamplight hung at the corner where a rotund lamplighter stood smoking a pipe. He nodded at them as the two men passed by.

Marshall glanced back at the sound of footsteps after they turned down the next street. The lamplighter was gone. However, two men followed them. His senses heightened, and the captain slowed. Before he could tell his friend of his suspicions, two dark figures rushed out of the shadows between two buildings. He reached for a weapon, but Marshall took a blow to his head. He fell to the pavement, then a kick struck him in the side of his face. Nearly senseless, the pirate felt his arms twisted behind his back. When he struggled, another blow hit in the head. Before he knew what happened, the assailants had his wrists bound. Then they lifted him to his feet.

The sound of hoofbeats drew closer while several men beat Leiras to the ground. A horse and its rider came to a stop in front of Marshall. The thugs hoisted him belly-first over the back of the mount. While the blood rushed to his head, he struggled to loosen his bound wrists. Another punch in his face dazed him, and he fell limp. The pirate felt the bag holding one relic tied to the saddle as they tied his legs together. Nearby, Leiras yell out, then the monk went silent after another round of men beating him. When the thugs finished, they tied Leiras behind the saddle of another horse.

After a brief discussion that Marshall couldn't understand, the gang galloped away. Quickly moving through the twists and turns of dark streets, the group finally came out on a wood platform by the river. When they pulled to a stop, Marshall felt the bag lifted from next to him. One kidnapper cut the rope, and the captain fell headfirst onto the wooden planks. Laughter filled the air while Marshall tried to shake off the blow to his head. He felt Leiras land next to him. A groan escaped from his comrade. Then the angel cursed at the bandits in French.

"You should have accepted my offer," Elisabeth's gloating voice reached Marshall. He looked toward the sound.

Marshall didn't recognize the woman at first. Her long hair pulled back and dressed in a frock coat over a vest and breeches, Elisabeth carried the look of a young gentleman.

"You weren't expecting that I had friends who knew about a faster way. Now, you will suffer the consequences."

"That's Ménart, who does the dirty work for Bishop de Hoensbroeck," the angel whispered when he made out the old man in the black robes beside Elisabeth. "It's strange, but I sense something else here."

"Who cares? Just get out of these bindings," Marshall growled under his breath.

Both men watched one thug approach Ménart with the two bags of relics as he leaned on his cane. He shook his head, then the man's servant stepped forward to retrieve the relics. From the dim light cast by a lantern, Marshall noticed a medium built redhead dressed in black breeches with a scarlet coat and cape. It was the same man who came with Elisabeth to the doctor's house in Namur.

"Put those things to a crate," he quickly ordered his servant. "At daylight, the barge to Antwerp will arrive. We'll have several items for them to take."

Marshall glanced over at the rest of the thugs near the dock's edge. Judging from their shabby attire and sidelong glances, Elisabeth and her partner hired them as paid enforcers. One man held Marshall's rapier. The sight infuriated the captain when he saw the crude knives they carried.

"Your social circle is sinking like a cracked ship with a foul wind," he snarled at the woman while he pulled hard on his wrists. Her face turned red. Ménart interceded before Elisabeth could reply.

"Stuff them into the crates. They'll come with us," her partner ordered the nearby men. "They should survive the trip in their own filth."

When the two bandits lifted Marshall by his arms, the leather painfully bit into his wrist. However, the captain felt the binding snap. The man groaned, then went limp in their arms. When the men reached down to lift his weight, Marshall lightly swung around his freed arm. He reached for the thin stiletto sticking from the thug's belt. Pulling it away, the pirate stabbed the man in the kidney.

His victim yelled out in disbelief while Marshall whipped his bloody dagger blade into the neck of the other thug holding him. Warm blood spurted out from his jugular. It struck the pirate in the eyes, temporarily blinding him. Marshall backed away, nearly tripping over a body as he wiped his face with his sleeve.

Another bandit came at the captain, carrying Marshall's sword. However, his attacker's clumsy efforts at swordplay allowed Marshall to get the upper hand. The pirate easily dodged the thrust of the blade. When he came close, he grabbed the handguard on the sword. Marshall pulled his opponent into him and stabbed the knife blade into the thug's side. He took his rapier back from the dying man, then looked for his next target.

With weapons in either hand, the pirate attacked Ménart. The priest stood stoically, only a couple of paces away. When Marshall rushed him, the older man suddenly moved aside with uncanny quickness. Marshall's trust with the sword missed him completely.

A shot rang out from behind Marshall. He felt a blow in his back, and the air suddenly left his lungs while he fell. The bandit holding a flintlock pistol grinned after shooting Marshall. As he took another from his partner, Leiras slammed his shoulder into the smaller man with a head-first tackle. Despite his bound hands, the monk quickly got to his feet above his stunned adversary. With a ruthless kick, Leiras struck the thug in the back of his head with his boot. He was still kicking the unconscious man when two nearby comrades tackled the monk.

Marshall pulled his Saint Gennaro dagger. Ménart slammed down his walking stick on Marshall's back as he tried to rise. Running on adrenaline, the man swung out his arm and sliced deep into the priest's wrist. Marshall lost the blood-covered weapon as he lifted from his kneeling stance.

"Damn you," Ménart cursed in a growl as he dropped his staff.

Focused on his wound, the man didn't see Marshall leap forward with his rapier held out. The long blade impaled Ménart through the chest. As the priest staggered backward, one kidnapper pulled away from Leiras to help. The beefy thug struck Marshall in the head with a club. Staggered by the blow, the pirate fell backward. The larger man landed on the captain.

During the melee, Elisabeth immediately went after the jeweled dagger she saw fall to the ground between Ménart and Marshall. She lifted the weapon from the deck as Leiras kicked away from one man, trying to hold him down. With his hands behind his back, the monk got to his feet and ran toward his comrade.

Elisabeth heard the pounding of footsteps closing on her. She glanced back to see someone nearly on her. The duchess instincts kicked in, and she held out the dagger. Leiras impaled himself upon the blade.

As they stood there, both the angel and Elisabeth stared at each other. The monk's fat form instantly changed. For a moment, he stood in front of Elisabeth in the handsome, muscular body of a youth. In the blink of an eye, his figure reverted back.

"Remiel!"

Leiras gasped out before he fell back on the planks of the wooden deck. In the moonlight, his wide eyes stared blankly at the sky. Elisabeth stood over the angel as the man chasing Leiras passed her. He went to help his partner finish off Marshall.

The duchess blinked in disbelief, then Elisabeth heard the men beating on the pirate captain with a vengeance. Stepping back, the woman almost fell over one of the dead men. Still dazed, she slid the bloody dagger into her belt before she retrieved an unfired pistol from the ground. Elisabeth came toward the thugs beating on the pirate captain.

"Stop killing the man," she demanded. "I need him alive."

The two men paused briefly.

"Vous n'êtes rien d'autre que la salope Ménarts!" one thug spat out.

Enraged, she pointed the flintlock at the man who called her a bitch.

"You work for me now. Throw the bodies into the river," Elisabeth ordered with a bravado that surprised her.

When the thugs didn't move, Elisabeth pulled back on the hammer of the pistol.

"By God, I'm in charge! You want your money, then get the job done!" She stepped close enough to see the man's eyes widen at the gun barrel pointed at his face.

"Move it or die, you le fils de garce," she cursed at them like a sailor.

With a scowl filling his ugly face, the man stood and told his friend to join him. As she observed them, the two men picked up the closest body. As the men hauled their dead companion to the river, Elisabeth went to the captain, who was face down on the wood. She kneeled, looking at his bleeding wound in the soft yellow light of the nearby lantern.

"How can you still live?" Her whispered comment brought a bitter laugh.

"You really do not know, do you?"

Glancing up to see her remaining men continued to get rid of the bodies, Elisabeth grabbed Blackbane's wrist, forcing it behind his back. He groaned from the forced movement, but he barely resisted as she tied his wrists again.

"Your partner can no longer get in my way." She informed him. Elisabeth rolled the man on his back.

Marshall's blood poured from his forehead. His face carried the ghostly paleness. With his beard matted with blood and dirt, his eyes bore into hers with startling ferocity.

"Congratulations, duchess! You've condemned your soul to hell. You used the blood of Saint Gennaro to kill. I hope you sleep well, you arrogant bitch."

His venomous sarcasm caused her to smirk. As she stood, Elisabeth glanced over at the men who dragged the body of Leiras away. A sudden, fearful pang of guilt filled her. She looked down at the dagger in her belt. The duchess tried to forget the images of fire she remembered from paintings showing the condemned swept into hell's pit.

The sound of footsteps behind her forced her to look around.

"You should clean that dagger and put it away. It's worth too much to flash around with our hired help," Ménart's servant came from out of the shadows to speak for the first time. To her surprise, the man talked in the woman's Eastern Lombard language. His eyes remained on the expensive weapon.

"You let your master die?" She backed away and raised the pistol.

"The bishop uses me to monitor Ménart," he explained. "I can assure you that I'm more than a mere servant. I'm Octave Dufrene, and I'm on your side. The winged one who informed me to help you as needed!"

A splash came from the rivers as the two men threw the body of the angel into the water.

The redhead servant smiled. His blue eyes twinkled.

"I suppose I should prove it to you."

Elisabeth watched the scarlet caped man as she felt her nerves fraying. The unexpected brutality was exhilarating while the events spiraling out of control left her anxious.

The servant spoke to the men for a moment. The men laughed at his apparent joke. As he pulled out a flask for them to drink, the bandits readily accepted. The red-haired man started back to Elisabeth while the men drank. By the time he reached the duchess, the thugs were on the ground. They couldn't hear the mumbled pleas from their foaming lips. Elisabeth watched with revulsion as the men died in twisting convulsions.

"Now, you'll do not need to pay those wretched imbeciles. We'll put our passenger into the crate with a few holes and have the trekschuit owner put it aboard for our trip to Antwerp." Octave said with a smile. "We'll claim there are an exotic species of an animal inside. Then, I expect we'll have an interesting journey to France."

~~~

As the sun rose, the bodies were already out of sight as Elisabeth looked down the river. Stuffed inside the wooden box next to her was Marshall. When they put the pirate into the crate, he attempted to resist them. However, Octave used the handle of his flintlock to knock the pirate senseless before they slid him inside the container. Before Octave gagged him, Marshall cursed Elisabeth.

"You're no better than the demons who come for my soul. I'll see you in Hell, whore!"

Not long after, a pair of dockworkers arrived from the town. While Elisabeth spoke with the men as Octave threw the canvas sack holding the broken Xeropotamou lamp into the crate. Then, he pounded nails into the edges of the wood to ensure Marshal would remain a prisoner. Octave wandered closer to the woman who carried the trunk with Saint Julia's heart. He smiled at the thoughts crossing his mind.

When the trekschuit arrived at the dock, light fog covered the flowing river. The graying owner with a wide brimmed black hat stepped off with his hired hands after the men running the dock tied off the vessel. Surprise registered on his face when the owner figured out that a woman in the gentleman's clothes waited as a passenger. He glanced over at the man standing by the large crate. The barge owner recognized the small badge on the servant's clothes, showing the emblem for the house of Bishop de Hoensbroeck.
~~~

"We have two passengers and this container," Elisabeth told him.

"As long as I get paid," the man grunted.

He directed his men to haul the container aboard. Nearby, the dockworkers exchanged the donkeys that followed the trail along the river.

Elisabeth stepped onto the barge, suddenly noticing a gentleman dressed in a scarlet coat eyeing her from the back of the vessel. The stranger's hazel eyes watched the duchess while she went inside the protective wooden shack used by the passengers. She placed her trunk on the bench next to her. Octave followed her into the room, taking a seat at the other end.

The passenger listened to the trekschuit owner shouting orders to the others. His cursing showed that he was behind schedule that day. The sound of boots approached.

Then, the red-coated stranger entered the shack. His impressive black breeches and black waistcoat stood out under his coat. Around his neck, the stranger wore a golden cravat while his white powdered wig had a pulled back ponytail over his broad shoulders. The gentleman's hazel eyes widen at the sight of the trunk next to the woman.

Elisabeth glanced over as the man's servant entered. Standing out among the others, the large dark-skinned man wore a dark, loose-fitting robe with full sleeves. The embroidered scarlet mosaics on the gown showed the escort came from the land of the Turks. He carried an odd-looking bag on his back and had curved daggers stuck in his waistband.

Before the tall man sat across from Octave, the gentleman bowed toward Elisabeth, who acknowledged him with a nod. Feigning her disinterest, the woman watched the stranger with interest. His face, with his hollow cheeks and thin lips, carried an exciting mix of sinister and enticing. She could almost feel the surrounding aura when he looked over with his piercing hazel eyes. The duchess noticed his continued glances at her trunk. Concerned with his interest, she casually slid the container back into the canvas bag.

When the vessel moved down the river, the stranger stood and came closer. He bowed again to Elisabeth, calling her by her full title.

"How do you know me?"

He smiled.

"I believe the winged one is making sure you're known. However, I cannot fully appreciate your beauty until I saw you. I hope you don't mind the company. I'm Ramhout van Dam, the captain of the *Tappan Sea*. My ship is awaiting to escort the most beautiful woman in France back to her home."

She blushed at the comment.

"A gentleman is most welcome. They're hard to find. You must tell me of your adventures."

With a nod, Ramhout took a seat on the bench, still an arm's length away. Without instruction, his servant sat down a bag he carried, then came over to Ramhout with a stringed instrument that the captain introduced as a mandore.

"Tales of my travel come in song," the stranger grinned as he strummed the instrument.

~~~

On the quick trip to Antwerp, Elisabeth found herself enamored by the Ramhout. He appeared to know many things about the woman and her recent experiences. Explaining that the winged one gave him full details during his journey. He treated the duchess with the upmost in decorum, befitting a lady of her status. However, she knew of his underlying sexual overtones in his tidbits of advice and observations. Ramhout seemed to know the woman's thoughts and desires before she spoke about them. While she enjoyed his comments, Elisabeth found some of his ideas unsettling. Still, his stories swept her away to far worlds,
~~~

and she acted like a young maiden on her first date. Her attention remained focused on the man. Ramhout told her of his sea adventures, showing himself as the captain, master of his fate, and leader of the men.

When the vessel tied up at a dock inside Antwerp, Ramhout and his servant left. The captain vowed his ship waited for her arrival, and he would gather supplies for their vessel. Octave came to Elisabeth, telling her he would ensure delivery of the crate containing Marshall to the *Tappan Sea.* He also suggested a seamstress for her to find appropriate clothing for the trip. The duchess readily agreed, her mind already looking forward to her arrival at the ship. After Octave sent her away in a carriage, he went back to the crate holding the captured pirate. He ordered men to put it on a wagon. He told them to hurry to the dock where Ramhout's ship waited.

"The cargo inside can take the rough road," the servant told them with a smile.

<div style="text-align:center">~~~</div>

Inside the box, Marshall drifted from sleep to pain and back again. The gag in his dry mouth choked him, and his bound wrists left his hands numb. Cramps from his legs caused him to pound his head on the wood to distract him from the agony. Eventually, Marshall drifted into nothingness.

The man drifted above the ground, looking down at the landscape around. He saw a ship in the distance. However, he couldn't control his spirit's direction. Instead, an unseen force pushed him away from the sea and toward the mountains. The needle-like sting of cold air struck his face while his body rose over the top of the range. Then, he swept down over the valley and across a long lake.

At one point, he heard a familiar voice come to him. Inside the nearly dark interior, he saw the face of Saint Julia. Her image was so close that he saw the start of wrinkles around her eyes.

She smiled at him, and the voice in his head told him to remain patient.

"Your punishment continues, but take heart. As stated by our father, I must purge sin either by punishment or by sacrifice. We will not forsake you."

The face slowly disappeared, replaced by the image of a small church.

"Go to Chiesa di Santa Giulia in Calino; let my heart soothe yours."

~~~

A blinding light shot into the crate, along with fresh, cold air that woke the bound Marshall. Two men with wool skull caps and wearing gray canvas shirts reached inside and quickly dragged the man from his box. The prisoner's numb legs collapsed when the men tried to make him stand. The cursing sailors dragged him across the cobblestone to the nearby ship.

Groggy and in pain, Blackbane noticed the name on the stern, *Tappan Sea*, as they passed by. The pirate captain shook his head, thinking he didn't see the title correctly. A notorious ghost ship carried the name, and no sailor in their right mind would name their vessel with a cursed name.

Marshall and his escorts reached the gangway as his legs started regaining their strength. The sailors forced the prisoner up toward the ship, where the captain waited. He had his hands clasped behind his back. The men stopped Marshall in front of Ramhout van Dam.

"I'm sure that you'll enjoy my accommodations, Blackbane. Going back to the sea should refresh you. Obviously, I've heard of your exploits."

The captain pointed to a hulking sailor who stood by the quarterdeck. The man had a cat of nine tails hanging over his shoulder. He ordered the sailors to tie Marshall to the aft mast. When they finish, Ramhout stepped close to the prisoner.
~~~

"While Madam Elisabeth finds suitable clothing for the upcoming trip, I'm going to see how long you can last under the lash. I believe the pain and scars should keep you quiet during our brief journey to France."

Ramhout backed away to give his bosun's mate room for the flogging.

"I'm quite knowledgeable about you, Blackbane. I'm curious to see how long you last under the whip!"

Chapter 8: The Captain and the Duchess

Two days out of Antwerp, Elisabeth paced the inside of her cabin. During her brief stay, she found she was the only passenger on board. With little to do and no one to talk with, the duchess found the regimented routine of ship life too monotonous. Worse, she expected Ramhout would pay attention to her. After all, she was a duchess and his sole passenger. Yet, she only saw him occasionally. The captain remained on the quarterdeck or inside his cabin most of the time.

When she approached the quarterdeck on the first day, Elisabeth invited Ramhout to her cabin. She mentioned her collection of relics that she carried back to France, which she wished to show him. He shook his head at the idea. Ramhout insisted that his duties as master of the ship prevented such familiarity with a passenger in their cabin. However, they met for supper together in his quarters that evening. The captain was courteous, playing a tune for her before kissing her hand as she left.

Stepping from her cabin that morning, the duchess still held a fondness for the evening before. Elisabeth felt a longing for the mysterious yet charming captain. As she enjoyed the warmth of the sun, the woman thought of her other lovers.

In her social circles, lineage and ambition created marriages, not satisfied lovers. Elisabeth followed the rules of her friends. Those who cheated on their husbands always remain discrete, and they avoided having children out of wedlock. Getting inside the court of Louis XVI meant Elisabeth would walk over the bodies of noblemen to get there. It was necessary to advance one's family name.

Fortunately, her rape would remain hidden from public knowledge. To some extent, she blamed Blackbane for the commoner to ravage her. The woman also added Remiel to the bitterness in her heart. Such an angel could have warned her of the danger. That her rape might be a trial for her, she quickly dismissed. To purge the terrible memory from her mind, the woman decided her revenge came from taking the relics back to France.

The milling crowd of sailors around the stern of the ship brought the woman from her thoughts. Curious, the duchess drew closer and noticed Ramhout standing by the aft mast. She looked across the deck as a pair of men brought Blackbane out of the hold. They forced him to the aft mast, where they stripped off his coat, then tied his wrists around the thick pole. To her surprise, Elisabeth noticed the remains of his tattered shirt was brown by dried bloodstains from earlier whippings.

Convinced she would enjoy watching the pirate's punishment; Elisabeth worked her way to a place for a better view. The woman smiled when Blackbane looked her way, their eyes locked in recognition. However, her smile faded as she watched the spectacle. She quietly counted the number of blows in time with the sailor who shouted the count out to the crew.

Blackbane's stare remained fixed on Elisabeth. The man took the first few lashes without a sound coming from his steely expression. However, the brutal whipping continued, eventually forcing him to grunt with each stroke when the pain overwhelmed him. Thin rivets of blood trickled down his back and shoulders, then splattered across the men closest to the display.

When the pirate captain finally passed out, the duchess suddenly worried if the pirate had any skin left on his back. She wondered if the punishment had finished. However, a grinning Ramhout ordered Blackbane doused with buckets of seawater.

During the efforts to revive the victim, Elisabeth noticed her aching hands. The duchess frowned when she realized her fingers clenched the wood tighter and tighter with each blow of the leather straps. She turned back to watch the rest of the lashings. Her eyes moved away from the captive. Elisabeth focused on Ramhout, who appeared to relish the abuse. The captain of the *Tappan Sea* looked to the unsettled woman, and Elisabeth's skin tingled. Her mind no longer cared about the whipping. Instead, her face flushed while she considered ideas to get Ramhout alone.

When the men finally hauled the nearly unconscious pirate back to his cell, Elisabeth paid little attention. Instead, she focused on catching Ramhout's eye. The woman rushed to his presence.

"Madam, you carry a hint of excitement in your manner. Was the punishment against that foul pirate to your taste?"

Elisabeth caught her frown, then nodded.

"It's harsher than I expected. However, I'm sure that he deserved it."

"The captain must punish the wicked. In some ways, we're not that different from the one who judges sinners."

His knowing grin briefly flared, then he looked at the sailors standing nearby.

"Please excuse me," Ramhout quickly told her. He stepped away, cursing out orders to his men as he sent them into the rigging above.

With a sigh, the duchess returned to her cabin. For the rest of the morning, the bored woman attempted to entertain herself. She carried little interest in watching the foul-mouthed sailors attending their duties outside the cabin. They reminded her too much of the cutthroat buccaneers in the Mediterranean. Like pirates, the sailors came from the same rabble who filled the stinking streets of the villages and cities.

As she sat on her uncomfortably hard cot, Elisabeth heard the approaching sound of footsteps came through the open porthole. A knock at the door brought a smile to her face.

"Come in!"

Ramhout's Arab servant entered. She frowned at first, but when the silent man handed her a small envelope, she happily accepted. With growing anticipation, she read the note inside, then turned back to the servant.

"Tell Captain Ramhout that I happily accept his invitation."

A few hours later, Elisabeth walked the quiet deck. Dusk settled over the calm ocean. As the sailor rang the bell on the quarterdeck, Elisabeth found the Ramhout's servant standing at the door of his master's cabin. He opened the door for her, then remained outside after she entered.

The captain stood by his desk; his piercing eyes made her uncomfortable.

"I'm glad the busy captain found time to see his passenger." Her pompous tone brought a smirk to Ramhout's face.

"At sea, a captain is master of men and passengers." He replied while he took off his black cocked hat, then his wig. She saw his dark black hair for the first time.

"I see your table remains empty. Was I mistaken about dinner with you?" She stepped across from the small piece of furniture, which had three chairs around it.

"Oh, we'll have something to satisfy our hunger. Your glances got my attention, so here you are."

The man pulled off his greatcoat. Elisabeth's eyes widened at his action.

"Is rudeness another part of your charm?" She turned away. The captain laughed as he threw his coat on the table.

"My lady, your coyness is charming but overdone." He came up to her and kissed her bare shoulder.

Elisabeth jerked away.

"Don't do that! I'm not a commoner!" She crossed her arms but remained a step away.

Ramhout grinned at the comment as he unbuttoned his vest. When he pulled off the garment, the captain stepped closer. His hands gripped her arms, and he felt her shiver at his touch.

"My lady, you can't throw me out. We have so much in common. You cannot cast away the feelings you hold. I can sense your desire waiting for release."

The duchess felt a surge of excitement fill her as his lips slid along her neck.

How can I do this?

As Elisabeth arched her back at his soft kisses, she heard the noise of the sailors who playing cards below the quarterdeck. The sailor at the wheel outside the captain's cabin several feet away smoked his pipe. She smelled the waft of tobacco smoke coming through the open porthole.

"You have no shame!" Her half-hearted response surprised her.

"None!" he agreed. "You'll find I have little reason for such trifles."

He slowly ran his rough hands along her shoulders.

"I'm married," the woman said.

Still, Elisabeth refused to move from her spot. The electricity of lust-filled her again when his hot breath stroked her ear.

This is too soon after that bastard blacksmith raped me!

Suddenly, growing anxiety filled her.

"You must leave," she turned around. When she looked into the man's eyes, her mind suddenly forgot her apprehension. Instead, Elisabeth felt her concerns wash away. Only a vague but growing lust filled her.

"I'm here to fill your desires," Ramhout said as his fingers slid along her bare shoulders. He pulled down the fabric past the corset she wore.

Deeply inhaling at the man's actions, Elisabeth smelled the hint of smoke and musk on his clothes.

"Your husband is nothing to you. You've made that clear," he whispered.

"I cannot have rumors," Elisabeth attempted to glance away. Ramhout turned her head to face him. She could read his expression.

It didn't matter!

His hypnotic eyes forced her into another world. Her breathing grew heavy when the man wrapped his arms around her body to unpin her dress.

"Hurry!"

The unexpected words came from her mouth. Then, Elisabeth pulled away from his help to speedily slid out of her dress. Ramhout laughed lightly when the woman nearly ripped off her undergarments. Finally undressed, Elisabeth came to him and wrapped her arms around his neck. They kissed with a growing passion.

"Take me!" She whispered. Her mind raced with a dazed excitement of expectations and anxiety. A tiny voice screamed for her to stop, yet some deep and primal emotion overrode her.

With a devious grin, Ramhout led her to the table. He forced the surprised woman to bend over, her chest pressed down on the cold, hard surface.

"I'll have my dessert now, and you'll soon forget your troubles," he declared in an ominous tone. Suddenly, the captain raked her back with his long nails, drawing blood.

Elisabeth screamed out in pain and shock. Yet, she didn't fight or try to escape. Instead, images filled her mind. Swimming visions of orgiastic pleasures overwhelmed her. The woman recognized that she was too far gone. She would give herself to every sadistic idea that she knew was coming. The man ran his nails over her back again, then he brutally forced himself into her.

Instead of fighting, Elisabeth groaned aloud. Scenes of naked men and women heaving and writhing in frenzied sexual pleasure swept through the woman. When she saw her vision filled with flames, the duchess shuddered in pleasure. The duchess yelled out for him to defile her. With a smile of growing ecstasy, Elisabeth grunted in time the man pushed into her. Amid the debauchery, the duchess heard the laughter coming from the sailors outside the cabin, who mocked her passionate cries. When her lover's animalistic growls scared her, only one rational thought came through.

Why don't I care?

~~~

The next afternoon, a wearily sore Elisabeth looked across the water. A stiff breeze whipped her hair into her face, but she didn't bother to pin it back with her hand. The duchess left the captain's cabin at daylight. When she reached her cabin, Elisabeth fell into a deep, nightmare-filled sleep.

After she rose from the bed, the woman paced in her room for a while. After growing bored, she walked across the bow of the ship in a trancelike state. As Elisabeth stood there on the bow, the duchess didn't notice the sailors. The men kept looking at her with their smirking expressions. It was the first mate whose whispered disgusting comments finally broke Elisabeth from her trance. She turned to glare at the bearded man. Instead of backing down, the man stepped close.

"Rumor has it that your breasts were as hard and cold as those on the figurehead."

The man pointed with the stem of his pipe toward the half-naked statue attached to the bow.

"You proved us wrong," he smirked with the smell of gin. "Aye, the captain's found him a nice sea wench."
~~~

Infuriated, she left him.

"I'll have you flogged," Elisabeth vowed. Her face filled with fury as she listened to the laughter.

The duchess went to the quarterdeck, where the captain looked out at the darkening clouds. When she tried to get his attention, Ramhout glanced over, then he went to the railing to issue orders.

"Damn your hide. I want those sails shortened. Can't you see there's a blow coming?" The captain yelled as he sent the first mate to order the sailors into the riggings.

"What do you want?" Ramhout turned to Elisabeth.

His ugly expression forced her to take a step back. Quickly composing herself, she pointed to the first mate.

"I insist you flog that man. His insults against me would land him in the stocks in France. I'm a duchess, not some common peasant."

The captain looked over at the crewman who stood watching the scene but was too far away to hear the conversation. When Ramhout's attention returned to the duchess, his grimace turned uglier. She saw his hazel eyes flash with annoyance.

"Woman, you don't realize that I'm the master. You dare come to me with your petty demands. Go to your cabin before I give you to the crew tonight!"

His ominous tone and deadly expression caused Elisabeth to take another step back. Her face paled as she hurried away.

When the woman got back to her cabin, Elisabeth sat on her hard bed, trying to understand what she had witnessed. After several minutes, her eyes kept going to the box, holding the gold-covered relic of Saint Julia. The duchess frowned. With growing unease, she decided the religious item inside shouldn't be inside of her room. She used the holy artifact to achieve revenge and to gain power.

"My dear saint, how can you help me?" Elisabeth rose, then began pacing back and forth.

The woman's thoughts kept running over her encounter. Worse, she remembered the loving acceptance of the pain and humiliation at the hands of Ramhout. She tried to reconcile his public shaming with the perception she carried about herself. Elisabeth recognized something was deeply wrong. Profound in her thinking developed inside of her since she arrived on the ship. At times, the duchess appeared to sleepwalk without considering the repercussions. While Elisabeth used sex to meet her ends, she never gave herself to a man so quickly and without thinking about the benefits to her position.

Why didn't I threaten Ramhout with consequences for his actions? I'm a duchess!

"Because he holds the upper hand," she whispered to herself.

Even worse for Elisabeth was his near dismissal left her with no options. When they reached France, she couldn't go to the authorities about the captain. Not without a scandal erupting. The captain could use their encounter to shame her and her husband with his sailors willing to testify on his behalf. Her thoughts struggled to accept that the captain controlled her once she let him have her. That she still wanted the man, both stunned and horrified her.

The Duchess of Sully must always remain a lady without a public scandal. She kept her husband's proclivity for men hidden from the public. She must follow his lead. With Ramhout's sudden change, Elisabeth decided she needed something to guarantee his silence. Determined to regain control, the duchess vowed to find the captain's weakness.

The growing swells in the afternoon left the woman seasick. Elisabeth came out of her cabin into the chilly breeze. She heard the first mate shouting at the watch. Elisabeth wandered toward the stern where the sailors gathered again to witness the punishment. The duchess stood behind the men while she wondered if they were bringing Blackbane back to the mast.

That would kill him!

The thought surprised her.

I want him dead!

Elisabeth watched an unknown sailor being dragged to the mast. As the men tied the unfortunate sailor's wrists together, Elisabeth stared at Ramhout, who looked on with some interest. However, the man's attention appeared focused on the clouds building in the sky. Then she felt someone staring at her. The duchess looked over to see Octave leaning against the railing. It was the first time Elisabeth saw him on the small ship. The servant smiled before he went to the quarterdeck before she could talk with him.

When she lost sight of him among the group of sailors, the duchess had an urge to search the deck below. While Elisabeth did not know what she could find that might influence Captain Ramhout, she saw the open hatch and took the ladder to the next deck.

The narrow corridor led her past closed doors as she traveled toward the bow. Carefully, Elisabeth opened the first door. The sailmaker's shop held stacks of canvas and assorted tools. Her search continued until she reached an entrance barred by a padlocked entrance. She peered through the iron straps of the door and saw two trunks strapped to the deck inside the room. On the wall were rows of swords and other weapons.

It must be the armory.

Elisabeth recalled when Ramhout interrupted their talk about their voyage when they departed. Armed uniformed men carried two small trunks aboard the ship.

"Pardon me, duchess, but we have a payment coming for your king. The merchants entrusted their gold to me for payment to Louis."

His mischievous grin brought a smile to her lips that morning. Now she smiled for a different reason. The gold or silver inside the boxes might become her way to ensure Ramhout never betrayed her. She needed an ally.

A tapping noise coming from a room nearby caught her attention. The duchess followed the sound coming from behind a door that was unlocked. Elisabeth stepped inside the room and found a cell holding Marshall. She stopped in shock from the odor and his condition.

Nasty black and blue welts covered the man's back, his chest, and shoulders. Dried blood covered a shirt that was nothing more than strips of clothing.

"Here to gloat at my lot, bitch? Or did the coming storm bring you down? That gray pallor won't do to show your husband. You feel the swells increasing, don't you?"

The duchess remained silent as she covered her nose because of the stench.

"Oh, yes. My servants keep forgetting to remove the chamber pot. You know how hard it is to get good help." He carefully leaned back against the wooden planks of the hull.

"Take a good look, duchess. Your Captain Ramhout is more than he appears. I'm sure I don't need to tell you, but I should warn you…"

Suddenly, he stopped talking, then leaned forward. He saw the long scratch along her neck and one side of her shoulder.

"So, the sailor's talk that I overheard is true. The captain already gave you his pole." He shook his head. "You do not know what kind of trade you made. All I can do is pity you."

There was no triumph in the statement. The duchess wanted to lash out, but she paused when she saw his expression. Instead of victory and mocking, she recognized a profound disappointment, almost resignation in his eyes.

Slowly, Elisabeth stepped in front of the cage, looking at the thick iron straps. The duchess looked around. Wood stacked along the hull held folded tarps of the extra sailing canvas. It appeared they primarily used the area for storage. The woman put her hand on the rough surface of the beaten iron.

"I want to know why you stole Saint Julia's heart from my husband."

He glared at her.

"You forget I tried to buy it. Instead, you let your wounded pride get in the way. It led us to this place and conversation."

"It wasn't my pride."

His mocking laugh infuriated her. He pointed across the room on the floor.

"Hand me that lamp that Leiras made. Your partners do not know the valuable item inside of it."

Elisabeth reluctantly went to the place where he pointed. She picked up the battered Xeropotamou lamp. The woman held it away from her like it stank before she placed it on the deck near the cage. With a grimace, Marshall crawled over and pulled the item inside. He checked and smiled at the sliver of wood from the cross of Jesus that remained inside. The captain straightened the bent metal around the opening where the glass once sat.

"Like hell, it wasn't your pride," he finally glanced up at her. "You carry your vanity around like a badge of honor. Everyone sees it. But it's not just that. Like me, you're pig-headed and let your temper get the best of you. Bound to follow a path, no matter where it leads. It took me a while to figure it out."

He went back to his work.

"Since we're asking questions, I have one for you. Did you spend the rest of your life as a slave wife to the Beyliek?"

After a moment, he cackled.

"Of course not. You remain silent because you know the truth. Yes, your family paid a ransom like many others captured for ransom by the Turks. Now you're a titled woman living in luxury. You might not like your lot in life, but nobody gives a damn. Madame Elisabeth, your arrogance in the world and focused contempt of me led you to the spot where you stand!"

The duchess turned away, then stopped.

"Something's happened to you. You speak of my arrogance. However, I recall a captain who carried more foul traits than I can imagine. Look at you. You sit as a beaten prisoner inside the hull of this ship. I would say our roles are different now."

"Aye, perhaps you're correct," Marshall grunted as he straightened another piece of riveted metal. "But you don't hear me blaming others for why I'm in this cage. I'm not begging the damned demon for my life. I know he wants my slow demise. Hell, I'm not blaming you for my lot in life, even though you led the demons to me."

He glanced back, seeing Elisabeth's half-turned face showing a look of cynicism.

"Woman, I have no reason to lie to you. I've earned every bit of my treatment. I have learned to open my eyes a bit since we first met. For a moment in the graveyard when we fought Mammon, I held hope that you might see reality when you rode with Leiras and me. Instead, you cut down a monk who was once an angel. As foul as Leiras was, he still sought the help of Remiel. You're in for a rude awakening when you finally realize you picked the wrong side."

Elisabeth turned back at the comment. Her flesh quivered, and she felt a knot in her stomach.

"You're insane," she insisted. "Leiras was no angel. I followed the instructions of Remiel. Think about that for a moment."

The pirate looked at her, then shook his head.

"Well, maybe now you'll understand that those damn angels have their own agendas. It doesn't pay to trust them."

"Just tell me the truth," the duchess implored him. "Admit that you only lust for the gold in that display."

Silence filled the stinking area. Finally, Marshall responded.

"No, I won't admit that. The value of that heart fair exceeds the value of gold. I guess it does no harm to tell you, although you won't believe me," the prisoner told the duchess with a sigh. "I had a vision of the saint. She led me on this path. Leiras carried a similar one."

The woman's expression of disbelief remained as she looked at him.

"Yes, I realize it sounds crazy, but Saint Julia came to me. Her spirit seeks the relic's return to her body in Lombard."

After a moment of stunned silence, the woman came closer.

"Do you expect me to believe a bloody-thirsty pirate talks to saints?"

He shook his head, then went back to his work.

"Woman, you can believe what you wish! I have a feeling you aren't asking these questions just for conversation. I suspect that there's an inner voice telling you that something's wrong. Still, you wish to place your troubles on your encounters with me. Sorry to disappoint you, but I don't accept the blame. You can lay that on some dirty bastards who swear they're angels. With the wind picking up, my guess is you'll discover the truth soon. Riding out a storm requires all hands on deck. Perfect time to check out your suspicions."

"You're a conceited ass who lives in his filth and misery," Elisabeth shot back. "And you'll never know what happened after they hang you for your crimes."

The duchess left the room.

"I'm still alive!" Blackbane called out with a chuckle.

~~~

Marshall's prediction about the weather proved accurate when Elisabeth stepped out of her cabin later that day. The wind pushed at her as she walked along, holding the railing. Sea spray struck her occasionally, but she didn't notice.

Her mind focused on Octave. She needed an ally, and the vast fortune on the ship might provide her with an opportunity. As she worked her way aft, the woman thought about the pirate captain's words. So much of what Blackbane told her was crazy, yet she had no doubts about what she witnessed in the graveyard. Then, her last moment with Leiras. She knew the man's image changed in front of her.

No, it had to be something else. I couldn't kill an angel.

She remembered the jeweled dagger she stabbed Leiras with. Maybe Blackbane was right.

No, he can't be telling the truth!

Ramhout's servant silently stood in the woman's path, and she nearly collided with him near the quarterdeck. The Arab bowed, then waved her to follow him.

An eerie silence welcomed her inside the darkened cabin of the captain. A single lit lamp swayed to the roll of the ship above the table. She peered into the corner shadows next to her, then took a step back as Ménart stepped into the light, along with Octave.

"Wait, I saw you killed."

Ramhout stepped into the light and removed his robe. His muscled, naked body carried a hint of scarlet in his skin color.
~~~

"My dear, those who follow me don't worry about death. Ménart is a revenant, a sorcerer who gave me his soul. I gave him strength and agility of a night hunter who lives on blood."

She backed to the door where the Arab stood. He pushed her back toward the captain.

"What are you?" Elisabeth finally sputtered out.

"My, you're a dull-witted woman. Haven't you seen me before?"

The captain suddenly transformed into the golden-eyed angel from the deserted church. Wings of white feathers extended; he opened his arms wide.

Stunned, the duchess started muttering to herself.

"No, no, this isn't happening. Remiel, you took me to bed?" She fell to her knees.

The creature before her laughed, joined by the others in the cabin. Then the beast kneeled in front of her, his form changing again.

"Dear naïve child, you gave yourself to a fallen angel! The lics and deceit plotted out on your road to my bed."

The red face of a two-horned demon looked upon the woman. She fell back with a tortured moan.

"Oh, but I guess you never witnessed my true form," the creature's mocking tone went with his smile. "Some call me the deceiver."

"Dear God, no!" her voice choked out. "Not Lucifer!"

"Don't say that accursed name in front of me," he growled, then quickly recovered.

The demon smiled at the look on the woman's face.

"Each step of the way since you left Augsburg, I've been keeping an eye on you." The creature stepped around the woman as she gawked at him. Her mind tried to rationalize and comprehend what he told her.

"Your path to me wasn't hard for me to influence. My offspring and supporters live all over the world. They told me of this cursed Blackbane and his quest for reclamation. Fortune showed its hand when the pirate heard of your stolen relics. While those fool saints thwarted me, it was your need for revenge that led me right to my prize. Blackbane is the real prize. His cursed immortality leads the demons to seek him." Lucifer stopped and cocked his head at the thought.

"Funny, you never learned why his deadly wounds healed. I suppose those with revenge in their hearts seldom stop to consider their actions. It was quite easy to send you to the destinations where you corrupted yourself."

"You had the blacksmith rape me!" She spat out.

Lucifer placed his finger on his long chin.

"Me? No, I had no intention of having someone rape you. I prefer my mortals to debase themselves with me. That's my talent. When I offered you a way back to Marshall, I told you to take the boy. I think it's obvious where you made your mistake. The blacksmith saw the coins you tried to hide. Your arrogant attitude no doubt helped the man justify his rape of you. Then, of course, that led to his soul falling into my lake of fire for eternity."

When he noticed her pleased expression at Peeter's demise, Lucifer kneeled by her. She tried to look away, but he forced her to look at him.

"Madam Elisabeth, I understand your pleasure at the downfall of Peeter's soul. No doubt, you found satisfaction in pounding his brains out. Justified as you were, I'll remind you that you happily gave up whatever virtue you had left to pursue revenge against Blackbane."

His ominous laughter made the woman's skin crawl as he stood.

"Don't worry, your soul will join Peeters and me in Hell."

The woman screamed while she scrambled to her feet. Elisabeth tried to get past the giant servant at the door. However, the man grabbed her, squeezing the struggling duchess in his arms.

"No, it's not my time!" She shrieked. Her frantic struggles grew more frenzied when the pain of the man's tightening grip struck her. Soon, her ribs cracked as they neared collapsing.

"No, don't kill her!" Lucifer ordered.

The Arab loosened his grip, allowing Elisabeth to slide to her knees. Her shoulders shook in a silent wail as the demon walked over. He grabbed her by the hair and forced the woman to look up at him.

"Oh, my little lover, you misunderstand. I sealed your fate before you gave yourself to me last night." The demon's eyes danced with delight at her reaction. "Men took you to bed long before Octave told me about you killing a monk. Then you let two men die to remove any witnesses of your kidnapping."

He pressed his finger to his lips when she tried to argue.

"Quiet! Woman, Octave can't lie to me. I know Ménart planned it. I can read your thoughts. Perhaps the monk wasn't your intention. Yet, you really didn't care that he died by your hand. It's the same as the hired hands who worked for you. You denied them any rites and threw them into the water to hide their discovery. Then you came to me with your free will and took my seed. Murder, adultery, bearing false witness, you've broken every commandment given to Moses."

He grinned.

"You're just upset at finding out that you brought about your destruction. All it took was a little guidance from me!"

He released her, and the duchess collapsed on the deck. He paid no attention to her sobs as he went to a mirror and transformed into the image of Ramhout. The demon put on his powdered wig.

"However, I don't intend to collect your soul right now. I enjoy my games with mortals. Put an idea in their head, let it fester along with the hatred, prejudice, envy, or revenge already inside. They'll follow me straight into my realm."

Lucifer appeared pleased at his reflection. Then he tied and adjusted the golden cravat. He picked up his hat and placed it on top of his head.

"Don't worry, you'll live to a ripe old age before your soul comes to my pit of fire," he told the woman. "In the meantime, I have big plans for you and your idiot husband. You'll live like a goddess, just as you always dreamed about."

His expression hardened when he looked down.

"Since I have my prize in this immortal Blackbane, you'll return in triumph with your relics for the king. Once you go to the court of Louis, you'll have Ménart join you and your husband as your new spiritual advisor. His abilities will prove useful to your needs. No doubt, he'll satisfy you while I'm away. He enjoys the taste of blood and pain."

Elisabeth turned her head away as she started sobbing again.

"It's too bad that a storm is brewing. I must see to my duties as a mortal captain. It would not look good for a Prince of Hell to wind up on the rocks of a beach," he told her with a sneer.

"Go back to your cabin, my whore. Once I ensure our safety, I'll seed your womb again."

~~~

Elisabeth paced back and forth in her cabin during the afternoon. After recovering from the initial terrifying shock, the woman's thoughts twisted like the pit of her stomach. Feelings of rage went to dark despair, then to hopelessness and thoughts of suicide.

I'm utterly alone!

Sitting on the bed, Elisabeth looked over at the boxes holding the valuable relics. She suppressed a sudden urge to grab
~~~

them, then jump over the side of the ship with her arms clutched around each wooden case.

Facing reality, she blamed herself, but the woman did not know how to remove herself from a new and horrifying world. Lucifer used her to get what he wanted. The demon guided the woman to her fall like a virtuoso. It played upon her vanity and fears while sending his agents to steer her. No wonder the creature was pleased; it got Blackbane and her as a package.

Blackbane told her about the demon and his offspring! The pirate assumed she made a deal with Lucifer and Ménart.

Of course he would! I never gave him a reason to believe otherwise.

She shook her head, silently cursing her stupidity. Wrapped in her world of revenge, the duchess failed to recognize her peril. Now, a duchess would remain a demon's plaything. Lucifer's plans for her involved his sinister cohorts, Ménart and Octave. They would make her life a living hell. Her dreams were gone.

Hands shaking, she went to the decanter of wine, swinging back and forth in its holder by a small table. The duchess didn't bother with a cup. She put down a third of the bottle in several gulps.

Returning to her bed, she sat there, looking at the relic case. As she looked for a way out of her trap, her thoughts went back to Blackbane. Marshall fought against one demon and survived.

Would he help?

Elisabeth shook her head. He had no reason to assist her.

As the rolls of the ship intensified, the duchess sighed. She heard the splatter of sea spray striking her door.

"I guess I should learn to live by the verses of Matthew," she told the box holding the saint's heart.

Chapter 9: The Storm

When Elisabeth silently left her cabin, she noticed the captain on the quarterdeck. Her heart sank. Then, she recognized Ramhout was staring up at the mast. As the demon screamed orders to the crew, she hurried to the hatch leading down. The duchess stopped when she heard snoring coming from the first open door. Carefully moving past the entrance to the sailmaker's shop, she glanced inside to see a small man lying back on his chair.

Elisabeth found Marshall staring at his hand. He held the Saint Simpert cross inside the small leather bag that the bandits failed to remove from his belt. He quickly closed his fist. Marshall wondered about her panic-stricken expression. However, the woman just stared at him, unable to speak for a moment.

"I come to you with an offer," she finally explained. "If I help you escape from this cage, will you help me get off this ship? Tonight!"

He scowled at her, sliding his relic back along his waist.

"I'd rather trust a viper, my lady."

"He lied to me. It wasn't Remiel, it was Lucifer to wanted me to find you. If I help you, I want you to get me off this ship. I have to get away from him and his people."

Before Marshall could reply, he felt someone standing outside the door.

"Madam Elisabeth, I thought I saw you coming down here. Are you planning on helping our enemy? Can you imagine what Lucifer will do to people who betray him?"

Octave's ominous voice filled the room. Fear filled the woman when she turned to see him standing at the entrance. The smug servant's smile remained as he walked into the room.

The duchess quickly backed away from the cage.

"No, I wouldn't. I swear to God!"

"Don't mention that name in my presence, foul woman."

Ramhout entered the room. Ocean spray covered his oiled leather coat, and his hat streamed droplets of the water. His golden eyes focused on his prisoner.

"With this gale blowing, it's a perfect time for me to introduce myself to my guest. As a captain, you know what happens after the rain stops, and we've shortened sail. Most of the crew are in their berths, so they won't hear your screams." The captain glanced at Elisabeth, who was inching toward the door.

"Woman, don't you wish to observe while we break this man that you so despise?"

Without looking at Marshall, the duchess pushed past Octave and ran into Ménart at the entrance. The priest grabbed her, his fingernails digging deep into her arms. While she struggled to pull away, his unbelievably powerful arms penned her against his body. Ménart's mouth opened, exposing his growing fangs. As the creature started to bite down on the screaming woman's neck, Lucifer interrupted him with a roar.

"Not now. You can feed on her later! Blackbane is our victim on this night."

With a disappointed scowl, the revenant let Elisabeth go. She hurried into the passageway while Marshall rushed to retrieve the broken lantern. Lucifer turned back to his caged prey and smiled.

"You fool, that unlit lantern is no good to you. I know about your tricks. There's nothing you can do to stop me from finishing you before we dock. The storm will cover your screams. When we're finished, you'll willingly give me everything I want."

Suddenly frozen in his stance like a statue, Marshall observed a small fire near his boot. Like a snake, the flames crawled up and wrapped around the captain, who could only watch in horror. Lucifer's dark thoughts filled his mind.

"Do you think your nightmares will end now? I'll break you, mortal man. I'll own your mind, then your soul. Your madness will give me what I want. Your soul I'll cast into the Lake of Fire to feed my demons with its energy."

On the dark main deck above, Elisabeth barely heard Marshall's tortured screams rising through the wood. The black clouds and falling sun, along with the sea spray coming over the bow, made it difficult to see. She saw only one of the massive sails flapping in the wind above her. Only a few sailors were on the quarterdeck nearby.

The pellets of water lashed the woman as she stumbled on the slick wood deck in a panic. She barely heard the yells ordering her to get inside her cabin from the men standing on the quarterdeck. Elizabeth looked back as they started cursing to see them fighting with the ship's wheel. As a hard wave struck the ship on the port side, she fought the wind to open the door to her cabin. Once inside, the drenched woman found everything on her table now scattered across the deck.

Her frantic thoughts returned to escape. Jumping the water was no salvation for her. She couldn't swim! Briefly, Elisabeth considered a jolly boat hanging near the quarterdeck.

I can't get that damn boat unhooked from the ship!

Overwhelming fear, along with the tossing and pitching ship, started the sick feeling of nausea sweeping through her body. Her hands trembled with a growing sense of doom.

There's no hope!

Another powerful wave struck the ship again, sending the vessel rolling. Saint Julia's relic slid into the woman's foot while she held the door latch amid the rolling of the watercraft. Almost instinctively, the duchess reached down and grabbed the artifact. While she stared at it, a growing resolve filled her.

Elisabeth hurried to the bed. Sitting the relic on the mattress, she pulled the sheathed jeweled dagger from its hiding spot, then she slid the weapon inside of the belt around her corset.

The screams and howls coming from Marshall were no longer heard outside of the room, where his three tormentors enjoyed their abuse. Now, the pirate's hoarse cries sounded more like pitiful croaks. The cage was open, and Ménart fed on the blood leaking from the various bite wounds he left on Marshall's exposed shoulder. Avoiding the cursed cross mark on the prisoner's neck, the creature slowly bled Marshall.

Helping in the torment, Octave twisted Marshall's arms, which were penned behind his back and through the bars. The servant's face lit up with delight each time the prisoner groaned from the pain.

However, it was Lucifer's mental image that caused the most suffering for Marshall. The image of fire in his mind long since changed over the agony of a flaying. Inside the prisoner's mind, creatures from Hell were slowly cutting away the flesh from his body. Searing, unfathomable anguish filled Marshall. No longer able to stand, his knees gave way, only to add to his pain coming from his trapped arms. As the demon stepped next to Octave, he inhaled the stench coming from Marshall's sweating body.

"It won't be long now, Blackbane. Already, your mind is seeking a means to escape the punishment of your body. You'll search for a place to hide, but there's no escape," Lucifer chuckled.

"Ménart, you may cut into his artery now for his blood. We'll see how long his body can hold out."

"I'll break his arms as well," the servant suggested with glee. The demon nodded.

"Your only hope is to give your mind to me," Lucifer whispered to Marshall.

Elisabeth slowly crept toward the room when she heard the pitiful wails coming from the prisoner. At first, she mistook the sounds for a suffering animal. The duchess almost dropped the saint's heart when she saw Marshall.

"Get away, you bastards from Hell," she cried. Holding the relic in front of her, Elisabeth entered the room.

The sight of the holy object startled Lucifer, and he backed away. Octave let go of Marshall, who fell to the deck. Ménart carefully exited the cage, stepping over the prisoner.

Gathering his strength, the pirate brought his numb hands to his belt as he fumbled for the Saint Simpert cross. His fingers ripping at the leather bag attached to his belt. He glanced up to see a grinning Octave approaching Elisabeth.

"You stupid whore, that damn thing don't work on people."

The servant attacked the woman, throwing her against the cage. With one hand, Octave pulled Saint Julia's artifact out of the woman's hands. His other hand clasped around her neck; the servant squeezed tightly around Elisabeth's windpipe.

She pulled the Saint Gennaro dagger and stabbed Octave in the belly. The servant fell away, dropping the relic to the floor. A white flash of light suddenly emanated from the display.

As Marshall struggled to his knees, Ménart grabbed him, then slammed him against the cell.

"I'm tired of you spawn of Hell." Marshall fumed as he jabbed one end of the Saint Simpert cross into the creature's eye. The energy surged through him from the power inside the relic as the demon offspring screamed in pain. The pirate captain slammed Ménart down on the deck.

Elisabeth scrambled over to join him, but Lucifer got there first. His transformed body showed his true form as the demon swiped his three-clawed hand at her. The claws dug into her back, sending the woman next to the wounded Octave. The blessed dagger landed close to Marshall, who remained locked in battle with the devil's priest. He grabbed the cross stuck inside Ménart's eye socket. When Marshall pulled out the relic along with the creature's ruined eye, the devil's spawn screeched out.

The Arab servant barreled into the room. In an instant, he was on Marshall. He stabbed his daggers into the pirate as the man lifted his arm to ward off the blows. One blade severed fingers on Marshall's hand while the other stiletto cut into his forearm. Ignoring his pain, Marshall kicked out with his boot. He struck the bigger man in the groin, doubling him over. The pirate cried out when he pulled out the blade still in his hand.

Out of the corner of his eye, Marshall caught Lucifer swinging at him. He partially avoided the clawed hand, but the mind control from the demon started to overpower him again. He held up the cross relic and underworld creature fell back just as the Arab tackled Marshall. Expecting another blade in his back, the pirate captain desperately swung out. However, he only heard a groan, then felt the full weight of the man on his back. Marshall crawled from under the man, glancing back to see Elisabeth standing over the body with the blessed dagger in her hand.

"Woman, put down that weapon, or I'll rip you apart."

The ominous warning from Lucifer showed Marshall that she had the demon momentarily cut off from escape. The captain stumbled over the blood slick deck and nearly fell when he reached the Saint Julia's heart.

Behind him, Ménart attacked Elisabeth from the side. Before she could defend herself, the priest wrapped his arms around the woman. He embedded into her shoulder near the neck as the duchess dangled in his grip. Unable to use the dagger against Ménart, she could only cry out as the creature bite deeper, greedily draining her blood.

Marshall stood with Saint Julia's relic as Lucifer rushed him. The captain slammed the artifact into the demon's chest.

The creature's flesh burned while it howled in rage and pain, then backed into Ménart. Marshall pressed his advantage. As the white light that expanded from the display in his hands, the captain forced the energy towards the demon's face. A massive blast of an unnatural white fire struck the beast full on. Suddenly covered in eerie flames, Lucifer's muscular body spun around as his own red energy surged outward. The supernatural energy struck Marshall along with the nearby hull as well.

Marshall, in his frenzy to extinguish the fire covering him, dropped the relic at the foot of the demon. The man broke away and grabbed one of the canvas sheets. He fell to the deck while wrapping himself in the tarp. The frenzied howls of Lucifer filled the room as the creature looked for an escape. Then the demon extended his fiery wings, sending parts of the room ablaze.

The blasts separated Elisabeth from her attacker. She scrambled to her feet, stabbing Ménart in the back as the Cambion went to help its master. A desperate frenzy filled the duchess as she continued to jab the creature.

Suddenly, a massive flame ball shot upward. The force of the blast ripped out the massive wooden beams above the fallen angel. His howls piercing the night sky. Lucifer sprung up into the raging storm while the wooden debris fell back on the people inside the room.

As the demon escaped, his wing-filled supernatural flames started fires on everything they touched. The fire on the canvas sails and hemp lines, charred by the heat and spurred on by the wind, quickly spread.

After a moment of disbelief, the men on the quarterdeck signaled the alarm. Within a few moments, sailors spilled out of their position and ran into the storm. Another substantial wave struck over the bow, sending men to the deck. Some sailors tried to fight the blown fiery debris that rained down while others hurried aloft to cut away the burning sails.

Below, Elisabeth came out of her stupor caused by the explosion. Charred and burning items surrounded her. Yet, to her amazement, she was untouched by the heat. The reliquary holding the heart of the saint lay next to the unmoving Ménart. She spied a gold metallic gleam amid the light of the flames. She hurried to retrieve the relic.

As she reached down, the severely injured Ménart turned over. However, the priest felt the power of the item next to him. Instantly, the Cambion rolled away, growling like a wounded animal. The creature got on its feet and rushed to toward the doorway, now blocked by broken timber and debris.

Elisabeth immediately pounced on the relic for protection. Then she scrambled across the deck, looking for the dagger while keeping a wary eye on the injured Ménart. The creature noticed a path above and quickly crawled through the burning debris toward the gaping hole in the deck where Lucifer blast through. In an instant, the howling creature was out of sight.

Unable to follow the creature, Elisabeth retrieved the dagger and slid it into her belt. She scanned the room for a way out. The ship took a heavy roll, and the duchess tripped over Marshall's feet while he struggled to pull himself out of the charred canvas.

With a groan, the pirate moved, his mind working but his severely injured body refusing his commands. At the moment, Marshall could only fight to avoid the sliding debris that slid with him with each heavy pitch and roll of the ship. The man's mind yelled out that something was wrong in the way the *Tappan Sea* fought the waves. A growing fear rose inside him at the smell of oily smoke.

The ship is on fire and foundering!

The duchess paid no attention. She noticed a path to escape. The remains of Marshall's cage pushed through the bulkhead into the next room. Part of the wrecked ironwork created a ladder through a gaping hole of splintered wood that ran to the deck above. As the woman stepped through the debris going up, the sea spray splashed down. The duchess saw flames on the sails, along with distant, fearful shouts from the sailors above.

Then she halted. The gleaming reflections coming from the next room caught her attention. Peering closer, the woman saw a golden gleam scattered on the deck of the room.

With a quick glance at the fire behind her, Elisabeth's greed overcame her fear. She slid through the shattered part of the wall into the room. She fell to her knees, quickly scooping the coins on top of a section of her dress. Amid the shouts coming from above and the growing smoke filling the room, her focus remained on the gold coins that the ship carried to France. With her dress filled as much as she dared, Elisabeth reached out for the relic next to her.

Marshall grabbed her forearm and took Saint Julia's relic away. Then he pulled Elisabeth to her feet as she struggled to escape his clutches. His singed beard was nearly gone; she recognized the pain on his face from his injured hand when he released her.

"You damn fool, get out of here," his hoarse voice snarled. Half pushing her on a crate, Marshall followed her. His injured hand clumsily gripped the relic while he carried one of the partially opened bags of coins. Using another massive roll of the ship to their advantage, the two finally climbed out of the room and crawled into the raging storm above them.

Like hell on the sea, the burning canvas and lines rained down on the deck of the ship. The wind-driven spray quickly extinguished some flames. However, the mainmast lit the sky, fully engulfed and sending down fiery debris. With the sailors driven away from the ship's wheel by the flames, the sailing vessel was at the mercy of the strong seas. The first mate howled out his orders as men started a bucket brigade to stop the growing inferno. Marshall recognized the desperate order. He forced Elisabeth forward. Marshall's eyes scanned the dark horizon for lights, which he saw on the port side.

"This is a doomed ship," he cried in her ear as they tried to avoid the falling flaming debris.

The ship shuddered from another wave. The duchess clutched her bundled dress fold as coins spilled on the deck. Yellow light filled the area around them as flames shot out of the hold.

"The cargo's burning!" He continued to drag Elisabeth with him.

Another wave slamming into the ship sent them to the deck. Unable to let go of her bundle, the woman slid onto the railing. Marshall came in behind her, nearly losing the relic in his hand. He felt Saint Simpert's cross dangling from his neck.

"Come on, saints! Don't leave me now!"

After another wave struck, Marshall pushed Elisabeth against the railing with the heavy bag and handed her Saint Julia's display.

"Wrap your leg around that belaying pin," he ordered. "Don't lose this relic!"

The captain grabbed one rope sliding across the deck like a snake. He tied off one end to another pin, then tied the rope around his waist. Another wave struck the stern of the ship, and he heard the cries of sailors who went over the side. Soon, flames covered the aft sails and mast. The vessel shuddered again as the sea struck the stern again. He glanced over to see whitecaps in the direction of the shoreline lights.

Marshall hurried away, barely avoided a sliding barrel careening across the deck. He followed it to the railing near the spot Elisabeth hung on. The cask struck with a hollow crash he heard over the wind. When he got to the barrel, he found it nearly empty of the rum inside. The captain slid it closer to the woman and hurriedly put the bag of coins and the relic inside. Marshall drew close and ripped at her dress. Confused, she fought him, then helped him get the dress off. She threw her bundle into the cask as he untied the rope around him and attached it to the barrel. Later, Marshall put the cover back on and waited for the next ship's roll before he hoisted it over into the water.

"Over you go," he told her.

Before the woman could argue, the ship took another hit at the stern from a wave that forced the vessel against the ocean floor rising to the beach. The sudden stop broke the fire-weakened main mast, sending it over into the water along with screaming sailors. The force collapsed the railing and sent both of them into the water.

Bobbing to the surface, Marshall still held the line to the barrel. Somehow, in the fading light, he noticed Elisabeth struggled in the water. He saw her go under again after coming up from falling in. He got to the duchess, pulling her up by one arm. Panic set in the woman, and she grabbed on to Marshall. Unable to break free, he slammed his forehead into her head.

"Grab the barrel!" He pulled away from the stunned woman's reach.

"I can't!"

She splashed around in place until the pirate floated the wooden cask toward her.

"Let me die!" Elisabeth cried out. "Lucifer owns me now."

"Damn it, are you a duchess or not?" The captain demanded.

Elisabeth glared, but she took the edge of the barrel.

"Just kick with your feet towards those lights," he ordered, then paddled along with her.

When the unlikely pair finally reached shore, they stumbled across the sand. After they lay on the wet beach in the stiff wind, the two people dragged their barrel into the relative protection of the trees. Marshall paced back and forth, trying to stay warm. Then, he stared at the fully engulfed ship. As they watched in silence, both wonder about their next steps.

Splashing several yards away caught their attention. The first of several sailors finally came out of the surf. The men collapsed on the beach, just as Marshall and Elisabeth did.

They watched the men, who eventually struggled to their feet. An argument quickly developed between several men. Their voices carried over the noise of the surf.

"Rot!" one man told the other. "You know I jolly well didn't see nothing. I sez you dreamed something and woke up when the fire blew through them futtock shrouds and gaskets."

"Hell and damnation, ye're a fule! Me fightin the damn wheel with the mate, and I'm asleep! Explain how're the main mast catches fire at the top?" The other shot back as they started walking along the beach.

"What about them others?" Another sailor spoke up.

Marshall didn't hear the answer as the men move off, heading toward the distant lights of a town. After a while, the surviving crew was out of sight.

Finally, Elisabeth's weak voice came over the sound of the wind and surf.

"You should have let me drown.

"Quit feeling sorry for yourself. It appears we're both carrying the curses of our actions."

"Then, why go on?

Marshall laughed.

"I have no choice. If nay demon has their way, I spend an eternity in pain and agony as they suck me dry for my damn immortality. According to Remiel, judgment day is my only hope."

He continued watching the dying vessel.

"But I plan on beating that son of a bitch!" His growl was unforgiving.

"How do you beat an angel?" Her voice trailed away.

Marshall shrugged, then looked at her.

"Why did you partner with Lucifer?"

She stared at the cask which held Saint Julia's relic.

"He came to me as Remiel. He was waiting inside at that church where you left me." She shook her head. "The bastard made me an offer I couldn't refuse. I swear to God that I didn't know it was Lucifer. He was always one step ahead of me. Octave and Ménart showed up to assist me at just the right moments."

Marshall remained silent as he watched her talk.

We're all easy targets for these bastards!

He turned back to the water. The frigid wind kept blowing around them. The captain knew they needed to find shelter soon.

"That vision you spoke about. Your fight against an archangel, yet you talk about crazy things you claim a saint tells you."

The pirate captain nodded.

"I suppose it looks that way," he glanced back. "Do you think anything I say now is crazy?"

She shook her head.

"Remiel claimed God cursed me," Marshall continued. "But he's the one that gave me this damn mark. Leiras taught me that angels carry their own ideas about what the Lord wants."

He stepped next to the cask while he continued to stare out at the water. No more sailors came out of the rolling waves.

"I've also learned that the visions of Julia guide me as well. There's a comfort to them," the pirate shrugged. "It beats suffering at the hands of the ghosts of people I've killed."

There was a long silence as the duchess silently wept. She used the wet cloth of her sleeve to wipe her eyes.

"I didn't mean to kill Leiras," Elisabeth finally spoke with a shiver. "I turned around, and he was there."

Marshall looked over at the woman. The pale light coming from the remains of the ship showed him her vulnerability for the first time. He frowned when he recalled how much she looked like Emma Watson.

"I still don't understand!" She tried to erase her memory of his instant transformation after she stabbed him. "He talked like he murdered and raped. How could he be an angel?"

The captain shook his head.

"It's a long story. Anyway, that's for you to come to grips with. However, I wouldn't write Leiras off yet," Marshall thought about the fat man. For a moment, he missed the crazy monk. "You saw damn Ménart survive losing his eye and wounds from the blessed dagger."

The woman touched at the wounds along her neck, where Ménart's teeth sunk into her.

"In my homeland, I've heard about things called a revenant, but I never knew what they were until tonight. Lucifer called him sorcerers who sucked the blood of victims. The damned don't stand a chance with him."

Marshall stiffly turned around, shivering in his wet clothes, then he looked in the barrel. The captain pulled out the display holding Saint Julia's heart, along with the bag of coins.

"All I know is that we need to leave here soon! The fires will bring farmers and villagers looking for spoils floating ashore from the ship."

"What will happen now?"

"You take what you can carry and return to your husband. You keep the Saint Simpert dagger. I'm betting that you'll need it. I'll take Saint Julia to her resting place."

Marshall looked over the sea, where the ship's fires slowly extinguished as the vessel sank.

"Wait, I should go with you!" Elisabeth stood.

He refused to look back.

"No, you damn well shouldn't!"

Marshall walked into the night.

~~~

Inside the quiet confines of the Church of Santa Maria Annunziata, Marshall sat on a pew with his head bowed. The serenity of the nearly empty chapel gave the man a sense of tranquility he enjoyed. In the three months since he left Amsterdam, the former pirate journeyed across the Alps into the lands of Lombardy. He followed the visions of his benefactor, Saint Julia.

After finding his way to Antwerp, Marshall used part of his small fortune for horses and a priest escort. He searched along the river where Leiras was killed but never found his body. Eventually, the captain traveled through the Hapsburg lands and across the Alps. The soft voice of the saint came to him each night to show him the path.

When he reached Brescia, he immediately went to the small church of Chiesa di Santa Giulia in a village of Calino. The stout priest inside nearly came to tears when he saw the relic. With assurances of many prayers on his behalf, William Marshall left the church.

His mission completed, Marshall rode without thought or ambition until he reached the town of Salò, along the banks of the Lake Garda. Looking over the peaceful water, the captain called the place as his new home.

From his small apartment overlooking the water, he could see the monastery founded by St. Francis of Assisi. He went to the church daily. Many of the parishioners considered the eccentric foreigner a devout man with his time there. However, Marshall came to his pew to find restful sleep.
~~~

Lost in thought, the man didn't hear the quiet footsteps that came next to his pew.

"Who are you trying to fool?"

The captain didn't bother to glance up. He recognized the voice.

"Your master, of course." Marshall's sarcastic reply didn't surprise Remiel.

"I expected you sooner. Did you have trouble finding me?"

The angel scowled at the captain as he took a seat behind Marshall.

"You expected me. Mortal, does your insolence ever stop?"

The captain shook his head. He looked around the sanctuary, and none of the other parishioners noticed the golden-eyed angel in a white robe wearing wings.

"I get it. Only I can see you. You forget I'm immortal now, thanks to you." He hissed.

No need to get the locals thinking I'm insane!

"Yet you wear a stolen relic around your neck. You're not immortal, my hunted friend," Remiel scoffed as he leaned back, his wings folded away.

"Don't call me your friend!" Marshall growled. "I also keep the Xeropotamou lamp Leiras built. It keeps your real friends from bothering me. Too bad I can't use it on you."

The angel's expression didn't change.

"Where is the heart of Saint Julia?"

"Ask her, I'm not your errand boy," the captain turned away. He felt the mark on his neck grew hot.

"Don't forget who you talk with," his visitor warned. "I might turn you into a blabbering insane man yelling out blasphemy against this church. Burning at stake follows that!"

Marshall glared back at the angel.

"Alright, have it your way. Saint Julia guided me to place her remains in the chapel at Brescia. I felt her hand across my cheek as he whispered her thanks. Perhaps Julia doesn't see the world as you do. I count my blessings for having her at my side."

"The saints can't protect you from what awaits. They also don't deal with rude mortals who question God!"

Marshall shrugged his shoulders.

"He gave us free will, didn't he? I don't suppose you came here to remove this damn mark on my neck?"

He stared at the angel for a moment.

"No, I suppose not! What brings an archangel to a cursed man? You knew where the relics were."

"There is no place of sanctuary for you. Hiding in a church does not stop your curse." The angel warned him.

"Perhaps, but at least I can get some sleep. Now, come to the point. I'm sure you need to cause the world more problems." The captain stood and slid out of the pew.

"You should become familiar with the works of Shakespeare. You approach the ides of March." The man told him as his wing shot out to stop Marshall.

"I might dress like a gentleman; however, I don't know Latin or Greek," Marshall sighed. "I certainly don't mix with those who talk of Shakespeare. What is that supposed to mean?"

The angel's nasty grin unsettled him as he stood and stood over the captain.

"You should be careful with your friends and allies. Your activities to lift your curse bring you more enemies."

"Is that a threat or advice?"

"It is your fortune." Remiel turned and disappeared.

As Marshall left the church, he heard Remiel's soft laughter. The mocking sound caused the cursed man to grumble out profanities against the angel.

Shielding his eyes as he stepped into the bright sunlight, Marshall walked across the street to a tavern. Inside, he saw

Filippo Baldissera, who stood by the bar. With an inaudible groan, Marshall went over to his new friend.

He met Filippo briefly when Marshall rented his apartment in the building the merchant owned. The nervous balding man was also one of the few in the area who understood Marshall's language.

During his short time with Filippo, Marshall found the merchant carried an unsavory reputation in the town. He was the black sheep of an important family in Milan, with a tendency to borrow more than he could afford to pay. The ex-pirate recognized Filippo saw him as a potential mark for one of the man's schemes.

"Ah, my friend, I've been waiting for you." The merchant smiled broadly. "You must come to my estate today. The guest I told you about arrived last week; you've not accepted my invitations."

Marshall ordered a drink using the little Lombard language he learned so far. He caught a nearby scent, which made him scowl. Knowledge won during his hard road wasn't lost in his memories.

"That's because I'm a busy man of leisure now! You're a well-respected member of society who seeks even more fame and fortune."

Still unable to fully comprehend Marshall's frequent use of sarcasm, Filippo's chest puffed out as the tavern owner slid over a mug of beer to Marshall.

"Well, drink up, my friend. I have a carriage waiting to take us to my home."

With a sigh, Marshall finished his drink.

"I guess I might as well get this over with," agreed as the captain followed his friend out of the tavern.

As the men traveled to Filippo's estate along the shores of the lake, Marshall sat across from the merchant who regaled him with his latest exploits. The carriage turned off to a side road sent the battered Xeropotamou lamp to cling against the side of the vehicle.

"Why do you carry that thing?" Filippo asked. "And you're always armed." He nodded at the broad saber strapped to the captain's waist.

"The lamp was from a friend, and you can never tell when you might need," the captain said. "Tell me about this person who we're meeting."

"We have to keep this endeavor silent since my new partner must stay anonymous. My family would banish me if they realized the importance of the person who came to me. But I trust you won't say anything."

"Considering that I've never met your family, and that you said they live in Milan, I can assure my silence," Marshall replied.

"Ah, that famous English sarcasm," Filippo grinned. "You'll learn to trust me someday."

When they arrived at the villa, his host led them into a library.

"I promise that my new endeavor should be quite profitable," the man told Marshall. "My partner is eager to meet you and wants to speak with you alone. There's a fine brandy on the table. I'll return shortly."

With a perturbed glare, Marshall watched his host close the heavy paneled doors. Then he heard a soft voice behind him.

"Captain, it's good to see you again. You may pull your new sword for your revenge now."

Marshall turned and looked behind the desk, where Elisabeth stood. She wore a white wig and a pale-yellow corset with a dark blue silk dress. However, her hollow eyes and paler complexion made him look closer. There was a faint trace of amusement on her lips, but her haunted expression caught his attention.

"Hunted by demons in the blinding snow and bitter cold of the Alps makes a man lose interest in the petty ideas of revenge." He gave her an awkward smile.

"At least the saints seem to pity me. Of course, the spirits of those I've murdered continue to haunt my dreams."

Marshall saw her force a grin at the comment.

"Your arrival means something, but I cannot understand the reason you're here."

He suddenly glanced back at the closed door. Marshall immediately crossed the room to look out of the window. He scanned the quiet grounds.

"You do not need to worry, William Marshall. I'm not your enemy." She scrutinized his movements, noting his renewed confidence while remaining vigilant.

"In fact, I'm here alone. Only Filippo knows that I'm here." She paused, slightly bemused at the man staring out the window. Then she frowned.

"I come for your help."

"Yes, I'm sure that you forgot how much you hate me. I smelled that damn Filippo. Now, what could you possibly..." He stopped in mid-sentence when he glanced over at her profile.

The pregnant woman refused to look at him. She already guessed at his expression.

"Yes, I'm here for your help. As you can see, I'm taking my medicine now. Isn't that what you said would happen to me?"

With growing apprehension, Marshall slowly came to the desk, his focus on her trembling lips. She finally looked at him with an expression of guilt and fear.

"Tell me why you're here, Elisabeth."

Her eyes dropped. She remained silent for a moment.

"I'm here because I'm too weak to kill myself," the woman admitted. Then the duchess looked at him. "If I go to a priest, they'll burn me at stake for the creature that will come from my loins. No physician will believe my story. I cannot risk going to a person to remove this thing."

"Are you telling me you're carrying a Cambion from Lucifer?"

Her face fell at his words.

"I'm not sure," she admitted. "Another man raped me before Lucifer took me." She stepped from behind the desk to stand in front of the captain. Elisabeth's grin was a poor attempt.

"However, I'm sure you must enjoy the irony. My superior bearing brought down before you. An aristocrat willing to beg a pirate for help."

Marshall shook his head.

"No, that's not true. Many of my resentments and twisted feelings withered away long before I met you again." He shrugged. "What I feel right now is sorrow for you."

Her eyes hardened.

"Don't! You once told me you deserved the pain that you went through. Don't you think I earned every bit of the agony this creature inside brings to me? No doubt, it'll come out as a breach."

"Then, if you don't want my sympathy, why come to me?"

"Because I can trust you. You damned cursed pirate, yet you're the only one who understands what I need. You have the strength to do what's necessary."

Marshall's confused look caused the woman to give him a wry smile.

"Don't play the fool," the duchess stated as she sat on the baroque chair next to her.

Finally, the woman sighed.

"Alright, I'll make it simple. In a few months, I'll go through the torture of birth. Once that happens, there's no guarantee that I'll survive. That's why you need to be there."

Marshall narrowed his eyes.

"What are you asking?"

Elisabeth's pretty face twisted with despair.

"You must kill the child that comes from my womb!"

About the Author

Gordon Brewer is the pseudonym for a professional geek, history buff, and full-time dad who took up a challenge from his son to finish his first novel and enter the world of writing. Raised on a farm in Kansas, the author spent nearly five years in the US Navy traveling to 12 countries during this time. After his discharge, he received his BS degree with majors in History and Political Science.

Over the next twenty years, Gordon focused on the business and IT world. His experiences left him with a need to explore wide-ranging interests in multiple genres, each with historical consideration given to the characters and settings.

Residing in Tennessee, he often uses his family and friends as un-fortunate guinea pigs, where they are forced to listen to his tales, no matter how poorly conceived they may be.

You can find out more about the author and upcoming books, along with his other works at www.gordonbrewer.com.